Neon Hemlock Press
www.neonhemlock.com
@neonhemlock

© 2021 Neon Hemlock Press

We're Here: The Best Queer Speculative Fiction 2020
Edited by C.L. Clark and Series Editor Charles Payseur

Cover Illustration by Sajan Rai
Cover Design by dave ring

Paperback ISBN-13: 978-1-952086-27-4
Ebook ISBN-13: 978-1-952086-28-1

WE'RE HERE
THE BEST QUEER SPECULATIVE FICTION 2020

Neon Hemlock Press

We're Here
2020

EDITED BY C.L. CLARK & CHARLES PAYSEUR

A Note From the Series Editor

Inever imagined I'd be co-editing a Best Of anthology, in part because declaring some group of works the "best" based on editorial preference is...well, not something I'm wholly comfortable with. But since the discontinuation of the Lethe Best Ofs (*Wilde Stories, Heiresses of Russ,* and *Transcendent*) that focused on stories with queer content, I've been missing the voice they brought to the wider Best Of conversation. And tracking, celebrating, and promoting queer speculative fiction has been something I've been engaged with for some time, either passively as a fan of it or actively through my monthly reading lists. So I'm not shy about being involved in the work, and this is perhaps just a continuation of my passions and my pursuits as a reviewer and critic. So here I am, writing this introduction, trying to find things to say about the best queer speculative fiction of the last year.

But that's not really the start, either. First, I think I have to ask myself, "What *is* queer speculative fiction?" I feel the need to define terms a bit at least in this first volume because nothing about queerness is simple (except that it's awesome). When I say queer speculative fiction, I mean work that features queer characters and/or themes. The writers of these works aren't required to be queer, or to be out as queer. The conversations around that aspect of writing, publishing, and criticism are difficult and nuanced, but for this collection, the criteria is on the queerness of the *content*. Though...who gets to judge? Certainly if it were just one or two people going around deciding what stories were "queer enough" to consider for this anthology, there'd be a bit of a problem. Thankfully, the best judge of whether a story should or should not be considered is the author of the work, and in that spirit works could be submitted for consideration. It's not a perfect solution, and I did my best to canvas publications and my own reading for further works to consider as well, but it is, I feel, the best solution available, and I can't complain about the response we received.

After all, I often find myself a bit frustrated seeing Best Of anthologies where the same few publications seem to feature prominently punctuated by exceptions. Where there's a general sense that the field isn't as wide as it is. For queer speculative fiction, this is complicated by what publications put out more or less queer stories, which is by no means equal. It's also shaped by my own preferences and biases, and those of my co-editor, like any Best Of. All told, I tried my best to look widely, and even so I feel there's room for improvement, as when compiling the short list I noticed I had multiple stories from *Strange Horizons, PodCastle,* and *The Dark.* Which wasn't bad at all, but I don't want to fall into a kind of complacency with my reading that might lead me to not consider as closely or enthusiastically works coming from all over. To that end, I've already added a lot of publications to what I'm reading in 2021, to go along with what I had already been reading in 2020. Plus, again, the open submissions will hopefully fill in some areas that I cannot, as a single reader, cover.

For this anthology, though, I've certainly found that queer SFF is alive and well, and we received close to 300 submissions, which brought the number of stories considered for this anthology probably over 500. And that's...well, amazing. That's something to celebrate, even as it's also something to contextualize before voices from certain quarters begin to claim that publishing queer speculative fiction is easy or advantaged in all levels of the field. After all, a number of the works came from publications that specifically put out queer speculative fiction. Short fiction venues like *Glittership, Prismatica,* and *Baffling Magazine,* as well as anthology projects like *Silk & Steel, Glitter + Ashes, Decoded Pride,* and more, all helped to really boost the numbers of queer speculative fiction being put out. And these represent some incredibly exciting, incredibly good projects that feature some of the most prominent and powerful writers out there. Most of these, though, are projects funded and fueled by small teams and the intense efforts of queer editors and creatives, all happening without an abundance of institutional support.

Not that there's not reasons to celebrate the queer speculative fiction coming out from larger, more established and more funded publications. *Uncanny Magazine, Strange Horizons*, the Escape Artist podcasts, and many more short fiction venues have put out a lot of queer stories. As do anthologies from even larger publishers. Queer SFF novellas in particular have had a phenomenal year at presses large and small, with major releases from Tor (like *Finna* by Nino Cipri), Tachyon (*The Four Profound Weaves* by R.B. Lemberg), Aqueduct (*City of a Thousand Feelings* by Anya Johanna DeNiro & more), Neon Hemlock (all four of their novella releases, including the phenomenal *Stone & Steel* by Eboni Dunbar), *Clarkesworld* ("Power to Yield" by Bogi Takács), Unnerving Books (*Offstage* Offerings by Priya Sridhar), and many more. But while queer stories are being published at the largest and most well-known venues, any idea that they are omnipresent or represent anything close to a majority of works published should be quickly dismissed. Rather, these stories and the landscape that allows for their publication exist despite a constant grumbling and prejudice, into whose face we must constantly stand and say "get used to it!"

Still, it breaks my heart that we can't include all the stories in this anthology, especially because there are some that I dearly loved that didn't make the cut, either because they weren't ultimately selected for inclusion or because they weren't eligible.

Case in point, the work of my co-editor, C.L. Clark, was phenomenal in 2020, and especially the Ignyte Award finalist "You Perfect, Broken Thing" (*Uncanny Magazine*). It's one of my favorite stories from last year, but because they are involved with editing this, it wasn't able to be included. And just because you should read all their stuff, "Forgive Me, My Love, for the Ice and the Sea" from *Beneath Ceaseless Skies* (which landed on the Locus Recommended Reading List) and "After the Birds and the Bees Have Gone On" from *Glitter + Ashes* are both also wonderful and feature messy and real and glorious queer relationships.

Though their fiction cannot be included in this year's *We're Here*, I'm honored to be joined by such a sharp and celebrated author and editor. Through their work at *PodCastle*, Cherae has been recognized with Aurora, Ignyte, and Hugo Award nominations, and last year won, along with the *PodCastle* team, the British Fantasy Award for Best Audio. As if all that weren't enough, their recent debut novel, *The Unbroken*, is a powerful and stunning epic that is also really heckin' queer.

So it's a great time to be a reader of queer speculative fiction, even if those lingering conversations about portrayal, audience, and identity aren't really going anywhere. With the increased marketability of queer SFF, with its increasing prominence in the field, the prospect of curating a Best Of is getting more complicated, more difficult rather than easier. So where does that leave me and this project that you're holding in your hands (or reading on a screen)? Well...

How I like to think about Best Ofs is that they represent a voice in a conversation. Or voices, as this isn't a solo venture. Of the editors, speaking from a place of power, yes, with the backing of a publisher. But still just one (or two) perspectives weighing in with joy and with excitement to engage with and celebrate queer speculative fiction. To do the awkward work of breaking the ice, so that what follows can be a conversation between multitudes of people all talking about, all engaging with queer speculative fiction. I'd love to see more people put out lists of their favorite queer speculative fiction. To spread their joy and their love of stories that moved them, that entertained them, that maybe made them feel less alone in a world that for the last year has certainly been isolated and difficult.

And I'll close with an entreaty. For writers, that if you get a queer SFF story out in the world, let me know. For readers, that if you come across a queer SFF story that you loved, let me know. Either through the open submissions for this project, or through Twitter (@ClowderofTwo) or email (quicksipreviews@gmail.com). I compile these stories into a list every month publicly on my Patreon, and I really just love finding new works of queer speculative fiction. Cheers!

Charles Payseur
May 2021
Eau Claire, WI

A Note From the Guest Editor

It's spring as I write this from my desk in London. I'm watching the occasional airplane fly by as I contemplate my own impending travel in the coming weeks because of the vagaries and injustices that are borders. It's strange; the sky used to be more crowded with them. I have lived as an itinerant for the last half-decade, traveling alternately in the footsteps of restless dissatisfaction and urgent curiosity. I find I'm always seeking. Much like in my reading and writing life.

I've found in the past few years that there are two main ways to travel. Either you have the means to travel self-sufficiently, with suitcases full of all that you need and the financial means to board in a discrete hotel room, with privacy and a small patch of sovereignty and the ability to keep yourself distant if you so desire. Or, you come with less. You rely on those who greet you when you arrive, who make room for you in their homes, in their communal spaces; you trust that they will share what you could not carry and in return, you give of yourself—your time, your stories, your labor, your care.

Eventually, you leave again—but one of these modes of travel leaves an indelible mark long after you've gone.

Perhaps there was something in the water as all of these stories came out, or maybe it was sheer coincidence—but allow me to draw these connections, even if they exist only in my own head. Maybe that's the truth of the correlation, anyway—I picked them because something in *me* is obsessed with the idea of movement, especially now that it has been restricted and loaded with danger and consequences in a way that casual travel wasn't before. But we are barreling through another year of the COVID-19 pandemic, and travel—the notion of it, the idea of free movement, the sharp, frightening and glorious idea of how close we all truly are to each other—it's been forever changed. And I think that most of the stories I've chosen for this anthology reflect this in some way or another, for all that they deal with speculative worlds.

More than a few aptly speculate on the distances that separate us as global catastrophe changes the very landscapes we traverse, like Waverly SM's flooded England in "The Last Good Time to Be Alive," where everyone outside of central London risks starvation as their homes are swallowed up, calling to mind the way the global north will weather climate change. Another is Brenden Williams-Childs "The Wedding after the Bomb," where our narrator hikes through the burnout zone of a nuclear bomb, all to attend the wedding of two people they're not sure are still alive.

In fact, there's a line in Childs' story that echoes a theme of travel that I love: "You won't be the same person you were when you went into [the woods]. This is true about everywhere you go." You may leave a mark on a place, but it will always leave its mark on you, whether you realize it or not—but it will change you the most if you're open to the transformation. It is a story many queer people know well, as we go on long journeys to transform ourselves and be perceived truly. Many of the stories in this anthology show this transformation literally, including Charlie Jane Anders's "If You Take My Meaning," where revolutionaries journey into the depths of a mountain to become hybrid beings that just might save humanity, and "Rat and Finch Are Friends," where two boys who can turn into animals find themselves crossing a chasm that is wider than them realize, and with painful consequences. And there is Anya Johanna DeNiro's "A Voyage to Queensthroat," where, through pilgrimage and devotion, a child can become the woman she was meant to be.

For others, travel is about seeking answers, seeking comfort, seeking truth or love—seeking the self. And these also are journeys queer people often take out of necessity, and they are worth taking even if, on the outside, you remain exactly as you are, because on the inside the trials and discoveries have made you into something stronger, sturdier, maybe even whole. A few stories in this vein include "Salt and Iron" by Gem Isherwood, where a woman cursed with iron fists and a blind woman fight in their own ways against a world that would have them kneel to others and "To Balance the Weight of Khalem," which...well, it truly defies description, but you will follow a scholar on their own journey through space and memory as delicate as the crinkled husk of an onion.

There are stories of escape. The flight of the refugee, the persecuted. Stories of entrapment, so that the only journeys you can take are in your imagination. Those, too, are stories that queer people know too well. There are even stories in the form of that oh-so-familiar quest, video games and super heroes, all queered.

In all of these journeys, it is love that carries the characters from one point of the journey to the end (do these journeys ever truly end?): love for their partners, love for their community, their family, even love for themselves, which is often the hardest love to give. It's the glue that will hold us together.

It would be easy in a time like this—in fact, it has been recommended—to close down, stay put, and seal ourselves off from others. It's safest. It protects us. But it will also damn us, if we are too locked within our strongholds to reach out to one another. And there are ways, healthy, safe ways, to keep ourselves open and available to make gifts out of each others' presences and resources, digital or otherwise.

As a people, humanity has a great capacity for generosity, a tensile strength that can hold together under the strongest beatings; marginalized people in particular know this well. More often than not, we have been all that we had, and so we cling to that.

But that generosity doesn't have to stay within the margins. Reach out. Come with me.

The only way we'll get where we're going is together.

C.L. Clark
May 2021
London, England

We're Here 2020
Table of Contents

Escaping Dr. Markoff

Gabriela Santiago

You love Dr. Markoff.

You have always loved Dr. Markoff, even before the film began.

He is unlike any man you have ever met. Have you met many other men? It is so difficult to remember. His hair is black as jet. His eyes are as deep as night. When he speaks in his low accented voice you hear red wine being poured slowly into a crystal glass.

*

"You are only my assistant," he says. He is a mountain in winter. "Never forget that."

Rewind to the beginning of the scene. He has taken you to the symphony, an exclusive concert by The Father, an acclaimed violinist. You are in the box next to The Beautiful Daughter and The Fiancé. The Beautiful Daughter and The Fiancé are so pale they blaze with light, threatening to chase away all shadows and contrast.

"Do you really intend to pursue this girl?" you ask Dr. Markoff. "Simply for a chance resemblance to a dead woman? After all I've done for you—the secrets I've kept—"

He grabs your chin. His hands are ice and fire; your blood sings towards his hand where he touches you. His eyes are dark electricity, storms brewing under the harsh cliff of his brow, ready to sweep you away, to shatter you without mercy.

"You are only my assistant," he says. He is a mountain in winter. "Never forget that."

Forget? Was there something to forget? There is only Dr. Markoff, and his hands, and his eyes.

＊

YOU ARE A scientist in your own right. You attended university. You must have, surely. Yes, here they are, the memories backfilling themselves with only a slight delay: the row with your father, who you thought would understand after all he had told you of oppression; the cold dormitory made warmer by the smile of the pretty girl who roomed with you your first year; the japes and sneers in the laboratory giving way to grudging respect.

There is no diploma on your wall, and your memory echoes the blank plaster as you count one, two, three, four, five—scene: a man walks into the laboratory, like no man you have seen before. His hair is black as jet. His eyes are as deep as night. When he speaks—

Cut to: Dr. Markoff's laboratory. You sit monitoring the elixir in the crucible. It must boil slowly. It will be ruined if it reaches its height too soon. Your hair is different, so it must be the past.

Cut to: the symphony. You wear a beautiful dress. You are beautiful, your black hair curled and tumbling down delicate sepia shoulders. Your eyes sparkle and cloud like flawed diamonds.

Dr. Markoff does not notice.

The Father, the acclaimed violinist, plays a string of undistinguished notes. The notes he plays do not match the position of his fingers on the strings. The audience applauds wildly.

＊

HOW LONG HAVE you loved Dr. Markoff? It is a love outside of time. He is the storm, gathered, the moment before lightning. He is the moment itself. He is potential.

He has never touched you.

You think, sometimes, of fairy bread and pomegranates.

You never remember why.

＊

FAST-FORWARD—THE gorilla pounds its fists against the cage's bars and howls; you scream, leaping backwards. One of the dogs Dr. Markoff keeps for his experiments leaps up to defend you. He barks madly until the gorilla cowers back against the far wall.

"I wish you'd get rid of that beast!" you sob.

"Be reasonable," Dr. Markoff says. His voice is dark honey; his smile never reaches his eyes. "He is very useful to my experiments. And as long as my henchman remembers to lock his cage, he can never harm you."

✳

THE HENCHMAN LIVES below the laboratory. Dr. Markoff lives in an apartment adjacent. You live in an efficiency above.

Why is The Henchman here? He is not in love with Dr. Markoff. His motivation is significantly less complex.

He is paid.

✳

"I HAVE ARRESTED the spread of acromegaly," Dr. Markoff cries in triumph, his eyes wide. "But this is not enough! Soon I will have perfected the elixir—I will be able to reverse the process! Can you imagine—the power—to be the only man who knows—"

"You're mad!" you cry. "To think of using it in that way! When you could ease such suffering around the world, you think only of gain—"

✳

REWIND.

"You're mad!" you cry. "She will never love you! How could she love you? How could she—"

Dr. Markoff advances—

✳

REWIND.

"You're mad!" you cry. "And ungrateful—all these years

I've kept your secret, that you are not the true Dr. Markoff— that you killed him in a fit of jealous rage and stole his life's work—"

"And why not?" Dr. Markoff thunders. "When he stole from me the love of my dear wife! Ah, but I had my revenge! I knew he did not love her—would not love her when acromegaly distorted the features of her fair face—" the briefest shadow across his face, a fleeting cloud barely glimpsed through a storm—"and stole her faith in me, so that she did not believe I could find the cure—so that she took solace instead in a plunge from the cliffs!"

"I won't let this go on any longer!" you declare. Your blood sings with lightning despite how many times you have made this speech...how many times have you made this speech? "I'll go to the authorities! I'll tell them what I know—"

Dr. Markoff advances, a panther with claws unsheathed. His eyes are as deep as night. His eyes are—

"You know nothing," he growls. "You remember nothing."

"I know nothing," you whisper. His body is so close to yours. You are falling. "I remember nothing."

He moves away from you. You feel the loss like an iceberg cleaving into the ocean. Something else cleaves with it, feather-light as snow.

"You are only my assistant," he says. "Never forget that."

Forget?

✳

INTERIOR SHOT: CLOSE-UP on Dr. Markoff's hand, lifting the latch of the gorilla's cage.

Interior shot: your room above the laboratory. You recline in a low-cut silk nightgown that ripples like silver down to your ankles, your feet bare against the soft sheets of your bed.

Exterior shot: the stairway leading to your room. The gorilla shuffles slowly into the night. Its feet pad clumsily across the ground; it pauses to sniff the air. It snorts, and begins to slope up the steps to your room, the wood creaking below its weight...

Interior shot: your room. You are curled beneath a blanket

thin as gossamer, your dark curls splayed on the white pillow. Your eyes are closed, but your forehead is creased; your lips purse in a soundless cry.

Cut to: the creak of a door, slowly opening. A shadow on the floor.

Cut to: you toss restlessly on the bed, as if visited by bad dreams. One strap of your nightgown has slipped from your shoulder.

Cut to: the gorilla looms in the doorway, nearly bursting its frame. The frame of the story creaks beneath its weight. It sniffs the air, and grunts.

Cut to: you toss restlessly on the bed, as if visited by bad dreams. A shadow covers the lower half of your body. There is the creaking of old wood. The shadow grows larger and larger—

✱

Skip scene.

✱

You enter the laboratory. Dr. Markoff starts, and then smiles. "Ah, my dear—did you sleep well?"

"Not at all!" For a moment, there are only the words; your mind hangs in the air halfway through a trapeze act. Then more words come: "That damn dirty beast got out of its cage! Thank heavens your dog was there to protect me."

The words spill in your mind like ink in water, blossoming into memories: yes, you awoke, you screamed, the ape advanced, and then that dear dog leaping forward, barking madly, driving the monster back into its cage where you latched it. Yes, this is how it happened.

This was always how it happened.

"Oh dear, that is most unfortunate," Dr. Markoff says. "Still, you are well, are you not?"

"Yes," you say, a reflex, your head bobbing like a puppet on a string.

✳

REWIND. YOU SIT monitoring the elixir in the crucible. Dr. Markoff has told you not to take your eyes off the elixir. Your hair is the same, so it must be the present.

Dr. Markoff enters. Your eyes flick to his broad shoulders, back to the bubbling liquids before he can see.

So it is this scene, then: The Father has come to the clinic to demand that Dr. Markoff cease his pursuit of The Beautiful Daughter.

Dr. Markoff presses the button that slides back the hidden panel in his bookshelf. He carefully takes out the jar marked Acromegaly.

✳

FAST-FORWARD: YOU have threatened one too many times to go to the police. Dr. Markoff slaps you, calls for The Henchman. The Henchman wrestles you to the next room, ties you to a chair.

✳

IF YOU CANNOT have Dr. Markoff, you will have his antagonist. You will have The Father.

Rewind to the night of the symphony. You slip between frames to his dressing room, after The Beautiful Daughter and The Fiancé have left. He is wearing only a robe.

You straddle him, gripping the still firm muscle of his broad shoulders. He laughs and calls you a "fast woman," but that does not stop his hands from moving under your dress. His hands are experienced on your nipples as you bounce up and down on his cock. You come together, crying out, clutching.

You revisit this scene several times.

He never remembers you in any of your subsequent scenes together.

✳

FAST-FORWARD: "YOU will marry me!" cries Dr. Markoff to The Beautiful Daughter.

"Never!" she cries, jerking her porcelain cheek back from the touch of his lips.

They are framed perfectly. The black of Dr. Markoff's suited arm crushing her to his chest, the white silk heaving over her breasts as she strains away. Power and weakness tight as a clenched fist, as soft as an arched neck. His hair as dark as jet, her eyes moonstone-bright with fear.

His eyes the heat of coals, her skin the flames of the sun...

This is the second before the lightning strike and cannot be sustained—he must ravish her or she must escape, and at this point in the narrative the film will allow neither. Any second now the camera will cut away.

Freeze-frame.

To live in this moment, you think, watching. But as whom?

As The Beautiful Daughter, a fragile blossom swept up by a thunderstorm, crushed deliciously by iron hands?

As Dr. Markoff, the power surging in the muscles of your body, seizing the sun itself and demanding its surrender...

Rewind.

✳

NOW THAT YOU think about it, there is something odd about Dr. Markoff having a large jar marked Acromegaly behind a secret panel in his laboratory.

Surely that can't be how acromegaly works?

✳

FAST-FORWARD. THE gorilla looms in the doorway, nearly bursting its frame. You toss restlessly on the bed, as if visited by bad dreams. A shadow covers the lower half of your body. There is the creaking of old wood. The shadow grows larger and larger—

You open your eyes.

There is a zipper down the gorilla's front.

You reach out and slowly unzip the gorilla suit. Inside is a lithe, attractive young man who is blushing deeply. He is entirely naked.

"It gets hot in there," he says, and blushes deeper.

You look down. He has a very nice penis.

"I think I like you," you say, and pull him into a kiss.

He sheds the rest of the suit and you shed your nightgown, and you have sex on top of the gossamer-thin blanket, while the sweet, confused dog whines at the side of the bed. About halfway through, one of you has to get up and take it outside, giving it a biscuit before locking the door.

✳

FAST-FORWARD: YOU have threatened one too many times to go to the police. Dr. Markoff slaps you, call for The Henchman. The Henchman wrestles you to the next room, ties you to a chair.

✳

REWIND. YOUR SHY attractive young man is already peeling off the oppressive suit. You spread it like a blanket on the floor of his cage and ride him until you come.

He never stops blushing. His smile is so lovely. He looks at you like you are the sun.

He always starts and ends with a little kiss on the cheek, as if he is picking you up for a milkshake at the pharmacist's.

"This is fun," he always says. "Come back soon?"

✳

"I SHALL GO to the police!" The Father thunders. He turns his back to Dr. Markoff.

Dr. Markoff's eyes are as deep as night. Lightning flashes inside them.

He grabs the marble bust of his dead wife from the mantelpiece, and brings it down upon The Father's head.

✳

YOU GET A little careless. A test audience catches half of your rendezvous with your shy attractive young man. Hush money is paid; the footage is burned.

It stays in your memory like a half-penciled sketch: the line of a back arching upward, the grip of your fingers against his shoulder.

How strange people are: they have come to see a film where beauty is held captive. The Father, infected with acromegaly— is acromegaly infectious? This seems more and more unlikely the more you think about it—his chiseled profile swollen into something at which they can gawp and cringe, secure in their faux velvet cinema seats, thinking themselves safe. The Beautiful Daughter, virtuous and pure, hostage to the carnal demands of the dark foreigner who can save The Father.

How strange people are: so outraged to see beauty free.

*

"YOU ARE ONLY my assistant," Dr. Markoff says. "Never forget that."

His eyes are deep as night. His hair is black as jet. His hair is brushing against the collar of his shirt, leaving black smears behind.

*

FAST-FORWARD: "YOU will marry me!" cries Dr. Markoff to The Beautiful Daughter.

"Never!" she cries, jerking her porcelain cheek back from the touch of his lips.

How long have you loved Dr. Markoff?

The Beautiful Daughter is very beautiful.

"Never forget that," Dr. Markoff says. His accent wavers.

Rewind. Rewind, rewind! The names scroll across the screen, white cursive against the dark backdrop of Dr. Markoff's eyes, made blacker and slanted by the kohl around them. There is no name like Dr. Markoff's. There is no name like yours. What is your name? Fast-forward—

"—forget that," says Dr. Markoff. His hair is black as jet. His hair is dripping shoe polish under studio lights. He is sweating makeup, streaks and pools of darker grey at his neck. He is wearing a false nose; its edges bite into his pale skin.

He has never been Dr. Markoff at all.

Was this the only reason you loved him?

That you thought there might be someone else in this film like you?

✳

FAST-FORWARD: YOU have threatened one too many times to go to the police. Dr. Markoff slaps you, call for The Henchman. He wrestles you to the next room, ties you to a chair.

You struggle against surprisingly soft ropes. The Henchman's hands are calloused and warm on your ankles as he kneels between your knees. He does not grab hard enough to bruise, only firm enough that you cannot escape to spoil the next scene. He looks a little like Dr. Markoff, but taller, darker. The lines of his face have been filled in by years rather than sketched sharply with greasepaint.

"Déjà vu," he murmurs. His voice low but rough around the edges, like stones worn not quite smooth by long travels through stormy water. "Hope it's not too boring..."

Like Dr. Markoff, but softly faded, like a photograph left in the sun...

Sudden heat pools between your legs.

Your left hand is still free, and you run your fingers over the rim of his ear.

He looks up, surprised eyes. Kind eyes.

"While you're down there..."

He sees what you mean, and grins.

✳

THE FIANCÉ USUALLY interrupts The Henchman halfway through tying you up. This time, when he walks in on The Henchman with his head under your skirt, your nails digging into the chair as you moan, he is so embarrassed he drops his gun, flees the laboratory, and never rescues The Beautiful Daughter.

The film shudders to a halt, uncertain where to go next, as your orgasm ripples across its span, sending sparks like scratches on the tape to flare in every scene.

*

"OH, FATHER, OH no!" The Beautiful Daughter cries. She is convulsed, bent double over his prone form. His fingers are thick and distorted; his face is like clay molded by a child.

"His heartbeat is very faint," you say.

Tears glisten like perfect diamonds on the marble of her skin. "Oh, please, please, isn't there anything you can do?"

"Why, yes!" And there it is, right in your brain, no waiting for the blank wall to slide aside and reveal the answer behind the secret panel. "Dr. Markoff found an elixir—"

The syringe is already in your hand, sloppy editing. The Beautiful Daughter smiles like the sun and you discover that you don't mind.

You slide the syringe beneath skin that gives like rubber and the layers of film melt against each other, superimposed. Pause scene—

A PA slips between the frames and escorts The Father to his trailer, where several technicians carefully remove the latex layers from his face and reapply makeup to hide the chafing and his allergic reaction to the glue.

—until the illness fades away from The Father's face and he is in the arms of The Beautiful Daughter again. They smile, and the Fiancé smiles, and you smile, and Dr. Markoff's body is on the floor in the background, and The Henchman is offstage, and the sweet young man will never be seen again, was never seen in the first place.

This is the end of the film.

*

YOU LOVE THE Beautiful Daughter.

You love her even after the film ends.

Your entire love is after the film ends: helping her ease The Father into the car ride home, offering your services as a visiting nurse, accepting a week later her spontaneous offer to move into her mansion to better care for him. He recovers quickly and goes back on tour, but she won't hear of you moving out. You play tennis and take in Broadway shows.

You say goodbye to your shy attractive young man, who is going back home to his family.

"It's rough in Hollywood," he says. "They never give me a part without a mask."

You miss him. You would miss him more if not for The Beautiful Daughter. Her smile is blinding. Her skin is blinding. She bounds down the stairs to greet you like a shooting star.

*

WHEN YOU TOUCH, finally, truly, it is in a bed that could be filmed like an ocean, silk sheets curling into waves. Your hands skim and stroke all her unfilmable places, soft nipples, light downy hair wet with desire, freckles on the backs of her knees. Where your hands skim blushes with—you have heard the words before, but now you *see* them, the pink of the blood under skin, the blue of the arching delicate veins, and you know you have never seen color before, that your world has never contained such hues— your hands burst shades and gradations into the world where they touch her, as if peach and cream, amethyst and sapphire, flax and copper, were living things that could blossom and quicken and thrive under heat like tropical vines that wrench the foundation of your world, shift its moorings until the two of you are spinning at the end of an unraveling roll of film and then even your grip slips—

For one moment, you live in another film entirely, and color is infinite as air.

*

You ARE KISSING The Beautiful Daughter when The Fiancé walks in.

"Oh, don't worry!" she cries, laying one hand on your arm as you start up from the sofa, pulling you back down. "He doesn't mind." She lays her other hand on his arm. "We both like you so dearly—I like both of you so dearly—and he doesn't have an interest in these things, you know."

You regard The Fiancé speculatively. You think of your shy attractive young man, and what a pretty picture they would make. "No interest at all?"

The Fiancé blushes; a hint of color lingering in the air from your kiss with The Beautiful Daughter tries to suffuse his cheeks but is rebuffed, turns the wall behind him a glowing peach for a split second instead.

"None at all," he says firmly. He smiles; his hand rests thoughtlessly against The Beautiful Daughter's shoulder. You try to imagine having that confidence, that square-shouldered resolve. "But I hope you will join us for a concert once in a while."

✳

REWIND TO THE penultimate scene. Interior: laboratory. Dr. Markoff and The Fiancé struggle for Dr. Markoff's gun. Dr. Markoff holds it tight in his grip, his finger flicking at the trigger, the black metal gleaming as deep as his eyes, but The Fiancé's strong arms bunch under his shirtsleeves, forcing the barrel to the side—

The Beautiful Daughter crouches next to The Father where he lies motionless on the operating table, presses her beautiful cheek against his ridged and swollen one—

The Fiancé slips, and the two men fall to the floor, obscured from the camera's view—

You are not in the scene. You are in the hallway, still halfway bound, helpless.

✳

SCENE: A MAN walks into the laboratory, like no man you have seen before. His hair is black as jet. Your hair is different again, so it must be farther in the past than you have ever been before.

His eyes, deep as night, skip over the diploma on your wall. Light on the bust you keep on the mantle; a fleeting likeness, but the best your inartistic hands could capture.

When he speaks, you hear arsenic being poured into a glass of wine. "So this is where my wife was spending all of her time."

Your heart thunders in your chest. You stay sitting. You are monitoring the crucible. It must boil slowly, or the effects will be lost.

He steps closer, the tread of a panther. His eyes light greedily upon the elixir, the notes beside it. "Could this have saved her?"

"I don't understand how she contracted acromegaly in the first place," you say. "That isn't how acromegaly works—"

"What kind of woman are you?" he interrupts. "You are beautiful. You could have a man. Why her—"

※

FAST-FORWARD: YOU are not in the scene. You are in the hallway, still halfway bound, helpless. You observe through the proscenium of the open door:

The Fiancé slips, and the two men fall to the floor, obscured from the camera's view—

※

REWIND: HE IS clenching and unclenching his fists. The official autopsy said the marks around her neck came from the rocks when she threw herself from the cliffs.

"I loved her," you whisper. "And she never loved you. No woman ever could."

He bares his teeth. "Look into my eyes and tell me that."

Without thinking, you do. His eyes are as deep as night. He looms before you like a mountain in winter.

*

FAST-FORWARD: YOU are not in the scene. You are in the hallway, still halfway bound, helpless. You observe through the proscenium of the open door:

The Fiancé slips, and the two men fall to the floor, obscured from the camera's view, and there are two kinds of films that this film could be, the kind where the gun goes off and Dr. Markoff crumples to the floor, or the kind where the gun goes off and scores a long groove into the wallpaper, and he is led away in handcuffs...

Freeze-frame. Your hands are unbound. They were never bound in the first place; you only thought they were.

*

"YOU ARE MY assistant." His voice rumbles like a gathering storm; you are falling into the eye of the storm, into his eyes. "Only my assistant. Never forget that."

"Only your assistant." The words choke in your throat like your tongue being pulled out of your mouth.

"You love me," he says. "Madly, deeply, with no hope of return, or escape."

You reach out a hand to steady yourself. It brushes the diploma on the wall, sends it crashing to the ground. A shard stings your eye, but you cannot look away from his eyes, his eyes are...

His lips brush yours, and the film slips into the projector, almost ready to begin.

His lips brush your ear as he withdraws, and for a second you see color, the deep red of pomegranates, as your love smiles. "Goodbye, Dr. Markoff."

*

FAST-FORWARD:

He crumples to the floor. Blood seeps out around him, as black and sweet as night.

＊

THE BEAUTIFUL DAUGHTER says, "You are unlike any woman I have ever known."

"Have you known many women?" you tease.

"You are unlike any woman I have ever known," says The Beautiful Daughter. "You move through life unbound by the laws of the universe. When you speak, I hear red wine being poured into a crystal glass. Your hair is as dark as jet. Your eyes sparkle and cloud like flawed diamonds..."

The Currant Dumas

L.D. Lewis

SAMSON ARRITA DUCHAMP stands at the coffee hutch at the edge of the blustery marketplace, watching the industrious little ballet of volunteers swapping the goods in their trailers and truck beds for the crates onboard the candy painted cars of the *Carlyle Limited No. 4*. The train itself rumbles between hydraulic hisses and belches steam that whips away on the wind.

She slugs a tin cup of objectively bad coffee, made worse by her recent, singular experience with good coffee. Her colony's Garden Master, Mr. Acres, had shared a pot with her made from a small pouch of whole beans he'd gotten as a birthday present. He'd doused it with hazelnut milk and a dusting of fairly ancient cocoa powder, and Sam went to work in the Stadium greenhouses that day more or less glowing.

That had been the sign. A dozen salvaged travel books, a thousand recipes, and four seasons of Anthony Bourdain on a borrowed thumb drive had built the fantasy of life as a traveling food writer, and a single cup of decent coffee had set her off.

There isn't much traveling anymore, though. Especially not overseas, not with the storm. This close to it, there isn't even a sky. And thanks to everything set in motion after it, there are barely even roads. There is, however, the *Carlyle*.

"The Currant Dumas occupies two railway cars of the *Carlyle* and the only mobile restaurant in the FSA," Sam says into her voice recorder. She shields it from the constant wind with a hand cupped like she's lighting a cigarette. But damn near no one smokes anymore. "The facade is a mulled red color—I assume—hence the name. DUMAS is painted in elegant, gold letters spanning its entire length. It's nested between a string of smoke-gray boxcars being loaded with trade goods, and a handful of green cars occupied by the performers of the Cirque

Carlyle, known to bring music and stories and feats of magic and general strangeness to the stops on their route."

The performers are distinct from the regular train crew in that there isn't a single faded hoodie between them. Lithe acrobats in wool coats and dancers with glitter-painted faces do light shopping from colony truck beds and disappear inside the warmth of the troup's green railway cars. Singers and musicians are identifiable by the gloves and heavy scarves they wore to protect the parts of themselves key to their instruments, and the beelines they made to the tea and wax traders. Brawny men with tattooed heads bark with laughter, lounging atop crates and steamer trunks. One of their number approaches the group with a crate of dark liquor hoisted onto his shoulder, and is met with cheers as it was pried open.

"There's something almost charmingly Victorian about them," Sam says into her voice recorder. "They're comfortable, as if life on the rails was something they'd have chosen in any other time in history."

She frowns, mouthing the sentence again to see if it feels as purple and self-important as it felt the first time.

"I don't know, maybe don't use that," she says aloud.

A young woman with short, dark curls and an alarmingly bright smile steps from one of the Cirque cars and carves a path through the players. Sam immediately decides she's interesting and follows her movements through the passing loading crew. The woman's boots are untied and her dark overcoat flaps open at the hem to reveal an emerald satin lining and Sam swallows hard to calm the fluttering that begins in her stomach when she sees the woman is approaching her.

Well, not me, obviously, Sam thinks with a snort. *The coffee stand.* Unsure how to register the impression, she clicks off the recorder and sips the terrible coffee to slake her sudden thirst.

"Hey," the woman says cheerily as she reaches the coffee stand. Her eyes sparkle and the copper apples of her cheeks have already begun pinking in the wind.

Sam nods and says an anxious "hey" into her cup. But at least the ice was broken.

"How's the coffee?" The woman pours herself a cup.

"Ever drink actual tar?" It's Sam's best stab at cleverness.

"No. Is today my lucky day?"

"We'll find out in a second."

Sam watches as she puts the steaming cup to her exceptionally well-moisturized lips, and counts the seconds until her face changes to something that borders both disgust and hilarity.

"Oh god." The woman gags.

"Right?" Sam reaches into her tattered messenger bag for a small jar. "Here. Maple sugar. That and a little water should take it down to a pleasant oil slick."

She pours her a proper dose and the woman stirs it with a long, lacquered finger before trying it again, this time frowning considerably less.

"This is less bad, thank you. I'm Layla," she says.

"Sam."

"I've never seen you here before. You're a trader? Really unfortunate barista?"

"Writer. Kind of," Sam says.

"Magician. Also kind of. Illusions for the disillusioned." Layla replied with a bit of a theatrical flourish.

"Really?" Sam raises an eyebrow. "Why can't I think of a single other female magician?"

"To be fair, they just called them witches." Layla winks.

"Brave new world." Sam lifts her cup and Layla toasts with her own.

"Brave new world."

This is going well, Sam tells herself. She finds herself taken with the little black stars in Layla's ears, the neatly painted navy color of her nails, that Sam notices when Layla turns to wave at someone in the marketplace. She's about to ask about the whole magician thing when Layla turns back with what shockingly seems like keen interest.

"So what do you write?"

"Food...journalism?" Sam chokes out. It feels like such a silly thing to say seriously now that everything's fallen apart.

"You sure?" Layla chuckles.

"For now. I work in the horticulture department for the Stadium settlement in South City. I'm being hosted at the

Currant, though, to interview people about how our food culture has changed since the end."

"Ah, a food nerd! Okay! That's how you know maple sugar is a thing, I take it."

"Only natural sweetener indigenous to the whole continent. Our Master Gardener is Mvskoke so we're re-learning all kinds of stuff."

You're showing off. Don't be weird, she scolds herself.

"Genius. The magic of giving the land back." Layla gives an impressed nod.

"That's what I said."

A tall, brown-skinned woman in a weathered Star Wars sweatshirt rushes by, rolling a hand cart stacked high with reusable bins that rattle on the uneven pavement.

"Door. Door, door, door. You," she says breathlessly, glancing in their direction.

Layla grimaces as she finishes what remains of her coffee and backs away.

"That's all you. I've got some shopping to do before Redd gets on the horn. Don't stray too far or he *will* leave you," Layla advises. "I'll see you on the rails."

"Wait! I want to know about this magic stuff. What do you do?" Sam calls after her.

"Come find me for an interview. I'll show you a trick."

"*Door.*" The tall woman barks, and Sam drops her smile a bit, leaving her duffel bag by the coffee stand to get the door for her. A flood of cinnamon and citrus rushes out of the open door and Sam activates a lift to get the trolley onto the right floor before moving aside and clicking on her recorder.

"The Currant is opulent by today's standards, with wood and brass finishes, a polished bar, and damask wallpaper the color of ripe pomegranates. Everything here seems to fit unlike everywhere else. The kitchen appears to be on the lower le— Oh." Sams stops when she notices the woman's irritated glare from the other end of the car.

"You're the foodie Acres sent us," she says.

"Something like that, yes. Sam Duchamp." Sam makes an effort to sound pleasant and self assured as she extends her hand.

"Yvette. Proprietor of this establishment." Yvette shakes her hand aggressively.

"Oh *you're* Yvette," Sam says, relieved if not for the gun she's only now noticed on Yvette's hip. "I'd love to interview you when you ha—"

"You a stranger to work, Sam Duchamp?" Yvette cuts her off.

"Not at all. I grew most of the collards on this haul."

"Good, because we don't have room here for anyone who doesn't work. You'll do all that writing business on your time, not mine. Understood?"

"Yes, of course. Thank you for having me."

"Good." Yvette sighs, grunting as she goes back to securing her bins. "You'll bunk with the kitchen staff six cars down that way past baggage. Cars beyond that are off limits to anyone but security personnel. You get space for two bags and whatever's on your back. Hope you brought sheets. Quartermaster is a Mr. Redd. You'll know him when you see him. You have any problems, you take them to him. Don't get caught out after he sounds that damn horn. They will absolutely leave you wherever you end up."

Sam waits in silent anxiety, not sure if she's dismissed or allowed to ask questions. She hasn't left the colony in years and the new rules are daunting.

"Is...that all?" Yvette asks finally.

"I just had a couple of questions. How long you've been here, why the name Currant Dumas, things like that," says Sam.

"Six years, four months. 'Dumas' because French author Alexandre Dumas's collected works were the only intact books onboard this particular car when we found it, and 'Currant' because there was a lot of this paint, too. Everything's random in the apocalypse. That all?" Yvette wipes her brow with the sleeve of her sweatshirt and blinks at her impatiently.

"For now," Sam replies, trying to keep the words in her head until she could record them without being weird about it.

Yvette huffs and heads back toward the door. "Good, because I have things to do. Redd will leave my ass behind, too. I'm only mean when I'm busy. He's an asshole all the time. Get what you're getting and get back here. See you on the rails."

Sam steps back off the train long enough to collect her things from where they wait for her beside the coffee stand, and walks five cars down, past the green Cirque cars and their sounds of practiced music and scent of cloves and incense, to a trio of steel-blue ones. A windowless black car separates the ones designated for passengers from two tankers and a caboose. Armed personnel stand guarding them.

Sam finds her bunk in the second blue car, marked by a torn scrap of paper pinned to the bed curtain. With not much else to do, she considers wandering off to look for Layla again. But a mountain of a man with an impressive red beard walks by the doorway yelling effortlessly and impossibly loud for everyone to board. They make the briefest eye contact and she's shocked by how furious he looks for what seems like no reason.

"Annnnd…that's Redd," she says aloud to no one and sits back on her gym mat of a bed, hoping she packed sheets.

*

YVETTE'S ROOM IS a private sleeper cabin in the performers' residential car. The hallway is filled with music and through the window, the afternoon sun is almost obscenely bright this far northwest, set in the first blue sky Sam has seen since she was fourteen. The storage shelf above her bench has been converted into a bookshelf, lined in part by Dumas's works. A collapsible table stands between them, doubling as workspace and keeper of the ashtray into which she taps her impeccably rolled Dutch.

"I always dreamed of owning a restaurant," Yvette says wistfully, exhaling smoke out of the open window. Sam's recorder ticks away the seconds of Sam's first interview as a food writer. They've been here for twenty minutes already.

"Then the bottom fell out. I mean, the way things were, I wouldn't have been able to afford it anyway. I taught high school and had 'Black people credit' so the money just wasn't ever going to be there. You dream anyway though. Then there's the storm, which…I mean, there's your physical threat to a sustainable society, right? It hit and just wouldn't let up. Half the eastern seaboard is gone, capital's drowned, so the shit folds even faster with the fallout. And then there's the existential threat. What if it's the end? What if it's just the end of *this* place? People panic. There's this exodus at the same time water runs the islanders out of their homes and into the mainland. And like that, boom." She snaps her fingers. "Fractured States. Everybody's scattered and trying to scrape together survival conditions and it's *hard*. Eleven years on, *it's still hard*. But there's no debt. No systemic oppression because there's no enforceable currency in a capitalist state. No government, no bank left to say no to your dreams. So you find a train and you do what you want with it."

Sam tries to see her as a high school teacher and wonders if all the gray streaking her French braids was there from dealing with children or carving out a life in the aftermath. "Sounds like you're making it work," she says. "Anything you're missing?"

Yvette nods and sips tea to settle a cough. "Tetanus shots. Infrastructure was shot to hell before the country collapsed but there's a thousand gross ways a train exterior will kill you if you're not careful."

Sam blinks. "Oh. Okay..."

Out in the hallway, a door slides closed with a bang and someone races up by, laughing.

"Fools won a crate of whiskey in a game of Uno," Yvette mutters. "They'll be lit for the next week."

"Uno?" Sam raises an eyebrow.

"Ever try to find a full deck of regular playing cards in the apocalypse? You can play Uno with damn near anything."

"What kind of food does the Currant serve that makes it so popular?" Sam asks. The recorder is on 30% battery and who knows where a charging station is on this thing.

"Soups mostly. Or whatever can be made from what we have on hand or through trades and whatnot. Not like we have too much competition for best restaurant." She suddenly sits forward as if excited. "We used to head out to these places with the menu on a sandwich board out front. One side was whatever was on the menu, other side was ingredients we had available for trade and the quantities we could let go. I started seeing how...excited these women were to get their hands on what we had. So I started opening the kitchen up to them when we stop

by and *that's* where the real magic happens. A lot of them don't
have access to full kitchens. Ovens, stoves, refrigerators, solid
cookware. My favorite thing is just stepping back, watching
aunties of every culture doing what they do in the kitchen,
feeling like they did when they were back home for a few hours."

Sam is suddenly excited, too. These are the food stories she
wants. These are the food stories Bourdain would get them to
tell."You think I'll be able to talk to them?"

"You'll have to ask them. I'm not here to volunteer anyone
else's time. Next station's in the Northern Lakes. We don't stop
in the mounta—"

There's a knock on the cabin door and a dark-skinned man
Sam is sure is someone's grill-enthusiast uncle is standing in the
hall.

"Did you put sweet potatoes somewhere?" he asks Yvette,
either too tired or too busy to acknowledge Sam.

Yvette rolls her eyes. "I brought whatever they loaded on that
dolly and I put it in kitchen storage."

"Kid's saying there's supposed to be some sixty pounds of
sweet potatoes and we can't find 'em."

"Well if they're not in the kitchen, I didn't get them."

"Dammit. Think they're in the back somewhere? Somebody
put them on the wrong dolly?"

"Tommy, I don't know."

"Well, come help me look." Tommy insists.

"Get one of the kids to do it! You see I'm doing something. If
I don't have them, somebody else knows where they are," Yvette
snapped.

"I'm just saying, Yve, you're supposed to be running this shit,
I don't see why—"

Yvette stands up and the curses start flying, each person more
done with this shit than the other. Without warning, Yvette
leaves the cabin and slams the door, both their voices fading as
they disappear down the hall.

"End of, uh…interview, I guess," Sam says into her recorder
and clicks it off. "Good talk."

The north passes outside the window in the form of
abandoned suburbs with their overgrown lawns. Each is now

little more than a place for colonists to loot for supplies if they haven't been picked clean already. Sam knows there isn't a house outside South City Stadium with so much as a bar of soap left in it. The horn blares on an overpass where she can see the decrepit roadways are clogged with vehicles first abandoned for want of gas, then looted for want of parts. It's this blockage everywhere that's made the *Carlyle* the only reliable way to traverse the countryside.

She threads through the Cirque cars, trying to find either Layla or a charging station for her recorder. Instead, she finds Redd entering the car through the rear door. His body nearly fills the entire corridor and Sam makes herself small, pressing against the windows to inch past him. He passes without a word, but Sam decides the world on a train is too small already and that she isn't going to shrink again needlessly.

"You're Redd," she calls out and he turns back with a look in his eye that says she's wasting his time. He has a tattoo of Dr. Teeth and the Electric Mayhem on his forearm, though, that makes him difficult to find terrifying.

"...yes?" he grunts. Neither is certain it was a question.

"Well, I'm Sam Duchamp. Just a writer covering the Currant. I thought I'd introduce myself so I'm not just a strange face in your hallways here. And so if you see me chasing the train when you pull off one day, you'll recognize me. Maybe stop. They keep telling me you leave people behind."

"You don't want to get left, don't be late." Redd shrugs.

"Right."

A moment of silence passes before she decides she's said what she came to say. But he speaks again just as she turns to leave.

"Who do you write for?"

"I don't. I mean...just me right now."

He looks at her then like she's given the strangest possible answer. "Alright."

"I did have a question for you. One maybe you can answer as quartermaster since it's not really food related."

Redd says nothing, but rolls his hand in an "out with it" gesture.

Sam clicks on her recorder. "Why is it the *Carlyle Limited*?

That means you don't make every stop possible, right? Seems like wherever there's people, they'd need supplies."

"We only stop the colonies with hubs. The ones sprouted up in the cities. About a dozen spots across the...countryside. Some places we don't stop because fuck 'em."

"Fuck 'em?"

"Yeah." Redd shrugs. "Some clusters of good ol' boys set up their little strongholds mosting in the mountain regions. They still hold onto that white supremacy shit while everyone else manages to rebuild together. The *Carlyle* is an antifa outfit. So fuck 'em."

"Damn."

"They're hurting for supplies, though. That's why you see security around here. They haven't tried us in awhile, but that just means they're overdue."

"...oh." Sam frowns. Being onboard during a racist bandit attack seemed less than ideal.

"Nah, it's fine," Redd adds, with the first hint of a smile Sam's seen. "We have a secret weapon."

"*Oh*," Sam replies with considerably less disappointment. She wonders if she should pry about the secret part.

"That it?"

Sam clicks off her recorder and smiles, grateful to have cleared the air. "That's it. Thanks."

Redd nods and responds to his crackling radio with a gruff "on my way" as he starts back up the hallway.

Sam steps through the door to the Cirque's prop car to find a handful of players around a table. Only a few of them glance up when she enters. The light is low in the windowless room, generated mostly by a string of twinkle lights strewn across the ceiling.

"Hey, it's Maple Sugar!" Layla is smiling when her head pops up from behind a beam. She is sitting atop a planetary model of Saturn with a fan of Uno cards in her hand.

"Hey." Sam's butterflies return. This time she's not sure if it's Layla or the assortment of strangers in the dark room of creepy carnival sets.

"Come, come, come. Everyone, this is Sam, the food writer

I mentioned. Sam, love, this is Vannish, our ringleader." She points to an ageless, beautiful sort of man in shirt sleeves and suspenders who tips a hat he isn't wearing in her general direction. "And this Jazz, Morty, and Farah, all very good at their respective circus things while being total shit at this game."

"Says the magician like she doesn't pull stunts with cards all damn day," quips the person Sam assumes is Farah.

"*What?*" Layla gasps in mock incredulity.

"You cheat!" says Jazz, probably.

"You lie!" Layla replies. "Do you play, Sam? We can deal you in. It would be hard for you to lose."

"Don't bait the children, darling. You'll be all they talk about when you leave," Vannish warns, in a bored sort of tone.

"Maybe later?" Sam says. "I'm actually looking for a charging station. My recorder's dying."

"They're in the bunks. I'll show you." Layla drops her hand onto the table and stands up.

Sam follows her through the next cars back toward the staff bunks, quietly thrilled about being near her again. Scents of coconut and cocoa butter drift in her wake, and Sam notices a tattoo of a bird on the back of Layla's neck that she will make a point to ask about later if she runs out of interesting things to say.

"Get anything good in your interviews so far?" Layla asks.

"Talked to Yvette before Tommy dragged her off to look for sweet potatoes. And just talked to Redd about fascists in the mountains."

"Oh he's a *real* chatterbox about the hills having eyes. He tell you there's a secret weapon?" Layla waggles her eyebrows as if it's some salacious thing and Sam laughs.

"Yeah. Didn't mention what it was, though."

"Sounds about right. Here you are." Layla shows her the outlet underneath in the windowsill of her bunk. "They prefer you use it during the day while the solar's still going. We need the stored power at night, especially for our shows."

"Thanks. So I believe I was promised a trick."

"Oh I *promised*, did I? My memory is there was supposed to be an exchange. An interview for a trick."

"Fair enough." Sam sits on her bed and clicks on the recorder.

Layla doesn't hesitate to join her.

"Interview with Layla…"

"Legend."

"Layla Legend? You're joking."

"Honest to God, it's my given name."

"I'm so sorry."

"Thank you."

"Interview with Layla No-Last-Name, Day One aboard the *Carlyle*. So how long have you been a magician?"

"The only correct answer is all my life."

"Is that what brought you to the *Carlyle*? You saw a hole in the Cirque's programming?"

"I was looking for somewhere to…be. Just like everyone else. There's always been a type of person who was always meant to run away with the circus. My turn just came late."

Sam knows this feeling of being born too late, destined to fill some void in a world that no longer existed. She'd been born a collector, and she tried collecting stories at Stadium but, after a long enough period of shared experiences, the stories in one place started to sound the same. There is an entire world out there, fractured, but still. The *Carlyle* is a step closer than she'd ever been to the rest of it.

"Where were you from originally?" Sam asks.

"Everywhere. I was a military brat. That's what military brats say. We were just south of the Capital when the storm hit. I was sixteen. I evacuated up north with my parents. They were ordered back to the coast when the riots started. It was too much for them like it was too much for everyone else, I guess." Layla shrugs and her eyes glisten in the passing sunlight. And Sam immediately regrets doing this.

"I'm sorry. We don't have to talk about this if you don't want."

"Relax." Layla sniffles. "I'm well-adjusted. What else did I think we were going to talk about?"

"Alright. So…you found a new home, a new family sort of, on the rails?"

Layla rocks her hand in a so-so kind of way.

"And you're the only one capable of '*magic*.'" Sam's air quotes flounder a bit as she wonders if it's an offensive thing to wave disbelief in a magician's face.

"Looks like it," Layla says, unbothered.

"Close-up or…"

"Oh this is you trying to get me to do the trick."

"Can you blame me?" Sam asks.

"Alright, alright, easy, tiger. Do you have a coin? Bigger the better. A quarter or something."

Sam scoffs. "I haven't had money since…"

"Figures. No one carries change these days." Layla digs into a pocket of her jeans and fishes out a silver dollar, flicking it at Sam. "Check it out. Observe there's nothing funky about it. Solid, good weight, a little dirty. Perfectly normal silver dollar, right?"

Sam turns it over in her hands. There is indeed nothing funky about it, and she says as much.

"Now place it on the back of your hand. Right there in the center. Good. Hold it up here. Now look at me."

With pleasure, Sam doesn't say.

"Promise me you won't freak out. I'm going to count to three and then I'm going to take my finger and I'm going to push the coin *through* your hand."

"*Through* my hand," Sam repeats in disbelief. "With the bones and everything in the way."

"Yep. You freak out and hit me, I'm going to be upset. Black people get all scary about magic but I have a show tonight and this face is what cashes the checks around here. So here we go. One, don't hit me…"

Sam watches her eyes, her other hand, anything to catch the trick of it all.

"Two, don't hit me…."

Now she watches the coin on her hand as Layla applies more pressure, careful not to blink.

"Three!"

And the coin hits the floor. It isn't a new coin. There was just the one. She hadn't felt anything but the pressure, hadn't seen anything but Layla's finger applying it.

"Wait…" Sam tries to piece together some explanation. She examines the back of her hand for signs of trauma (there was none), and then screams as she turns it over to see a perfectly painless, perfectly circular, gaping, silver dollar-sized hole in her palm through, which Layla is now winking at her.

Terrified, Sam shakes her hand so vigorously she hits the bunk above her. But when she stops, the hole is gone. Her hand is normal, intact, but her heart is racing.

"How...what…"

Layla casually retrieves the coin off the floor."See? Magic."

✳

THE NORTH LAKES settlement is in yet another football stadium about three miles from the train station so Sam doesn't get to see it; and three miles is too far to wander if Redd decides it's time to leave. She's heard most of the settlements are in stadiums, though, for their high capacity and resilience to the elements and their parking garages easily become neighborhoods. The North Lakes stadium is domed, and its residents can't grow food on its field with natural sunlight, so the *Carlyle* distributes to them first en route west. The train is greeted warmly from nearby parking structures, leaving the small lot for loading vehicles and trade merchants.

Cirque performers ready their attractions quickly as an audience gathers in the vast, gated parking lot of some abandoned university on the other side of the station. They light the dark with torches and mirrors and solar lanterns strung from garlands. The city is impossibly dark beyond them.

"Lucia Velez-Avila. I'm from the islands. Jayuya."

She is an older woman, sixty give or take, and one of the two guest chefs in the Currant kitchen tonight. She takes a break from humming while peeling a mountain of plantains for mofongo to enunciate into Sam's recorder.

"And I am Marcia Batista. I am from the islands as well but have lived in the Capital the last thirty years." the second woman declares. She is a small, brown-skinned woman with glasses set in red cat-eye frames. She preps trout for frying on a counter further down the line. It's the only ingredient the *Carlyle* hasn't had to bring.

Sam has volunteered for the knife work, chopping chilis and onions, okra and heirloom tomatoes between them. The rest of the kitchen cheered when they were dismissed, because a night off is still a night off, even in the apocalypse.

"Can you tell me what it was like when you left the islands? Was it before the storm?"

"It was close. We were all leaving. Most people barely paid attention to where the boats, planes, whatever were even going. Every storm left behind less and less to rebuild. We were tired already. I came north through Louisiana with one suitcase. The southern coast was too dangerous. By the time I got there, they weren't even asking for paperwork anymore. Some tornadoes scared the shit out of border security and they were long gone."

The women laugh loudly.

"It's always the paperwork that matters," Mrs. Batista adds. "Until it doesn't, you know?"

"You know?" Lucia agrees.

"I left the Capitol during one of those early breaks in the storm when they thought it was going to be over. Something told me not to stay. Jimmy and I packed up the car. We were two blocks from being too flooded to go anywhere."

"Who's Jimmy?"

"My husband, child. Where did you think I got the 'Mrs.?' He's somewhere out there. Thinks he's a pitmaster but couldn't grill a hot dog back when there were still hot dogs so I don't know what he's doing now."

"So, both of you were here for the collapse."

"Yes. I was living with my sister not too far from here when the exodus started. The shortage of everything. People going west to catch planes out of the country then couldn't go west anymore unless it was on foot because there was no more gas. I ended up here headed to the border before they shut down it down," says Mrs. Batista.

"I was in the city for the last State of the Union address what's-his-name gave before the power grid went down. The rest of the world was still out there, though. Watching. Waiting for their turn, I think," says Lucia.

"I still think about how it took years for things to just...end.

You think it all falls apart *so slowly* that it'll never be completely done." Mrs. Batista sighs. "And then you're standing in the ruins and it takes all of five minutes to explain how you got there."

A moment of silence passes between them, and Sam can hear the cheering for the Cirque outside. The cooking has started in the kitchen, though, and her eyes begin to burn from either their somber stories or the exposure to the onions and chopped chilis.

"Anything you miss?" she asks them both.

"My kitchen," Mrs. Batista laughs.

"Just roots," says Lucia. "The people, you find again. The music, the joy, the culture you bring with you. But everywhere that isn't home feels...temporary. I think we all know we are refugees. For now it doesn't feel like we will have to run again. And that's nice. But we *will* have to."

Sam thanks them for their time and excuses herself for fresher air before her vision's too blurry to get her up the stairs. The night is cool this close to the water that separates what's left of the city from the old national border. She watches from the overpass as the Cirque performs, checking her hand intermittently for strange holes.

The musical performances that start the night are lively, mostly classical covers of hits most everyone is old enough to remember. By the time food is served, acrobatic acts, a puppet show, and one unfortunate clown have all given their contributions to the night, each introduced by Vannish, elaborately dressed and occasionally eating fire. Spotting Layla in the wings ("wings" here being a couple of tented parking spaces between two dusty HVAC vans) as she's ready to be introduced, Sam begins to make her way down the hill of broken concrete to be closer to the show.

"Where are *you* going?" Yvette's voice chided from behind. Sam turned to see her silhouette backlit by the red, bare bulbs of the Cirque's signage, arms crossed over her chest, undoubtedly something disapproving on her shadowed face.

Sam barely opened her mouth.

"I hope those ladies dismissed you and you didn't sneak just sneak off."

Well, she had, she thought guiltily. But she wasn't going to miss Layla's show. "I didn't want to be in the way."

"I bet." Yvette turned to leave. "Get this out of your system and be back for dishes. Cooks don't clean in my car."

"Yes, ma'am," Sam replied, bowing for some reason before deciding that was ridiculous and turning to find a seat on a grassy hill opposite the rapt audience.

Layla begins with a series of close-up magic tricks aimed at the children present. Sam isn't close enough to hear the set up, but she's pretty sure none of them will have holes in their hands.

One small but fearless kid in a purple unicorn t-shirt raises her hand at the front of the audience and Layla asks her to whisper a wish in her ear.

Layla immediately leaps back with an impressed gasp and cries "to *fly?*" Then there's the muttering of instructions, something to do with spinning around as fast as she could while the crowd counts down from ten. Sam finds herself counting in a whisper. And by the time everyone gets down to three, a curious pink mist has solidified around the girl's shoulders. By two, the mist unfurls, and by one, reveals itself to be massive, glowing butterfly wings. The crowd gasps and Sam is on her feet as the girl appears to float a full six feet off the ground before settling back down again to uproarious applause.

"Impossible." Sam climbs down the short wall into the parking lot. By the time she reaches Layla, the magician has fireworks issuing from finger guns she's casting into the sky. They burst forth in shades of violet and gold. Every eye is filled with wonder, mouths agape as the sky lights up in the finale.

Layla bows and takes Sam's hand as they head back to the makeshift corridor made of mismatched panels from the prop car.

"Did you enjoy it?" Layla's glistening with sweat, but smiles brightly and undoes the red bowtie at her neck.

"Layla, how. *HOW,*" Sam manages. "Did she really fly? Was she some kind of...prop...child...I don't..."

And to her pleasant, heart-tripling surprise, Layla lifts her hand and kisses it. "Not now, love. I'm starving."

*

THE *CARLYLE* STEALS away in the night, heading westward. Half the Cirque staff are well and tuckered out, the other half make good use of their prize whiskey. Layla decides she will copy her interviews from the recorder long-hand before the next city where she'd collect more stories, take part in new recipes born of the cultural merging of refugees. In the meantime, she and Layla play Uno in the bunk, which Sam has decided is cozy if only for the right company. They share slices of tangerine and laugh quietly at their own jokes so as not to disturb the sleeping kitchen staff around them. Somewhere, a radio crackles with muffled commentary from the security team transitioning their shifts.

"When you said earlier that female magicians were just witches, did you...mean something by it?"

"What would I have meant?" Layla asks, flicking a Draw 4 onto the pile.

"I mean, were you trying to tell me something? About you. Or when you said you belonged with circus people."

"Something like what?"

Sam bites her lip. She could only play coy so long. Frankly, Layla's lucky Sam likes her so much.

"Well...are you a witch?" she asks outright. "Or a mutant or something?"

"That's a hell of a question, isn't it?" Layla replies between bites of tangerine, but her attention is clearly elsewhere. There's a flurry of activity between the cars as security gathers. The rumbling of the train tracks barely disguise the words coming over their radios. Sam makes out "lights ahead," "scout," and "convoy." Her pulse races as Layla leans out of the bed and whistles to a guard at the far end of the car. Sam looks back to see him gesture for her to join them.

"What is it? What's happening?" Sam insists.

"We got trouble." Layla slides her feet back into her untied boots and heads to the end of the car. Sam, for want of something smarter to do, follows.

They are led to the black box car before the tankers. It's an armory. Sam's stomach drops.

Redd is watching monitors, pensively poking his bottom lip with the antenna of his radio. He does a double-take when he notices Sam is present.

"Why is she here?"

"She's with me. It's fine. What's happening?" Layla's voice is different, more authoritative, less of a jokester.

"Drone's picked up four vehicles. They're en route to intercept us after this bridge up here."

"Looks like a well-regulated militia to me," Layla says.

Redd snorts. "Security's got their orders. I'll get the crew to tuck in."

"I'm up top," Layla declares before turning to Sam. "You gonna fall off the train or anything if I take you outside with me?"

"Outside...where? What, *while we're moving?*"

"Yeah. It's cool if you're squeamish. You can head back to the bunk car, just make sure you're on the floor away from the windows for like ten minutes."

Sam's mind races. This feels like it should be an urgent moment, brimming with imminent danger. But somehow the huge security guy and the magician are calm. "I just...can you help me understand for a second. What does a circus magician have to do with defense strategy against a…"

And it dawns on her. Redd's bored stare and Layla's pleasant but impatient one.

Layla's the secret weapon.

"*There* you go." Layla pats her on the back as if seeing the lightbulb go off over her head. "She's got it. You good?"

"I...yeah…" Sam hesitates.

"Then up we go."

They don harnesses at their waists and climb a narrow, steel staircase into the windy dark where a guard waits to tether them to the rooftop. Sam can barely make out more than the edges of things touched by moonlight, or the blinking lights on drone helicopters buzzing overhead. They lean into the wind as they cross to the forward end of the train. Sam's face stings and her eyes burn as she tries to keep them open. Layla seems barely bothered by any of it.

They stop and face south, unable to go further without crunching solar panels. Sam can see a short bridge over glittering water, and the flicker of headlights rushing to meet them on the other side of it.

"What will you do?" Sam shouts into Layla's ear.

Layla makes an O with her hand and pokes a finger through it. "Magic!" she shouts back.

Sam is trembling. She feels it first in her knees and thinks for a moment she might pitch herself over the side after all. In a matter of seconds, they will be within firing range of whatever guns these people have with them. And if they are going after a train, it won't be with pea-shooters.

"The front guards will engage first, don't worry," Layla shouts as if she hears Sam's thoughts. Sam wonders if that's a thing she can do. "You, I have a job for."

"*Me?*" Sam shrieks. "*Job?* What job? Why does everyone want to give me jobs?"

"We all have jobs. I can't do mine until I see the spot first. So you're going to count me down."

"What spot?"

"The Impossible Spot," Layla yells. "The last second of space between us and them. It's loud, it's dark, I have to focus. You just say when, alright? A three-count will do. Don't get fancy on me."

Sam's mind races with a thousand questions, none of which there seem to be time for. "I don't know if I can," she blurts.

"Count from three?" Layla raises an eyebrow.

"On top of a speeding train in a hail of bullets? No."

In an instant, Layla lunges and presses her lips against Sam's, warm hands cradling the sides of her face. She smells like coffee and theater smoke and gunpowder. The sound of rushing blood in Sam's ears is lost in the wind and the drone of the train. The sparks from bullets plinking off the iron surface might as well be starlight in her periphery.

Layla pulls back, holding Sam's gaze in hers as she speaks loudly, slowly. "You feeling confident now? Because we're in the shit, kid, and that was a goodbye kiss if we die here tonight because you can't do this."

"I… what?" Sam is still dazed, her adrenaline peaking with no idea what to do with itself. "Yes. Okay. Yes. I'll count."

"Three-two-one, yeah?"

"Yeah." Sam nods vigorously.

"Smashing." Layla winks at her. She turns away and lifts a finger, drawing a widening spiral on the back of her other hand as the *Carlyle* begins to cross the bridge. Sam searches the tree line ahead of them for signs of this Impossible Spot but there's nothing there but rapidly moving darkness. *Pings* and *thwips* of bullets fly through northern flora and pepper the atmosphere and the train's guards return fire. It's hard to focus when she feels like she should be dodging.

I should be doing dishes right now, she pouts. *I would* love *to be doing dishes right now.*

Halfway across the bridge, she gulps as lights bounce through the dark trees on a headlong trajectory, it seems, to meet the train.

That's it. That's them.

She takes a deep breath, trying to time the pace of her count so as not to kill them all. "Ready?" Sam calls out.

"Yeah!" Layla's voice catches on the wind.

The horn blows; Sam holds her breath and instinctively flattens herself against the train. It's hard not to blink with the wind in her eyes, but she holds fast, marveling at Layla's tall, focused stance atop the car.

"Three!" she shouts as they cross the bridge completely. The lights are brighter, the moments between the bullets are fewer.

"Two!" A road reveals itself behind the trees, illuminated by the moon and exposing a convoy of six vehicles, maybe seven, all speeding toward the railroad crossing ahead of them. At the last possible second, the moment before the first car reaches the track, she screams: "One!"

She doesn't blink as Layla raises an outstretched palm. The other side of the sky is visible through a hole in the center of it. Her shoulders dip back suddenly, as if absorbing some recoil. And with a pulse and a pop of atmosphere, like the sensation of sound being sucked from the air just before a thunderclap, a gaping black hole develops in the road just before the tracks, a perfect circle the precise diameter of a six-maybe-seven-vehicle convoy.

The train speeds by in time to see the bandits drop one by one into the pit, each driving much too fast to slow down. And as the last vehicle falls completely out of sight, the hole closes again, the old road complete with its cracks and ancient potholes, the forest trees back in their place beside the river.

*

SAM IS SPEECHLESS when they return to the armory car. She wants to tell Redd his flat "well done" is insufficient praise for whatever it was that just happened. She wants to ask Layla if she's okay, if she maybe needs to lie down, what had the kiss been about, and maybe if she'd liked it. But they walk back to her bunk as if they'd just come from a late dinner at the Currant, and Layla seems all too pleased to find the half a tangerine she'd forgotten about.

"Vitamin C," she says, chewing thirstily on a wedge. "*So* vital to putting holes in things. Who knew?"

Sam clicks on her recorder and places it on the bed between them. Layla inspects her Uno hand for next moves and Sam watches her.

"You get your…power…from oranges?" Sam asks.

Layla pauses thoughtfully. "Not exactly, but I'm more effective with them than without them. Ever try to do magic with scurvy?"

"I…no?" Sam mutters, only half certain the question was rhetorical. Her face is raw, cheeks buzzing with wind-burn and mild embarrassment. She chews at a dry spot on her bottom lip, wondering if it'd been this rough when Layla kissed her.

"Do you want to re-cap what happened up there? For posterity?"

The kiss. The plummeting of pirates into a gaping abyss. She'll let Layla decide.

"Me? No. Magicians and our secrets, after all. Do you?"

Sam narrows her eyes. There is elusive and then there's Layla.

A cook with an impish grin and a generally pungent air squeezes past someone climbing into a bunk and bumps Sam with a lumpy, mesh bag of potatoes. There is whispering and snickering as the cook stops in the aisle behind her, allowing other members of the kitchen staff to take them and hide potatoes in shoes and under pillows and mattresses.

"Oh. There they are," Layla muses. "You're not hiding from Yvette, are you? She'll be through here looking for lost produce sooner or later."

Sam sighs. "*Hiding* is a strong word but you're right. I should probably get to the kitchen. One question, though. Just the one."

Layla sighs, seemingly resigned, and Sam feels victorious. "Alright. What is it?"

"Where did that hole go?"

And here Layla shrugs, plying a slice of fruit into her mouth and dropping another Draw 4 on their stack.

"Hell, naturally."

The Ashes of Vivian Firestrike
Kristen Koopman

LISTENERS, YOU MAY have noticed that in this week's episode of *Murder and Mayhem: Stories from the Intersection of Magic and True Crime with Amy and Christy*, your hosts had a bit of a debate on the death of the Internet's favorite elementalist, Vivian Firestrike. It's not a big enough case for its own episode, but our aside sparked some discussions in the Facegroup page that were almost as contentious as the one on the pod. Since it's my week to do the minisode (Christy here), I figured I'd put together a primer for the case so you can all decide for yourselves whether you're Team Faked Her Death For No Apparent Reason or Team Sorry, She's Totally Dead, That's Just How It Is.

Not that I'm biased.

Tl;dr version: Three years ago, in 2015, Vivian Firestrike, arguably the most famous fire elementalist of our generation and definitely the most gifted, was attacked by an amateur practitioner named Bradley Clovenhoof. This was towards the end of that three-year period where everyone was dueling everyone—started, ironically, by Firestrike herself. Unsatisfied with then-current City Chief Elementalist Anthony Currentsrun's performance and frustrated at the lack of electoral recourse (note: since Firestrike's death, the position has gone from an appointment by the mayor to an elected post), Firestrike found an obscure law that had never been revoked that allowed her to challenge Currentsrun to a duel for his position. He hella lost and retired from the public eye to wallow in his humiliation probably, and suddenly everyone was challenging everyone else to duels again.

And lots of people, of course, were challenging Vivian Firestrike to duels. Clovenhoof did exactly that and of course Firestrike won, but she disappeared the next evening as the result of what authorities later figured out was his death curse.

So, here are the details. For the pictures, videos, and other media resources, check out our show notes; everything's numbered there, and I'll be specifying what I'm referring to if you want to follow along.

1.

LET'S START WITH the duel itself, and a content warning. The cell phone footage of the whole duel, including the gruesome parts, is on uVideo under the (tacky as hell) title "this duel really gets my goat." It all went down at about quarter to eight on Tuesday, October 21, when Firestrike emerged from the subway on her way to her first appearance on *Daily Coffee & Conjuration with Lee and Marie!* They'd been trying to get her on the show for a year, but it took her first major initiative in the City Chief Elementalist position to get her to agree to do it at all: the Color of Magic campaign. The tabloid Elementaweek later published her planned talking points:

- *More practitioners' licensing centers in low-income neighborhoods*
- *Change licensing exams to be less all European magic all the time*
- *Arrest rates for unlicensed magic are 34% higher for ethnic/racial minorities and that's messed up*
- *Last time Currentsrun was on, you asked him about his favorite magic tricks for Fourth of July parties, so maybe next time you call yourselves the "voice of the people, speaking truth to power" maybe think about asking some uncomfortable questions???*
- *Why do you care more about the assholes challenging me to duels than the people who would actually benefit from your attention and visibility?*
- *This is such bullshit.*
- *No I won't talk about my diet.*

Clovenhoof's friend Alexis Livinggreen took the footage, and the beginning of the clip shows Clovenhoof's satyr legs and hooves when he lifts one leg of his baggy cargo pants and says, "Let's see how she likes this! Dangerous duels, mofos!" Livinggreen posted the footage on their #dangerousduels challenge series on uVideo supposedly in honor of his friend, where the explicit content sparked a firestorm (no pun intended) of controversy. You can see the tree roots erupt through the sidewalk and spike through Firestrike's feet (which was Clovenhoof's first spell), and Clovenhoof's death seconds later can be seen in gruesome detail. Firestrike conjures a net of fire to contain him with light burns—one of her signature moves—but instead the net scorches its way through his flesh, lighting the sap in his veins and shooting flames through his open mouth as he releases his final curse. Livinggreen's retching is clearly audible. (And, yeah, dude. Me too.)

2.

OBVIOUSLY, NEXT, THE news went into overdrive. My personal favorite after-school special inspired by this case has to be the Investigation Hour episode on Clovenhoof's transformation. He was the first high-profile case of deliberate and willing self-transmogrification. Since most magic relies on the connection between a practitioner and their chosen element (in Clovenhoof's case, earth), a weak practitioner can become more powerful by being transformed into an elemental creature, such as an earth-aligned satyr. Though this has its own risks and drawbacks—transmogrification being considerably more difficult than pure elemental magic—once Clovenhoof brought the idea into the public consciousness, it sparked a brief trend that in turn led to this special report. The top-rated comment thread on the video, "Self-Transmogrification: What Are Your Kids *Really* Turning Into?", reads in its entirety:

"#kidglovesareoff ?"

"Satyr is the lowest form of wit."

"that's sarcasm, dumbass"

3.

Above, we have the crime scene photos of Firestrike's footfalls burned into the sidewalk. As we mentioned in our debate, such effects wouldn't have been uncommon for a fire elementalist like Firestrike. Channeling an elemental spell brings the practitioner closer to their element, and because of Firestrike's strength, she had no reason to suspect Clovenhoof's curse had turned her magic against her.

Because everything seemed fine aside from Clovenhoof, first-responders failed to secure the scene beyond where the duel occurred. Sections of concrete, carpet, and flooring stepped on by Firestrike later sold at auction, creating a considerable market of forged Firestrike footprints and associated footprint assessors.

4.

PAPARAZZI PHOTOS OF the crime scene and associated headlines, published in the day and a half between the duel and Firestrike's death. Our favorites include "FIRESTRIKE'S LATEST FLAMES PROVE FATAL: FULL SCOOP ON FORCED DUEL WITH SECRET SATYR" and "FOE, FAN, OR FATHER? PROOF OF FIRESTRIKE AND CLOVENHOOF'S SIZZLING HALF-SATYR SON." In the background of the photos, fans of Firestrike stand between the police tape and the studio where her appearance was scheduled. Why none of these fans realized that it might be in poor taste to display signs reading "I Burn for Firestrike!" and "Immolate Me, Vivian!" remains unexplained.

5.

THESE STILL IMAGES from subway security footage show Firestrike entering the station on her way home, against law enforcement's recommendation. Firestrike's (irrational) love of the subway was well-known, since she first gained national recognition when videos of her illusions for children and minor curses for rude behavior on the subway went viral.

(Note: Due to copyright issues, we've had to take down the image of Caleb Ivans's autobiography cover. On her final subway ride, Firestrike cursed Ivans to have, for the rest of his life, his knees stuck as far apart as they were on the train. As of this posting, Ivans's *Knee-Jerk Reaction: My Life as Vivian Firestrike's Last Victim* sold over 200,000 copies worldwide and became the cultural touchstone for discussions of manspreading everywhere.)

6.

MORE PAPARAZZI PHOTOS, these of Firestrike arriving at her apartment building after the fight. Although none of the paparazzi heeded her yell of "Could you give me some peace and *goddamn* quiet, for *once*," her hands spontaneously bursting into flames dissuaded them more successfully. The last photo in the set shows the fire-engulfed hands reflected in Firestrike's wide, staring eyes, although she quickly shook her hands out.

This was step one towards death, y'all. Or, sorry, *mysterious disappearance*.

7.

POLICE PHOTO OF marks on Firestrike's apartment door. A clear handprint grasping the knob and a small circular dead-mark on the door suggest prolonged contact of Firestrike's hand and head, respectively. This may be a sign that she stood at her apartment door, holding the knob and watching the metal soften red-hot under her fingers, her forehead smoldering an oval into the surface of the door.

Obviously, looking back, we know how early things got dire, but by this point it must have been clear to her that something was wrong.

8.

POLICE PHOTO OF Feinstein's *Compendium of Fatal Curses* found in Firestrike's apartment, open to the page describing the Golden Curse. Note the gentle trail of gray leading down the side of the paragraph describing how the curse turns the victim's own magic against them, amplifying it. Amy put it best in the episode (timestamp 37:24 for those of you listening along at home): "This curse is basically the Crocodile Dundee of death curses. It looked at Vivian Firestrike and said, '*That's* not fire magic. *This* is fire magic!' and then tried to burn her alive."

While the book damage can't be definitively attributed to Firestrike, it seems likely. She was alone in her apartment for several hours after the duel since her wife, Paloma Seer, had three panel discussions to moderate at the city's annual soothsaying convention, ConVoyance. In addition, Jared Ironroot later described this level of damage to borrowed books in his eulogy for Firestrike as "classic fuckin' Viv" while shaking his fist at the sky.

9.

EVIDENCE PHOTOS OF multiple flame-repelling tarps, standard

equipment for fire elementalists such as Firestrike, found in disarray across the floor of her apartment. Police reports also list additional cloth and underwire fragments found in the apartment indicating that she burned through ten shirts, four pairs of jeans, two skirts, three bras, and six pairs of shoes. Later in the day, spectators spotted her wearing clothing treated with flame-repelling charms. These notoriously uncomfortable suits are also known by fire elementalists as "instant unisex yeast-infections, just add elementalist."

So to recap at this point: Firestrike was definitely cursed and was definitely having fire magic problems as a result of that curse. #TeamSheDied.

10.

PHOTO OF LOT #622 at the Bid Against Dueling Charity Auction in 2017. Firestrike and Seer had dinner at Ceridwen's Cauldron the day of the duel, after news of Clovenhoof's death went public. This lot consists of the remains of items Firestrike damaged there: a water glass, four wine glasses, a highball glass, a plate, and a utensil set in addition to the seven cloth napkins she accidentally set ablaze. Ceridwen's Cauldron has since accumulated an additional Michelin star to go with the two it had on the evening in question, making it the perfect venue for a last meal—not to editorialize.

Seer, a noted eccentric, claims that they discussed her latest batch of predictions for Firestrike's weekly magical circular, *Firestrike Fridays*. The predictions Seer provided to police included "Taurus: 5 Across is 'Millard Fillmore'," "Gemini: Your mail will be delivered at 3:46," "Libra: You will be pulled over for an expired vehicle registration in two days even though this column reminded you to renew it," and "Sagittarius: Your keys are on the floor behind your desk, but you can't reach them without the grill tongs."

Phone records show that Seer called another mutual friend of theirs while at dinner: the master transmogrifier Simon Formcaster. When asked about this call by police, Seer stated that it was a drunken prank call in which they asked if his refrigerator was running and, when he answered yes, suggested he should turn something into a net to catch it.

Formcaster corroborated this story to the police with a deep and aggrieved sigh.

11.

THE SOLE SURVIVING photo of Seer and Firestrike leaving Ceridwen's Cauldron that night, showing Seer visibly off-balance and Firestrike sprouting massive flames from her extended left middle finger. It was taken on a cell phone, since Firestrike turned all of the paparazzi cameras into swarms of bees.

(For a more in-depth discussion of whether turning inanimate material into swarms of bees shows that Firestrike could transmogrify, let alone self-transmogrify, listen to the episode. Suffice it to say, we don't know because it depends on the bees.)

Photographer Neil Maricon, notorious for his photos of Firestrike's sister leaving the hospital after a miscarriage in 2012, filed his second police report against Firestrike over the loss of the camera even though she had been declared legally dead at that point (we'll come back to the conspiracy theories in a sec). The first lawsuit accused her of placing a curse on him that singed off all the hair on his body overnight, every night, leaving only enough to spell out "OBJECTIVELY AWFUL" across the back of his head. Courts dismissed the lawsuit after Firestrike's death, and before that she gave only one public comment on the case: "Maybe his hair wants everyone to know what scum he is."

12.

STILL PHOTO OF the *Lee and Marie!* interview with Amanda Karlsen, the barista who served Firestrike, Seer, and their colleague Jared Ironroot the next morning at Beelzebub Coffee and Bakeshop. According to Karlsen, Firestrike twice attempted to take her coffee in paper to-go cups, both of which burst into flames at her touch and were immediately doused with the coffee itself. After that, she took a porcelain mug.

Estimates of the heat required to light a to-go cup aflame are consistent with projections of the effects of Clovenhoof 's Golden Curse, culminating in an official time of death of approximately 11:50 that night.

It's generally accepted that Firestrike consulted with Ironroot about the limits of Clovenhoof's abilities as a satyr, since Ironroot specialized in earth magic. It's still debated whether Clovenhoof's self-transmogrification made him powerful enough to deliver a fatal curse. Though Ironroot has not publicly discussed the case, police listed a heat-damaged copy of *The Secrets of Elemental Beasts: From the Silent Speed of the Kraken to the Quiet Voice of the Phoenix* belonging to Ironroot in their inventory of Firestrike's apartment.

Now, this is where the conspiracy theories—sorry, *alternate explanations* about Firestrike begin. As Amy pointed out in the episode, Firestrike was famous for three things: her temper, her talent, and her fuck-you attitude. That combination made her City Chief Elementalist, and it also made her a celebrity, and a lot of people argue that it also made her the last person who would sit around and wait for a death curse to come to pass. To which I say, you can accomplish anything if you work hard and believe in yourself...except overcoming a death curse through sheer force of will.

13.

POLICE PHOTO OF a notebook and pen found in Firestrike's apartment. The note on the page reads: "This is the last will and testament of Vivian Firestrike. If you're reading this, then I'm dead and don't care, so: Paloma Seer is my executor. Do whatever."

14.

THE RECEIPT FROM Baba Yaga's Big-Box Sorcery Supply Co. found in the apartment. Although Seer's credit card purchased the items, some believe they were intended for Firestrike as Seer also returned with lunch for two from Chupacabra's Kabobs and Gyros.

The receipt lists chameleon scales, caterpillar cocoon silk, the baby teeth of a hare, rosebuds, a vial of Western Wind, and phoenix feathers. These are common materials for transmogrification spells, although more typical components are missing (such as dyes, leftover coins, and copies of Kafka novels).

This led to the rise of conspiracy theories that Firestrike faked her death by transmogrifying her own face. Her discomfort and displeasure with her celebrity-elementalist status, and the duel challenges it brought with increasing frequency since the #dangerousduels movement began, is well-documented. (For more on that, her two best biographies are *Sometimes the Phoenix Doesn't Rise: The True Story of America's Favorite Flame* and *Firestruck: The Downfall of the First Social-Media Celebrelementalist*.) Our discussion in this week's episode goes into this in more depth. It shouldn't be too hard to figure out which of us is on which side, but for the sake of balance, I'll just note again that while Firestrike was a very strong practitioner of magic, there is no evidence that she ever engaged in heavy-duty transmogrification, bees notwithstanding.

But the fact remains: what does it matter if she disguised herself using magic when there's no sign she managed to break the curse? There were witnesses—not perfect or eyewitnesses, but still expert witnesses—who told police that they felt the curse take effect. That means she's dead.

15.

PHOTO OF THE Elvis impersonator claiming to be Vivian Firestrike in hiding. This claim was refuted by DNA, fingerprint evidence, and dental records. (Yeah, sounds pretty dumb when I say it like that, doesn't it, *Amy*?)

16.

PHOTO OF SEER's tattoo, done on the one-year anniversary of Firestrike's death. As Seer told Moonglow Magazine in their 2016 profile of her, "The last time we touched skin-to-skin, she kissed my hand. She worked so hard and in such a short time redefined what a Chief Elementalist could do, but when that curse came for her, her priority was making sure I knew how she felt. This tattoo over the burn scar reminds me of all the ways she's always with me, even if it's different from what we had before." Tabloid *The Daily Magician* ran this photo on its cover with the headline "TORRID LOVE ENDS IN FLAMES: PALOMA SEER ONE YEAR LATER" Seer reposted the cover to her Picturebook account with the caption "It's not torrid if you're married, jackasses," the hashtag #galsbeingpals, and an eyeroll emoji.

17.

POLICE PHOTOS OF the roof of Jared Ironroot's apartment building, where Firestrike is believed to have died. Note the faint smoke still rising from the black footprints from the access door to the very center of the roof, and the streaks of soot bursting from their endpoint. Her flame-repelling clothing can be seen untouched in the center of the blast radius, and her emptied backpack was found on the other side of the water tank from where this photo was taken. Several empty vials, jars, and pouches were found scattered by the explosion, but no other sign of the contents of the backpack. One paparazzo who photographed Firestrike on her way into Ironroot's building noted the clinking of glass when she entered, but Firestrike loudly and slurringly proclaimed, "Haven't you heard? I'm about to invent tequila-pong!"

There were no direct witnesses, although the magicians at Ironroot's full-moon celebration below sensed the essence of her magic and of fire too strong for any human to survive, even one as talented as Firestrike. Neighbors reported a crackling explosion resounding from the roof, and one called the police to suggest someone was setting off fireworks. A particularly large piece of flaming debris was seen soaring, unfurling like a set of wings, across the roofs of the city toward the moon. This was likely the largest piece of Vivian Firestrike that remained after the curse took hold, and it was never recovered.

18.

AMY INSISTED THAT I include this one, and she wrote out what I should say:

Maybe Vivian Firestrike is dead. Maybe Bradley Clovenhoof and every other edgelord that tried to take her down a notch won in the end. Or maybe Vivian decided that she was done playing the game, and that nobody had a right to watch her every second of every day and challenge her to duels on the street and plaster her face on the covers of magazines while talking about her "enchanting style" instead of the values that she fought so hard for.

So here's a photo of Seer and her adopted pet phoenix, which she named Vivian. The silhouette of Seer stands on a beach, bracketed in the dusky stripe of Earth's shadow by sand below her and the pink-touched sunset sky above. The incandescent form of the phoenix Vivian, only partially captured while in motion, burns a line across the exposure.

Most phoenixes are capable of speech, but Seer claims hers is "just camera shy" and "will talk in public when she's good and ready." Still, she reposted the photo to her personal Picturebook account, where Jared Ironroot commented, "If phoenixes had middle fingers (talons?), she'd be giving it. Classic fuckin' Viv."

Seer's caption was only one word: "Freedom."

Portrait of Three Women with an Owl

Gwen C. Katz

S OME ARTISTIC MOVEMENTS are not fully appreciated until after the artists' time. Some enjoy immediate fame, only to fade from the spotlight as the years pass. And then there are the movements that, through no fault of the artists, never quite have their moment in the sun. Into this third category falls the subject of the Musée National d'Art Moderne (MNAM)'s excellent new exhibition, *Surradia: A Retrospective*.

Surradia has frequently been misclassified as a subgenre of surrealism (*Gardner's Art Through the Ages* still makes this mistake as of the 16th edition). Thus, the surradists, when they are shown at all, are often relegated to a small "female artists" corner of a larger surrealist exhibition.

Many critics and historians are predisposed to dismiss female artists out of hand. Women's art is often seen as small, personal, and unambitious, with little to say about the outside world. Surradia, with its themes of self-knowledge, may initially seem like an easy target for such criticisms. However, within the intimacy of the surradists' art we find incisive and groundbreaking attitudes in stark contrast to the modest domesticity expected of female artists.

But the greatest barrier the surradists have faced is undoubtedly the movement's abrupt and enigmatic ending. Disappearing as they did in the midst of the German occupation of France, they left no heirs, few connections in the art world, and a long list of unanswered questions. Who is the artist of the unsigned canvas known as "Portrait of Three Women with an Owl?" Were they responsible for the fate of the SS officer who occupied Vidal's house? Do they have any connection to the legendary Fox Girl of Fontainebleau? We may never know. But the MNAM exhibition provides tantalizing new clues.

Like many art movements, the boundaries of surradia
are difficult to define, and some have argued that surradist
scholars are too prone to classify artists by the manner of their
death rather than the content of their art. MNAM, however,
chooses to focus on the three artists who are almost universally
acknowledged as the heart of the movement: Alice Penderwood,
Corine Moriceau, and Amaya Vidal.

The auburn-haired Penderwood came to Paris from
Connecticut in 1936 as the lover of André Breton. She received
much critical acclaim for her early work, such as *The Debutante*
(1937), which already featured the recurring motif of a fox.
But though she was fascinated by the psychological side of
surrealism, she often clashed with the opinionated surrealist
leader. When asked her opinion about woman's role as the male
artist's muse, her reply was one word: "Bullshit." Unsurprisingly,
she soon left Breton and began developing her own style. An
avid cook, she abandoned oil paints and began making her own
egg tempera using natural pigments, creating paintings with
jewel-like tones that evoke medieval art. Later, beginning with
Procession at the Penderwood Estate (c. 1938), leaves, twigs, dirt, and
other natural materials began to enter her work. The MNAM
exhibition has done an admirable job establishing a chronology
out of these often-undated pieces.

The Dominican-born Moriceau also began her art career
among the surrealists, who she initially met as a model. But
unlike the brash Penderwood, 19-year-old Moriceau felt
intimidated among so many famous names. She rarely spoke
at gatherings. While she painted prolifically, she hesitated to
show or sell her work, much of which she gave away to friends or
family. MNAM has managed to locate two of these previously
uncatalogued works: *A Young Girl Discovers the Phases of the Moon*
and *The Invention of Music* (both c. 1936). Close friends with
Penderwood, she left the surrealist group shortly after her friend
did.

Moriceau is easily the most overlooked of the surradists, and
it's refreshing to see an exhibition finally acknowledge her central
role in the movement. Her work is deeply personal, featuring lone
individuals in fantastical versions of homelike settings. Moriceau's

large eyes and heart-shaped face appear on the subjects of her paintings, whether male or female. Her most common motif is a white stag, appearing either as a whole animal, a human with antlers, or, as in *The Pantry of Grandmother Night* simply a pair of antlers in the background. Several excellent essays have already explored the question of why Moriceau's animal avatar was a stag and not, as might be expected, a doe; however, the MNAM exhibition does not touch on this question.

Vidal, a French-born artist of Argentinian descent, was unique in her refusal to associate with the surrealists, though their influence is nevertheless apparent in her work. The eldest of the surradists, she already had a successful art career by the mid-1930s. Most of the writing about Vidal has focused on her eccentric lifestyle, wearing elaborate feathered gowns and allowing her beloved Persian cats to eat off her plate, and MNAM does fall into this trap, exhibiting several of her surviving outfits. But it also features a broad selection of her dark, eerie paintings with their themes of death and decay. The animal that appears most frequently in Vidal's work is, curiously, not a cat, but an owl.

Vidal was the inventor of the split-canvas motif that would become so distinctive over the next two years. A wall, tree, or other barrier divides the canvas into two scenes which are interrelated, yet subtly different. *Memory of Autumn* (1933) depicts a forest that is in leaf on one side of the painting and bare on the other. In *Portrait of Alice Penderwood* (1939), Penderwood passes through a gateway and comes out wearing a steel breastplate. Are the two sides past and present, or dream and reality? Or, perhaps, are both sides equally illusory? All three surradists would delve deep into this enigma during their time together.

In 1938, Vidal invited Penderwood and Moriceau to leave Paris and come stay at her house in Fontainebleau, and over the following year, surradia truly came into its own. There has been much speculation about the nature of this living situation, particularly between Penderwood and Moriceau, and several affectionate letters between the two featured in the exhibition will no doubt add fuel to the fire. It was here that Moriceau coined the name "surradia," which, she claims, came to her in a dream.

Art lovers may find the next room of the exhibition difficult to stomach. After the French surrender, the surrealists scattered, relying on American friends or even arranged marriages to get out of Europe, but the surradists lacked their connections and were forced to remain. A division of SS officers led by the brutish Oberführer Baer occupied Vidal's house, where they forced the women to cook and clean for them and defaced their artwork. I admit I was unable to maintain scholarly objectivity at the sight of the paintings that had been slashed with knives or painted with crude Nazi slogans. Saddest of all, the exhibition includes several photos of Penderwood's lost masterpiece *Who Are You, Silent One?* (c. 1939), which was burned in the bonfire of July 27, 1942 in the gardens of Jeu de Paume.

We don't know what incident proved to be the breaking point for the surradists, but we do know that in early 1940, the three women abandoned their house to the Nazis and fled into the woods, leaving their artwork behind.

Most of the locals assumed Baer had killed the women, and this opinion is still held by some in the art world to this day. But the postwar discovery of a small log lean-to in the woods reveals a different fate. The lean-to had apparently been abandoned for some time. It was in disrepair and, based on the strong animal smell, various creatures had used it as a den. Several types of scat were found inside, as well as an abandoned birds' nest near the fire hole. It contained a cooking pot, an axe, three moss-lined sleeping pallets, and the crown jewel of the MNAM exhibition: The unsigned painting *Portrait of Three Women with an Owl* (c. 1940), painted on a wooden panel using only natural pigments.

The three women in the painting are unmistakable. But which one was the artist? Wisely, MNAM takes no position on this question. The owl, of course, suggests Vidal. The use of natural materials points to Penderwood, though it may have been a matter of simple necessity. And the setting—a kitchen that resembles a medieval alchemy lab—most closely aligns with Moriceau's work. The three women surround a cauldron, clad only in leaves and lichen, each holding a long spoon handle. A vaulted archway divides the room. On one side are Penderwood and most of Moriceau in a dark brick room stocked with bottles of mysterious substances. On the other side is Vidal with her owl on her shoulder, but now the kitchen is made entirely of old, knobby trees, one growing into the next.

The surradists, it seems, survived in the woods for several months.

What became of them? The final room of the exhibition is devoted to this question. Three artworks of uncertain provenance that have been attributed to the surradists are on display. One, a landscape that showed up at an auction in Chicago, attributed to Penderwood, is almost certainly a hoax, but the two Vidals—one found in an abandoned house in Fontainebleau, the other recovered from the basement of a church—are much more intriguing. Found in 1949 and 1952 respectively, each set off a wave of speculation that the artist was still alive. Forensic experts have verified the works' authenticity, but it's impossible to determine when they were originally painted.

Here the otherwise strong exhibition finally falters, devoting the entire back wall to an overly credulous display of mysteries and enigmas that have been linked to the surradists over the years. There are several newspaper articles covering the rash of unusual animal encounters in the Seine-et-Marne area in the postwar years, including multiple sightings of leucistic deer and one case of an owl that flew into a house and refused to leave. One amusing (if unconvincing) inclusion is the original drawing of the Fox Girl of Fontainebleau, a cryptid sighted by a 14-year-old girl in 1976. She claimed she was walking in the woods when she saw a woman with wild red hair, dressed in a tunic made of animal skins. The woman ran into a copse of trees and, when the girl reached the copse, she found nothing but a fox fleeing into the underbrush. The story has been widely discredited—the reporter who first broke the story was a notorious hoaxer—but there are still scattered claims of sightings to this day.

The centerpiece of this final room, however, is an exhibit on the death of Oberführer Baer. Baer was found dead in the living room of Vidal's house on December 4, 1940. His body was covered in bruises and contusions, there were bite marks on his arms, and his face had been gouged by a bird's talons. The windows and doors of the house were thrown open, the floor scattered with leaf litter that had apparently blown in.

The coroner ruled that he had been mauled to death by wild animals, and though the ever-paranoid Vichy police classified it as a murder and investigated the whole town on the suspicion that someone might have somehow lured the beasts inside and set them on him, they were unable to determine who could have staged such a bizarre crime. Baer's death remains unsolved to this day. The exhibition features Baer's torn SS uniform, as well as the original police photos of the crime scene, laid out for the viewer to piece together.

Surradia is a beautiful and deeply underappreciated movement, one that was cut short before its time by its creators' sudden disappearance. One can't help but speculate how the history of 20th-century art might have gone differently had the artists survived the war and gone on to take their rightful place in the art world. This extensive and well-curated exhibition is sure to spark renewed interest in these extremely interesting women and their art, as well as in the natural world they loved so much. I myself, while I was composing this review, was struck to see a large gray owl perched on the fence outside my window, fluffing its feathers and staring at me.

Surradia: A Retrospective will be on display until June 20.

If You Take My Meaning

Charlie Jane Anders

They woke up stuck together again, still halfway in a shared dream, as the city blared to life around them. The warm air tasted of yeast, from their bodies, and from the bakery downstairs.

Mouth lay on one side of Sophie, with Alyssa on the other, sprawled on top of a pile of blankets and quilted pads. Alyssa couldn't get used to sleeping in a bedpile out in the open, after spending half her life in a nook—but Sophie insisted that's how everybody did things here. Sophie herself hadn't slept in a bedpile for ages, since she went away to school, but it was how she'd been raised.

"I guess it's almost time to go," Sophie whispered, with a reluctance that Alyssa could feel in her own core.

"Yeah," Alyssa muttered. "Can't keep putting it off."

Sophie peeled her tendrils off Mouth and Alyssa carefully, so Alyssa felt as if she was waking up a second time. One moment, Alyssa had a second heart inside her heart, an extra stream of chatter running under the surface of her thoughts. And then it was gone, and Alyssa was just one person again. Like the room got colder, even though the shutters were opening to let in the half-light.

Alyssa let out a low involuntary groan. Her bones creaked, and her right arm had gone half-numb from being slept on.

"You don't have to," Sophie whispered. "If you don't…if you'd rather hold off."

Alyssa didn't answer, because she didn't know what to say.

Mouth laughed. "You know Alyssa. Her mind don't change." Mouth's voice was light, but with a faint growl, like she wished Alyssa *would* change her mind, and stay.

The tendrils grew out of the flat of Sophie's ribcage, above her breasts, and they were surrounded by an oval of slightly darker skin, with a reddish tint, like a burn that hadn't healed all the way (just a few inches upward and to the left, Sophie's shoulder had an actual burn-scar). Someone might mistake the tendrils for strange ornaments, or a family of separate creatures nesting on Sophie's flesh, until you saw how they grew out of her, and the way she controlled their motion.

Whenever Alyssa's bare skin made contact with that part of Sophie's body, she could experience Sophie's thoughts, or her memories. Whatever Sophie wanted to lay open to her. But when the three of them slept in this pile, Sophie didn't share anything in particular. Just dream slices, or half-thoughts. Mouth still couldn't open herself up to the full communication with Sophie most of the time, but she'd taken to the sleep-sharing.

All three of them had their own brand of terrifying dreams, but they'd gotten better at soothing each other through the worst.

"So that's it." Mouth was already pulling on her linen shift and coarse muslin pants, and groping for her poncho. "You're going up that mountain, and the next time we see you, you'll... you'll be like Sophie. The two of you will be able to carry on whole conversations, without once making a sound."

Mouth looked away, but not before Alyssa caught sight of the anxiety on her face. Alyssa could remember when she used to have to guess at what the fuck Mouth was thinking, but that was a long time ago.

Sophie noticed, too, and she sat up, still in her nightclothes. "You don't ever have to worry about a thing." Sophie's voice was so quiet, Alyssa had to lean closer to hear. "No matter what happens, after all we've been through, the three of us are in this together."

"Yeah," Alyssa said, punching Mouth's arm with only a couple knuckles. "No amount of alien grafts are going to mess up our situation."

"Yeah, I know, I know, it's just..." Mouth laughed and shook her head, like this was a silly thing to worry about. "It's just, the two of you will have this whole other language. I'll be able to listen, but not talk. I wish I could go through that whole transformation, but that's not *me*. I need to keep what's in my head inside my head. I just…I want you both to fulfill your potential. I don't want to be holding the two of you back."

Alyssa leaned her head on Mouth's left shoulder, and Sophie's head rested on the right. "You speak to us in all the ways that matter," Sophie said.

"It's true," Alyssa said. "You already tell us everything we ever need to know."

Alyssa had grown up with romances, all about princes, duels, secret meetings, courtships, first kisses, and last trysts. She'd have said that real life could never be half as romantic as all those doomed lovers and secret vows…except now, those stories seemed cheap and flimsy, compared to the love she'd found, here in this tiny room.

For a moment, Alyssa wanted to call the whole thing off. Climb the Old Mother later, maybe just go back to bed. But then she shook it off.

She pulled on her boots.

"It's time."

✳

ALYSSA HAD HANDLED all kinds of rough terrain in her smuggler days. She'd even gone into the night without any protective gear one time. So she figured the Old Mother would be nothing. But by the time she got halfway up, her hamstrings started to throb and her thighs were spasming. Next to her, Mouth spat out little grunts of exhaustion. Only Sophie seemed to be enjoying pulling herself up from handhold to handhold.

"Shit shit shit. How the fuck did you ever get used to climbing this beast?" Alyssa wheezed.

Sophie just rolled her shoulders. And mumbled, "It wasn't a choice at first."

Behind them, Xiosphant had gone dark and still, just a valley of craggy shapes without highlights. Except for one light blaring from the top of the Palace, where the Vice Regent could never bring herself to obey the same shutters-up rule that all of her people lived by. Alyssa didn't want to risk falling, so she only half-turned for an instant, to see the storm damage, still unrepaired. And the piles of debris, where the fighting between the Vice Regent's forces and the new Uprising had briefly escalated to heavy cannon fire.

Everyone knew Bianca couldn't last as Vice Regent, but they had no notion whether she would hold on for a few more sleeps, or half a lifetime. Alyssa tried to avoid mentioning her name, even though her face was impossible to avoid, because Sophie still nursed some complicated regrets, and Mouth still felt guilty for helping to lead Bianca down a thorny path. Alyssa was the only one in their little family with clear-cut feelings about the Vice Regent: pure, invigorating hatred.

Alyssa wanted to stop and rest mid-climb, but the cruel slope of the Old Mother included no convenient resting places, especially for three people. And it would be a shitty irony if they almost reached the top, but slipped and fell to their deaths because they wanted to take a breather. The air felt colder and thinner, and Alyssa's hard-won aplomb was being severely tested.

"My fingers are bleeding," Mouth groaned. "Why didn't you mention our fingers would bleed?"

Sophie didn't answer.

They reached the top, which also formed the outer boundary of nothing. Ahead of Alyssa were no sights, no smells (because her nose got numb) and no sensations (because her skin was wrapped in every warm thing she could find). No sound but a crashing wind, which turned into subtle terrible music after a while.

Alyssa's mother and uncles had sent her off to the Absolutists' grammar school back home in Argelo, when she was old enough to walk and read. That was her earliest distinct memory: her mom holding one of her hands and her uncle Grant holding the other, marching her down around the bend in the gravel back road to the front gate where the school convened at regular intervals. That moment rushed back into her head now, as Sophie and Mouth fussed over her and prepared to send her away to another kind of school.

Mouth was pressing a satchel into Alyssa's hands. "I got as many of those parallelogram cakes as I could fit into a bag. Plus these salt buns, that taste kind of like cactus-pork crisps. And there are a few of your favorite romances tucked in, too."

"Thank you." Alyssa wrapped her arms around Mouth's neck. She couldn't tell if her eyes stung due to tears or the wind, or both. "I'll be back soon. Don't let Sophie take any more foolish risks."

"I'll do my best," Mouth said. "Say hi to the Gelet from me. And tell them…" She paused. "You know what? Just 'hi' is plenty."

Then Sophie was hugging Alyssa. "I can't get over how brave you are. You're the first person ever to visit this city, knowing exactly what's going to happen."

"Oh shut up." Alyssa was definitely starting to cry.

"I mean it. Your example is going to inspire a lot more people to go there. I think Mustache Bob is close to being ready." Sophie choked on the mountain air. "Come back safe. We need you. I love you."

"I love you too. Both of you." Alyssa started to say something else, but a massive, dark shell was rising out of the darkness on the far side of the mountain. "Shit. I need to go."

Alyssa let go of Sophie, clutching the satchel, and gave Mouth one last smile, then turned to face the writhing tentacles of the nearest Gelet. These two slippery ropes of flesh groped the air, reaching out to her.

*

As soon as they swathed Alyssa in woven moss and lifted her in their tentacles, she freaked out. She couldn't move, couldn't escape, couldn't even breathe. Her inner ear could not truck with this rapid descent down a sheer cliff, and somehow she wasn't ready for this disorientation, even though she'd talked through it with Sophie over and over. Alyssa wanted to yell that she'd changed her mind, this was a mistake, she wanted to go back to her family. But the Gelet would never understand, even if she could make herself heard.

She kept going down and down. Alyssa tried to tell herself this was just like being inside the Resourceful Couriers' sleep nook next to Mouth, except that she was alone, and she couldn't just pop out if she wanted to pee or stretch or anything. She held herself rigid as long as she could, and then she snapped—she thrashed and screamed, twisting her body until her spine wrenched.

A random memory popped up in Alyssa's head: huddling with the other Chancers in the hot gloom of a low-ceilinged basement on the day side of Argelo, after the Widehome job had gone flipside. (Because they'd burned down the wrong part of the building.) Lucas had squatted next to Alyssa, listing chemical formulas in a low voice, his usual anxiety strategy, and Wendy had fidgeted without making any sound. Every bump and croak above their heads instantly became, in Alyssa's mind, the Jamersons coming to murder them for what they'd done. This was the most terrified Alyssa had ever been, or probably ever would be, but also the closest she'd ever felt to anybody. These people were her indivisible comrades, any of them would die for the others, they were safe together in horrible danger.

Alyssa would always look back on that time in her life as the ideal, the best, the moment when she had a hope-to-die crew by her side, even though she could see all the flaws and the tiny betrayals. Honestly, she'd had way better friend groups since then, including the Resourceful Couriers, but that didn't change how she felt.

Alyssa did not do well with helplessness, or chains, or trusting random strangers. But wasn't that the whole point of this leap into darkness? Alyssa would get this mostly untested surgery, and then she would be able to share unfalsifiable information, and have massively expanded threat awareness thanks to the alien sensory organs. Sometimes you have to be more vulnerable in the short term, so that you can become more formidable later.

They must've reached the foot of the Old Mother without Alyssa noticing, what with all the turbulence. She had a sensation of moving forward, rather than downward, and her position in the web of tentacles shifted somewhat as well, and then at last they came to a stop and the Gelet unwrapped her tenderly. She landed on her feet inside a dark tunnel that sloped downward. This was almost scarier than the aftermath of the

Widehome job, or at least it was scary in a different way.

They led her down the tunnel, patient with all her stumbles. She couldn't see shit, but at least she was moving under her own power.

Alyssa kept reminding herself of what Sophie had said: she was the first human ever to visit the Gelet city, knowing what awaited her there. She was a pioneer.

The air grew warm enough for Alyssa to remove some of the layers of moss, and there were faint glimmers of light up ahead, so she must be entering the Gelet city proper. They needed to find a better name for it than "the midnight city." Something catchy and alluring, something to make this place a destination.

"I'm the first human to come down here with my eyes open, knowing what awaits," Alyssa said, loud enough to echo through the tunnel.

"Actually," a voice replied from the darkness ahead of her. "You're not. You're the second, which is almost as good. Right?"

*

HIS NAME WAS Jeremy, and he had worked with Sophie at that fancy coffee place, the Illyrian Parlour. Ginger hair, fair skin, nervous hands, soft voice. He'd been in the Gelet city a while already, maybe a few turns of the Xiosphanti shutters, but they hadn't done anything to alter him yet. "I can show you around, though I don't know the city very well, because large areas of it are totally dark." He sounded as though he must be smiling.

"Thanks," Alyssa said. "Appreciate any and all local knowledge."

Jeremy kept dropping information about himself, as if he didn't care at all about covering his tracks. He'd been part of the ruling elite in Xiosphant, studying at one of those fancy schools, until he'd fallen in love with a person of the wrong gender. Fucking homophobic Xiosphanti.

So he'd gone underground, slinging coffee to stressed-out working people, and that had been his first real encounter with anyone whose feet actually touched the ground, instead of walking on a fluffy cloud of privilege.

The Gelet had cleared a room, somewhere in the bowels of their unseeable city, for human visitors, with meager lighting, and some packs of food that had come straight from the Mothership. Alyssa and Jeremy opened three food packs and traded back and forth, sharing the weird foods of their distant ancestors: candies, jerky, sandwiches, some kind of sweet viscous liquid.

They bonded over sharing ancient foods, saying things like: "Try this one, it's kind of amazing."

Or: "I'm not sure this stuff has any nutritional value, but at least the aftertaste is better than the taste."

Alyssa chewed in silence and half-darkness for a while, then the pieces fell into place. "Oh," she said to Jeremy. "I just figured out who you are. You're the guy who tried to get Sophie to use her new abilities as a propaganda tool against the Vice Regent. She told us about you."

"I know who you are, too." Jeremy leaned forward, so his face took on more substance. "You're one of the foreign interlopers who helped the Vice Regent to take power in Xiosphant. You stood at Bianca's right hand, until she had one of her paranoid episodes. We have you to thank for our latest misery."

Alyssa couldn't believe she'd shared food with this man, just a short time ago.

"I'm going to go for a walk." Once she'd said this out loud, Alyssa was committed, even though it meant getting to her feet and walking out into a dark maze that included the occasional nearly bottomless ravine. At least the Gelet would keep an eye on her.

Probably.

Alyssa tried to walk as if she knew where she was going, as if she felt totally confident that the next step wouldn't take her into a wall or off the edge. She swung her arms and strode forward and tried not to revisit the whole ugly history of regime change in Xiosphant, and her part in it. She had trusted the wrong person, that was all.

What was Alyssa even doing here? All she wanted was to bury her past deeper than the lowest level of this city, but soon she would have the ability to share all her memories with random strangers. And she knew from talking to Sophie that it was easy to share way more than you bargained for—especially at first.

Alyssa might just reach out to someone for an innocent conversation, and end up unloading the pristine memory of the moment when she'd pledged her loyalty to a sociopath. The moment when Alyssa had believed that she'd found the thing she'd searched for since the Chancers fell apart, and that she would never feel hopeless again. Or Alyssa might share an image of the aftermath: herself wading through fresh blood, inside the glitzy walls of the Xiosphanti Palace.

"This was a mistake," Alyssa said to the darkness. "I need to go home. Sophie will understand. Mouth will be relieved. I should never have come here. When they offer to change me, I'll just say no, I'll make them understand. And then they'll have to send me home."

She almost expected Jeremy to answer, but he was nowhere near. She'd wandered a long way from their quarters, and there was no sound but the grumbling of old machines, and the scritching of the Gelet's forelegs as they moved around her.

*

"I'm not sure I can go through with this," Alyssa told Jeremy, when she'd somehow groped her way back to the living quarters. "I can't stand the idea of inflicting my past on anyone else."

"I'm definitely going ahead with it," Jeremy replied after a while. "When Sophie showed me what she could do, I couldn't even believe what a great organizing tool this could be. This is going to transform the new Uprising, because people will be able to see the truth for themselves, without any doubt or distortion."

Alyssa had wanted to avoid Jeremy, or shut out his self-righteous nattering. But they were the only two humans for thousands of kilometers, and she couldn't go too long without another human voice, as it turned out.

"So you're about to become one of the first members of a whole new species," Alyssa said, "and you're just going to use it as a recruiting tool for another regime change? So you can take power, and then someone else can turn around and overthrow you in turn? Seems like kind of a waste."

"At least I'm not—" Jeremy barked. Then he took a slow breath and shifted. His silhouette looked as if he was hugging himself. "It's not just about unseating your friend Bianca. It's not. It's about building a movement. I spent so much time in that coffeehouse, listening to people who could barely even give voice to all the ways they were struggling. We need a new kind of politics."

"Bianca's not my friend. I hate her too, in ways that you could never understand." Alyssa found more of the rectangular flat candy and ate a chunk. "But if enough people become hybrids, and learn to share the way Sophie shares, we could have something better than just more politics. We could have a new *community*. We could share resources as well as thoughts. We could work with the Gelet."

"Sure, sure," Jeremy said. "Maybe eventually."

"Not eventually," Alyssa said. "Soon."

"What makes you think a lot of people will buy into that vision, if you're not even willing to go through with it yourself?"

Alyssa groaned. "Look. I'm just saying…You have to be doing this for the right reasons, or it'll end really badly. You'll lose yourself. I saw it again and again, back in Argelo, people burning up everything they were just for the sake of allegiances or ideology or whatever."

They didn't talk for a while, but then they went back to arguing. There wasn't anything else to do, and besides, by the sound of it, Jeremy had been a good friend to Sophie, back when she'd really needed someone. So Alyssa didn't want him to wreck his psyche, or his heart, or whatever, by turning his memories into propaganda.

"I can be careful." Jeremy sounded as if he was trying to convince himself. "I can share only the memories and thoughts that will make people want to mobilize. I can keep everything else to myself."

"Maybe," was all Alyssa said.

These Xiosphanti believed in the power of repression, way more than was healthy. Or realistic.

"I wish we could ask the Gelet." Jeremy was doing some kind

of stretches in the darkness. "It's a terrible paradox: you can only have a conversation with them about the pros and cons of becoming a hybrid, after you've already become a hybrid."

Alyssa went for another walk in the chittering dark—she shrieked with terror, but only inside her own head—and when she got back, Jeremy said, "Maybe you're right. Maybe I'm going to regret this. Maybe I should stick to organizing people the old-fashioned way, winning their trust slowly. I don't know. I'm out of options."

Alyssa was startled to realize that while she'd been trying to talk Jeremy out of becoming a hybrid, she'd talked herself back into it. She needed to believe: in Sophie, in this higher communion. Alyssa kept dwelling on that memory of cowering in a hot basement with the other Chancers, and pictured herself sharing it with Sophie, or Mouth, or anyone. What would happen to that moment when it was no longer hers alone? She wanted to find out.

*

THE GELET SURROUNDED Alyssa with their chitinous bodies and opened their twin-bladed pincers, until she leaned forward and nuzzled the slick tubes, the slightly larger cousins of the tendrils growing out of Sophie's chest.

An oily, pungent aroma overwhelmed Alyssa for a moment, and then she was experiencing the world as the Gelet saw it. This Gelet showed her a sense-impression of a human, being torn open to make room for a mass of alien flesh that latched onto her heart, her lungs, her bowels. Alyssa couldn't keep from flinching so hard that she broke the connection.

But when they offered her a choice between the operating room and safe passage home, Alyssa didn't even hesitate before peeling off her clothes.

Alyssa had always said that pain was no big thing—like the worst part of pain was just the monotony of a single sensation that overstayed its welcome. But she'd never felt agony like this, not even on all the occasions when she'd been shot or stabbed or shackled inside a dungeon. Sophie had made this operation sound unpleasant, pretty awful, a nasty shock. But Alyssa started screaming cursewords in two languages before she was even half-awake, after surgery.

The pain didn't get any better, and the Gelet were super-cautious with their hoarded sedatives, and Alyssa was sure something had gone wrong, perhaps fatally. All she could do was try her best to shut out the world. But…she couldn't.

Because, even with her eyes closed and her ears covered, she could sense the walls of the chamber where the Gelet had brought her to rest, and she could "feel" the Gelet creeping around her, and in the passageways nearby. Her brand new tentacles insisted on bombarding her with sensations that her mind didn't know how to process. Alyssa had thought of Sophie's small tentacles as providing her with "enhanced threat awareness," but this was just too much world to deal with.

Alyssa screamed until her throat got sore. Even her teeth hurt from gnashing.

She looked down at herself. The top part of her chest was covered with all of these dark wriggling growths coated with fresh slime, like parasites. Like a mutilation. Before Alyssa even knew what she was doing, she had grabbed two handfuls of tendrils, and she was trying to yank them out of her body with all her strength.

Alyssa might as well have tried to cut off her own hand—the pain flared, more than she could endure. Searing, wrenching. Like being on fire and gutshot, at the same time. And even though her eyes told her that there were foreign objects attached to her chest, her skin (her mind?) told her these were part of her body, and she was attacking herself. She nearly passed out again from the pain of her own self-assault.

The Gelet rushed over, three of them, and now Alyssa could sense their panic even without any physical contact. Her new tentacles could pick up their emotional states, with more accuracy than being able to see facial expressions or body language, and these Gelet were very extremely freaked out. Two of them set about trying to stabilize Alyssa and undo the damage she'd just caused to her delicate grafts, while the third leaned over her.

Alyssa looked up with both her old and her new senses. A big blunt head descended toward her, with a huge claw opening to reveal more of those slimy strips of flesh, and Alyssa felt a mixture of disgust and warmth. She didn't know what she felt anymore, because her reactions were tainted by the sensory input from her tentacles. The Gelet leaning toward her gave off waves of tenderness and concern—but also annoyance and fear—and this was all too much to process.

"I would very much like not to feel any of what I'm feeling," Alyssa said.

Then the Gelet closest to her made contact with her tendrils, and Alyssa had the familiar sensation of falling out of herself, that she'd gotten from Sophie so many times now. And then—

—Sophie was standing right in front of Alyssa, close enough for Alyssa to look into her eyes.

"What are you doing? How are you here?" Alyssa asked Sophie, before she bit her tongue. Because of course, Sophie wasn't present at all. This was a memory or something.

Sophie was looking at herself, with her tendrils as fresh as the ones Alyssa had just tried to rip out of herself, and she was reaching out with her tentacles to "feel" the space around her, and Alyssa was doubly aware of Sophie's happiness, thanks to her facial expression and all the chemicals she was giving off. *At last*, Sophie seemed to be saying. *Thank you, at long last my head can be an estuary instead of just this reservoir.*

Alyssa wanted to reach out for Sophie, but Alyssa wasn't even herself in this memory. Alyssa was a Gelet, with a huge lumbering body under a thick shell and woolly fur, with a heart full of relief that this operation might be working better than anyone dared hope—

—Alyssa came back to herself, and looked at the Gelet leaning over her. The disgust was gone, and she "saw" every flex of the segmented legs and every twitch of the big shapeless head, as if they were the tiny habits of a distant family member.

"I'm sorry," Alyssa said, hoping they understood somehow. "I didn't mean to do that, it was just instinct. I hope I didn't ruin everything. I do want to understand all of you, and go home to Sophie as her equal. I really didn't want to, I'm sorry—I didn't want to, it just happened. I'm sorry."

Maybe if her tendrils weren't damaged beyond repair, she'd be able to tell them in a way they understood. As it was, they seemed satisfied that she wasn't going to try and tear herself apart again, and that they'd done everything they could to stabilize her.

Alyssa lay there cursing herself and hoping and worrying and freaking out, until she heard shrieks echoing from the next room. Jeremy. He'd gotten the procedure too, and he'd just woken up, with the same agony and loathing that had struck Alyssa. She wished she could think of something to say to talk him down. Or at least they could be miserable together, if she could talk to him.

This operation was supposed to help Alyssa to form connections, but she was more alone than ever.

The pain ground on and on. Alyssa would never get used to these stabbing, burning, throbbing sensations. Alyssa couldn't tell how much of this discomfort was from the operation, and how much was because she'd attacked herself when she was still healing.

Alyssa rested on a hammock of moss and roots until she got bored and the pain had lessened enough for her to move around, and then she started exploring the city again. This time, she could sense the walkways and all the galleries, all the way down into the depths of the city, and she was aware of the Gelet moving all around her. She started to be able to tell them apart, and read their moods, and all their little gestures and twitches and flexing tentacles began to seem more like mannerisms.

One Gelet, in particular, seemed to have been given the task of watching over Alyssa, and she had a loping stride and a friendly, nurturing "scent." (Alyssa couldn't think of the right word to describe the way she could tell the Gelet's emotions from the chemicals they gave off, but "scent" would do for now.) This Gelet stayed close enough to Alyssa to provide any help she needed, and Alyssa found her presence reassuring, rather than spooky.

Alyssa's new friend had survived the noxious blight that had killed a lot of her siblings in the weave where all the Gelet babies grew. (But she was still a little smaller than all the older Gelet.)

When she was brand new, the other Gelet had made a wish for her that boiled down to "Find reasons for hope, even in the midst of death."

That thought reminded Alyssa of a nagging regret: she and Sophie still hadn't succeeded in helping Mouth to figure out a new name, mostly because Mouth was impossible to please.

And this Gelet, whom Alyssa started calling Hope, had devoted most of her life so far to studying the high wind currents, the jetstreams that moved air from day to night and back again. Hope's mind was full of designs for flying machines, to let people examine the upper atmosphere up close, and find a way to keep the toxic clouds away from the Gelet city. But Alyssa's communication with Hope still only went one way. Her new grafts, the tendrils she'd tried to rip out, still hurt worse than daylight. She tried to shield them with her entire body, as if exposure to air would ruin them further.

What if they never worked right?

What if she could never use them to communicate, without feeling as if hot needles were poking in between her first few ribs?

That moment when she'd grabbed with both hands, tearing at her new skin, kept replaying in Alyssa's head, and she wanted to curse herself. Weak, untrustworthy, doomed—she cringed each time.

Hope kept offering her own open pincer and warm tendrils, which always contained some soothing memory of playing a friendly game with some other Gelet, or receiving a blessing from the Gelet's long-dead leader, in some dream-gathering. Alyssa kept wishing she could talk back, explain, maybe learn to become more than just a raw mass of anxiety with nothing to say.

At last, Alyssa decided to take the risk.

She raised her still-sore tendrils to meet Hope's, and tried to figure out how to send, instead of receive. Alyssa brought the awful memory to the front of her mind: her hands, grasping and pulling, so vivid, it was almost happening once again. She felt it flood out of her, but then she wasn't sure if Hope had received it. Until Hope recoiled, and sent back an impression of what Alyssa had looked like to everyone else, thrashing around, and the

Gelet rushing in to try and fix the damage.

Alyssa "saw" them touching her body, in the same places that still hurt now, and felt their anxiety, their horror, but also their...determination? Bloody-mindedness, maybe. She had the weird sensation of "watching" the Gelet surgeons repairing the adhesions on her chest, while she could still feel the ache inside those torn places. And the strangest part: as she watched the Gelet restore her grafts in the past, Alyssa found the wounds hurt less fiercely in the present.

*

THE PAIN DIDN'T magically fade to bliss or anything like that, but Alyssa found she could bear it, maybe because she could convince herself that they'd repaired the damage. She started thinking of it more like just another stab wound.

And once Alyssa decided she could use her new organs (antennae?) without wrecking something that was barely strung together, she started opening up more. She shared the memory of this caustic rain that had fallen on her in Argelo, which had seemed to come from the same alkali clouds that had doomed some of Hope's siblings. And the moment when Sophie had first given Alyssa a glimpse of this city and the Gelet living here, suffused with all of Sophie's love for this place. And finally, the first time Mouth, Sophie and Alyssa climbed onto the flat shale rooftops of the Warrens while everyone else slept, the three of them holding hands and looking across the whole city, from shadow to flame.

In return, Hope shared her earliest memories as a separate person, which was also the moment she realized that she was surrounded by the dead flesh of her hatchmates, hanging inside this sticky weave. Tiny lifeless bodies nestled against her, all of them connected to the same flow of nutrients that were keeping her alive. The crumbling skin touching hers, the overwhelming chemical stench of decay—with no way to escape, nothing to do but keep sending out distress pheromones until someone arrived to take away the dead. And then later, when Hope had left the web, and all the other Gelet had treated her like a fragile ice blossom.

Alyssa felt sickened in a deep cavity of herself, somewhere underneath her new grafts.

She tried to send back random scraps of her own upbringing, like when her mom and all her uncles died on her, or when she got in her first serious knife fight. But also, cakes, cactus crisps, and dancing. And kissing girls and boys and others, in the crook of this alleyway that curled around the hilt of the Knife in Argelo, where you felt the music more than you heard it, and you could get trashed off the fumes from other people's drinks. Always knowing that she could lose herself in this city, and there were more sweet secrets than Alyssa would ever have enough time to find.

Soon, Alyssa and Hope were just sharing back and forth, every furtive joy and every weird moment of being a kid and trying to make sense of the adults around you—and then growing up but still not understanding, most of the time. The intricacies of the Gelet culture still screwed Alyssa's head ten ways at once, but she could understand feeling like a weird kid, looking in.

Alyssa started to feel more comfortable with Hope than with 99 percent of human beings —until a few sleeps later, Hope showed Alyssa something that sent a spike of ice all the way through her. They were sitting together in one of those rooty-webby hammocks, and Alyssa was drowsing, finally no longer in so much pain that she couldn't rest, and Hope let something slip out. A memory of the past?

No—a possible future.

In Hope's vision, hybrid humans were moving in packs through this city, deep under the midnight chill. Dozens of people, all chattering with their human voices, but also reaching out to each other with their Gelet tendrils. This throng seemed joyful, but there was this undercurrent of dread to the whole thing, which made no sense to Alyssa.

Until she realized what was missing. Hope could see a future where the midnight city was filled with human-Gelet hybrids— but the Gelet themselves were gone.

*

"I HAVE SOMETHING I need to show you," Alyssa said to Jeremy.

He jerked his head up and gaped at her, with his new tendrils entwined with those of two Gelet that Alyssa hadn't met yet. He blinked, as if he'd forgotten the sound of language, then unthreaded himself from the two Gelet slowly and stumbled to his feet.

"Okay," Jeremy said. "What did you want to show me? Where is it?"

"Right here." Alyssa gestured at her tendrils.

Jeremy pulled away, just a couple centimeters, but enough so Alyssa noticed.

"Oh," he said. "I hadn't…I didn't."

"Don't be a baby," Alyssa said. "I know you bear a grudge, you blame me, I get it. You don't want to let me in."

"It's not even that," Jeremy stammered. "I don't even know. This is all so new, and even just sharing with the Gelet is unfamiliar enough. Being connected to another human being, or another hybrid I mean, would be…plus I heard that you…I heard you *did* something. You tried to damage yourself. They won't show me the details."

Fucking gossip. Alyssa shouldn't be surprised that the Gelet would be even worse than regular humans about telling everyone her business. The look in Jeremy's eyes made her feel even worse than ever, and her scars felt like they were flaring up.

"This isn't anything to do with me," Alyssa said. "I promise, I won't even share anything about myself, if you're so worried about mental contamination."

"I don't mean to be…" Jeremy sucked in a deep breath. "Okay. Okay. Sure. Go ahead."

Among the thousand things that the hybrids were going to need, some kind of etiquette would be one of the most important. A way to use their words to negotiate whether, and how, to communicate with each other non-verbally.

Jeremy leaned forward with his tunic open, and Alyssa concentrated, desperate to keep her promise and avoid sharing anything of her own. But of course, the more she worried about sharing the wrong thing, the more her mind filled with the image of herself inside the Xiosphanti Palace, tracking bloody footprints all over the most exquisite marble floor she'd ever seen.

No no no. Not that. Please.

"Wait a moment." Alyssa paused, when they were just a few centimeters apart. "Just. Need to clear. My head."

Curating your thoughts, weeding out the ugly, was a literal headache. If only Sophie was here…but Alyssa didn't want to open that cask of swamp vodka, or she'd never conjure a clean memory.

Breathe. Focus. Alyssa imagined Hope's scary vision, as if it was a clear liquid inside a little ball of glass, cupped in her palms. Separated from all her own thoughts, clean and delicate. She gave that glass ball to Jeremy in her mind as their tendrils made contact, and felt Hope's dream flow out of her.

A few strands of thought, or memory, leaked out of Jeremy in return: a slender boy with pale Calgary features and wiry brown hair, pulling his pants on with a sidelong glance at his forbidden lover. Bianca and her consort Dash, smiling down from a balcony as if the crowd beneath them was shouting tributes, instead of curses. A woman holding a tiny bloody bundle on a cobbled side street, wailing.

"Ugh, sorry," Jeremy said. And then Hope's vision of a possible future sunk in, and he gasped.

"That's…" Jeremy disconnected from her and staggered like a drunk, leaning into the nearest wall. "That's…"

"I know," Alyssa said. "I don't think…I don't think I was supposed to see that."

"We can't let that happen." Jeremy turned away from the wall and sobbed, wiping his eyes and nose with his tunic sleeve.

"Our ancestors already invaded their whole planet. This would be worse." Alyssa looked at her knuckles. "Way worse than when I helped those foreigners to invade your city. I'd rather…I'd rather die than be a part of another injustice."

The two of them walked around the Gelet city for a while. Watching small groups of children all connected to one teacher, puppeteers putting on a show, musicians filling the tunnels with vibrations, a team of engineers repairing a turbine. A million human-Gelet hybrids would need centuries just to understand all of this culture. Sophie had barely witnessed a tiny sliver of this city's life, and she'd spent way more time here than either Alyssa or Jeremy had so far.

"We can help, though." Alyssa broke a silence that seemed near-endless. "They didn't turn us into hybrids for our own sake. Right? They need us to help repair the damage that our own people did. Hope showed me some designs for new flying machines that could help them figure out how to keep the toxic rainclouds away, but they can't stand even partial sunlight."

Jeremy covered his face with one hand and his tendrils with the other. His new tentacles retreated behind his back, wrapping around like a pair of arms crossed in judgment. He shivered and let out low gasps. Alyssa wasn't sure if he was still crying, or what she ought to do about it. She just stood there and watched him, until he pulled himself together and they went and got some stewed roots together.

"We're not going to make it, are we?" Jeremy said to his hand. "We can't do this. We won't change enough people in time to help them. I know you did something terrible, right after they changed you, and I…" He couldn't bring himself to say what came next. "What I did was much worse. I can't. I can't even stand to think about it."

Between her new tentacles and all her ingrained old skills of reading people, Alyssa felt overwhelmed by sympathy for Jeremy. She could feel his emotions, maybe more clearly than her own, almost as if she could get head-spinning drunk on them. That sour intersection between fellowship and nausea. At least now she knew that she wasn't the only one who'd had a nasty reaction after the Gelet surgery.

Jeremy was waiting for Alyssa to say something. She wasn't going to.

After a long time, he said again, "We're not going to make it." Then walked away, still covering his mouth and tendrils, shrouding himself with all of his limbs.

*

ALYSSA DIDN'T SEE Jeremy for a few sleeps.

Meanwhile, she was busy gleaning everything she could from the Gelet, even though her brain hurt from taking in so many foreign memories, and concepts that couldn't be turned into words. She learned way more than she would ever understand. She kept pushing herself, even when all she wanted to do was to be alone.

Hope kept turning up, but Alyssa also got to know a bunch of other Gelet, most of them older but not all. Some of them had come from other settlements originally, and she caught some notions of what life was like in a town of just a few hundred or few thousand Gelet, where everybody really knew everyone else by heart. She got to witness just the merest part of what a debate among the Gelet would feel like.

In her coldest moments, Alyssa caught herself thinking, *I need to learn everything I can, in case one day these people are all gone and my descendants are the only ones who can preserve these memories.* That thought never failed to send her into a rage at herself, even angrier than when she thought she had ruined her own tendrils.

She thought of what Mouth had said to her once, about cultural survival. People died, even nations flamed out, but you need somebody left behind to carry the important stuff forward.

"You were right."

Jeremy had caught Alyssa by surprise when she was dozing in a big web with a dozen Gelet, waiting for their dead Magistrate to show up. Jeremy seemed way older than the last time Alyssa had seen him, his shoulders squared against some new weight that was never going to be lifted away. He faced her eye to eye, not trying to cover any part of himself or turn aside.

"Wait. What was I right about?" Alyssa said. "The last time I won an argument, it involved handfuls of blood and a punctured lung. I've stopped craving vindication."

"There's so much more at stake than who sits inside that ugly Palace back home in Xiosphant." Jeremy shook his head. "I came here hoping to find a new way to organize people against the Vice Regent, but we have more important work to do. You were right about all of it: being a hybrid isn't just a means to an end, it's way more important than that."

"Oh."

Alyssa looked at Jeremy's shy, unflinching expression, and a wave of affection caught her off guard. They'd gone through this thing together, that almost nobody else alive could understand. She couldn't help thinking of him almost as a sleepmate—even though they'd only slept near each other, not next to each other.

"We can't just send people here and expect them to handle this change on their own. Anyone who comes here is going to need someone to talk them through every step of the process, someone who understands how to be patient," Jeremy said. "So…I've made a decision. I think it would be easier to show than to tell."

Alyssa understood what he meant after a moment, and she let her tendrils relax, slacken, so his own could brush against them.

She was terrified that she would show him the moment when she tried to rip these things out of her body—so of course that's what she did show him. The screaming panic, the feeling of her fingers grasping and tearing, trying to rip out your own heart.

Jeremy stumbled, flinched, and let out a moan…and then he accepted Alyssa's memory. And he gave back a brief glimpse of his own worst moment: Alyssa was Jeremy, lashing out, with a snarl in his throat, the heel of his hand colliding with the nearest terrified Gelet, a blood-red haze over everything. *I'll kill you all* repeating in his head, *I'll tear you apart, kill you kill you.* The new alien senses flooding into Jeremy's brain, bringing back all the times when he'd needed to look over his shoulder with every step he took.

"It's okay," Alyssa said, wrapping her arms around Jeremy under the roots of his tentacles. "It's really okay."

"It's not okay." Jeremy trembled. "I'm a monster. At least nobody was badly hurt."

"You're not a monster. You were just scared. We both were." Alyssa clutched him tighter, until he clung to her as well. "We prepared ourselves, but we weren't ready. We need to make sure it goes better next time."

"That's what I was going to tell you about." Jeremy relaxed a little. "This is what I decided." He sent Alyssa another vision, this time of a future he'd envisioned.

Jeremy was here, still inside the midnight city, studying everything the Gelet could teach him. And then, when more humans arrived from Xiosphant, Alyssa saw Jeremy greeting them. Guiding them around the city, preparing them, talking them through every step of the way. The Jeremy in the vision grew old, but never went back to the light.

Alyssa had to say it aloud: "You want to stay here? Forever?"

"I...I think it's the right thing to do," Jeremy whispered. "I can organize, I can be a leader, all of that. Just down here, rather than back in Xiosphant. Humans are going to keep coming here, and there needs to be someone here to help. Otherwise, more people will..."

"More people will react the way you and I did." Alyssa shuddered.

"Yeah."

Alyssa found herself sharing a plan of her own with Jeremy. She imagined herself going back to Xiosphant, back to Sophie and Mouth—but not just helping them to convince more people to come here and become hybrids. She pictured herself carrying on Jeremy's work: finding the people who were being crushed by all the wrong certainties, helping them to form a movement. Maybe opening someplace like that coffee shop where Sophie and Jeremy used to work. Giving people a safe place to escape from all that Xiosphanti shit.

"You were right too," Alyssa told Jeremy. "People in Xiosphant need to come together. If they had someplace to go in that city, maybe more of them might be open to thinking about coming here."

"Can you take care of Cyrus, though?" Jeremy sent a brief impression of the biggest marmot Alyssa had ever seen, purring and extending blue pseudopods in every direction. "I left him with a friend, but he needs someone reliable to look after him. Sophie already knows him."

"Sure," Alyssa said, hugging Jeremy with their tendrils still intertwined.

Alyssa stayed a while longer in the midnight city, healing up but also keeping Jeremy company. After she left, he might not hear another voice for a while—and weirdly, the longer Alyssa had these tendrils, the more important verbal communication seemed to her, because words had a different kind of precision, and there were truths that could only be shared in word-form. Alyssa introduced Jeremy to Hope, and explained in a whisper about everything she'd been through, and Jeremy introduced Alyssa to some of his own Gelet friends, too.

Her surgical scars settled down to a dull ache, and then slowly stopped hurting at all, except for when she strained her muscles or slept weird. The new body parts and what remained of the pain both felt like they were just part of Alyssa, the same way the Chancers and the Resourceful Couriers would always be. "I guess it's time," Alyssa said to herself. She walked up towards the exit to the Gelet city with Hope on one side, and Jeremy on the other, though Jeremy planned to turn back before they reached the exit.

Almost without thinking, Alyssa extended her tendrils so she was connected to both Jeremy and Hope, and the three of them shared nothing in particular as they walked. Just a swirl of emotions, fragments of memory, and most of all, a set of wishes for the future that were just vague enough to be of comfort. They stayed in this three-way link, until the first gusts of freezing air began to filter down from the surface of the night.

A Voyage to Queensthroat

Anya Johanna Deniro

*

LET ME TELL you how I first met Seax-of-Peony, Empress of the Known Moons. That, of course, was not her name at the time, when she was a teenaged girl—she had that name ritually keelhauled upon her ascension. And though I am beyond old now, and the Empress has not spoken to me in many years, bringing her to Queensthroat has proved to be one of the treasures of my life.

*

MANY DECADES BEFORE that, after the Empire of Marigolds collapsed, I had fled to a nondescript moon and built a home in an expanse of wastrel marshes in order to cultivate an orchard of plum trees. Though I had very little, I brought my own plum tree grafts from imperial orchards that had burned soon after my flight. I knew the plums would grow well and peculiarly in the place I chose. In spring, the orchard would flood from the estuary, and the silt and brine would turn the plums white in the summer. Their sweetness was amplified by the salty tang, and traders who came to the village closest to me had buyers from distant moons who prized them—rarely for eating, but rather for pickling and preserving for decades, if not centuries, in the holds of thousand-year-old caravels that plied the emptiness between the moons.

On the day my careful life unraveled, five teenaged boys walked into my orchard. I saw them from a bit of a distance. They ranged from about fourteen to seventeen years of age. I could hear their drinking rum and cursing and singing half a mile up the path. When they reached the orchard, I stopped my work and waited for them.

They wore their grandparents' armaments, which their parents had likely also worn as hand-me-downs. Everything had been handed down for a long time. I could see the tarnish on their ill-kept sorrow-blades and the rust on their greaves. They no doubt took these from their families' memory chests, the sparse treasure troves that their grandparents—if they were still alive— would peer into and cry over, after a long night of sherry, on account of the battles that they had survived.

After they stopped in front of me, I said, "What can I do for you?" I wiped the sweat off my forehead with my blouse sleeve.

"We've come," the oldest said, "to take your plums and burn your cottage down."

"And kill your dog," the second oldest said.

My dog Couplet was still sleeping on the steps of the cottage.

I nodded and leaned on my walking stick, which was about the height of a broadsword. "All right," I said. "Do you want water? Before you try? I have a pitcher close by, a few trees over."

All of their faces, except for that of the youngest, were lumpen, wide-browed, and with sullen brown eyes. I could scarcely tell them apart, and figured them to be cousins, or even brothers. The youngest, by contrast, had strawberry blonde hair and a lanky body, with wide green eyes which made him look a little bit terrified. Which he probably was.

"I had heard," the third oldest said, with an exaggerated whisper, "that you used to be a man."

"Oh. Did you hear that in the village?" I said. I could smell the rum on his breath. The village didn't have a name, but it was the second largest village on this moon, so it was usually called "the other village." But these boys would have known nothing else than this one place.

"And that means," the oldest said, "that you *are* a man, in a dress. And that you defile the Pure Laws."

"I thought you were here for my plums," I said. "But it appears you have the *law* in your hearts. Who do you serve, knightlings, and who do your kin serve?"

"We serve the Pure Laws!" the second oldest shouted, holding the hilt of his short sword and scraping it halfway out of the scabbard. "And their emissary in this age, Lamb Villanelle!"

I was afraid of that but not surprised.

The fourth oldest strode forward and showed me his neck, which had a black crude V tattooed there. This was not the tattoo of a glitched-up, off-moon corsair. It was clear, as the others showed their own tattoos on the arms and neck—even the youngest—that they had done it themselves with sharp reeds and mussel ink from the estuary.

"Our parents are dead," the youngest at last said, perhaps intending to test his courage just a bit. There was something familiar about him that I couldn't quite place, but my mind must have wandered too far, because the next thing I knew, the two oldest had rushed at me with their swords drawn in a caterwaul that I knew was an imperfect imitation of the battle cry of Lamb Villanelle's Pure Army.

I sidestepped the first's wild swing, and I parried the second's stab of the broadsword much too heavy for him, pushing it aside with my stick. The other three had their weapons drawn and were trying to encircle me, including the fourth with a laser crossbow. However old, it was cocked. The second swung again at my head, and I leaned forward, twisting my body so this blade missed my ear by a finger's width. From a high position, I smacked his poorly helmeted skull with the end of the walking stick. The helmet clanged, and he fell down. I reminded myself, as the first ran at me yelling his friend's name, trying to run me through, that the ranks of most armies swelled with children such as these.

I was in a horrible position, and I tried to steady my feet when Couplet ran him down from behind and tore at his shoulder.

That was when the fourth oldest aimed his crossbow at Couplet.

"No!" I shouted, but the bolt thunked into my dog's skull, and his head exploded, sending red mesh and wet chrome everywhere around us, onto us.

If nothing else, I consoled myself that it was a quick death.

The boy dropped the crossbow and started heaving in deep shallow breaths. I lost my comportment.

"What in the gods' name did you do?" the youngest one said to the fourth oldest. It was because he said this, and was the only one to say anything, that I didn't thrash him after I lost my patience.

After I hobbled all of them—bruised, mostly, but also with some cracked ribs and shattered cheekbones—I watched them stumble to the path back to the village. I hit the youngest once along the back so the others would not think he got off easy. He was about to call out something to me when he was at a safe distance away, but I glared at him and he disappeared past the bend, following the others.

Panting, I leaned heavily on my walking stick—more heavily than I wanted to—and turned back to bury what was left of my dog.

*

COUPLET AND I had been companions since he started following me in the narrow, lurching alleys of Crane Velib, as a puppy. He had probably escaped from one of the vats in the plundered animal-grower markets. And I was destitute on a moon that had suddenly become unfriendly to me. The Empire had broken apart, losing moon after moon to rebellion, to people who were sick of the Priceless Court and those who served it, like me. Women who used to be men, like me.

I could not pretend that we weren't ruthless at times.

And people ran amok. Some moons became lost to any outside contact, and some went completely dark. We fled after the Contessa, Seax-of-Marigold's political Arbiter, was beheaded.

In fact, Lamb Villanelle had beheaded the Contessa himself.

If it were not for Couplet, in those days I would have been utterly alone. He deserved far more grieving than I was able to offer him after his senseless death.

But the next morning I smelled smoke from the village, and I knew right away that Lamb Villanelle's dragoons had descended, breaking through the moon's half-broken defense sigils with ease. Whether the boys had overheard gossip on the quay and had conspired to pledge themselves to the Law Lordship in drunken anticipation, or it was an ungodly coincidence, I could not say. But I knew the Pure Army would not content themselves with this village. They would be landing all over the moon and pushing inward, and my orchard would burn by sundown.

✳

I WAS NEARLY about to pass deeper into the marsh, where I could probably evade any sorties until I made my way upcountry. I was ready to find the bunker in the volcanic highlands where I had hidden my own imperial caravel all those years ago, and I would start over again, alone, as difficult as it would be.

But I thought of the youngest of the failed brigands. I did not think he was meant to be with them; he seemed pressed into their band for reasons I could not fathom. I thought about how likely it was that he would be murdered during any landing by Lamb Villanelle's dragoons, and I couldn't bear the thought of it, for reasons I could only guess at. Perhaps I saw something of myself in him, unfair as that might be at first glance—and far more unfair in retrospect.

So I went into my cottage next to the orchard and took my pack, loading it with white plums. I knelt down next to my own memory chest, and I took in the smell of *aquae koboli* and a tinge of blood. Sighing, I put on my gouged aquilla, and my sword, which I had named Learned Helplessness, its transpiric steel forged in the Contessa's own Ninth Refinery. Then I took my walking stick and followed the path that led toward the village, passing the grave I had dug for Couplet only a few hours before.

✳

BY THE TIME I reached the outskirts of the village, most of it had already been burned to the ground or toppled over by the dragoons. And most of the looting had already taken place. The village had little treasure of its own. Lamb Villanelle, in the Pure Laws that he concocted, called the despoiling of any moon "The Sacrament of Priceless Lust."

I had known him once. I spat into the blood-dirt.

I drew my sword, turned it on, and stepped around the landing shuttle, which had crushed a boarding house, into the market square. The shuttle, of course, was a leftover from the Empire of Marigolds, painted crudely red. The air was thick with charnel smoke. I had no idea how to find the boy.

"Oh, ha ha!"

The voice came from the back of the village's lone tavern. I moved closer and listened.

"You speechless dog," he continued. "You bear the mark, but do you deserve to be in the Pure Army?"

"Yes," a shaky reply came. Though I could only see him as a loose shape through the smoke, I knew right away it was the second oldest boy. "My heart is the fallow field where the law can bear … bear the tree of certainty …"

The smoke cleared for a few seconds, and I saw that he knelt in front of a lieutenant with gray spikes affixed to his helmet.

"Stand up, wicked child," the lieutenant said.

The boy stood up, uneasily, still weak from my thrashing.

The lieutenant turned a bit, and that was when I saw the youngest of the five, also kneeling in the mud. He was crying and looking over at his friend.

"He is too weak to march with us," the lieutenant said, pointing at the youngest. "You must prove your worth to the Pure Law and drive him down into the earth. You must—"

I couldn't bear to watch this spectacle any more. A blaze of smoke blew around me, embers crackling against my lacquered armilla. I walked towards the lieutenant through the grimy air, and I pushed the point of Learned Helplessness through the base of his neck and his throat, through the seams in his plate.

"Shut the fuck up," I said as he slid off the sword and onto the ground. The sword had melted him from his chin to his collarbones.

I pointed at the older boy. "I never want to see you again."

He nodded weakly and dropped his grandfather's sword, running around the corner of the tavern.

(As it happened, I *did* see him again, as well as the other three boys, years later. They had steadfastly followed their hearts' ambition to become thieves, cutthroats, and casual murderers in the space between the moons. And then they became captains of casual murderers. And then their fortunes broke, and the new Empress, after taking the peony as her sigil, hunted them down without quarter.)

The youngest boy looked up at me. I still had no idea who he was, but I was beginning to know. I held out my hand and helped him up. I noticed the graceful tattoo on his wrist, which was real, but didn't say anything yet. The "V" on his neck turned out to be from a stick of charcoal, and it had smudged. I almost laughed.

"Do you want to come with me?" I said. "I'm escaping."

"Where?" he said quietly.

I pointed north. The mountains could not be seen, but he had to have known what I meant. The mountains were away from all of this carnage.

"I have a ship there," I said, "that I have hidden."

He didn't seem surprised. He nodded.

We left the village as quietly as we could. The lieutenant's first assistant tried to stop me, but I dodged his first swing through the smoke and pierced his heart, melting it.

The boy didn't speak again until a half-day later, after we had at last pushed past the brackish marshes. He hadn't complained, not once, not with his legs muddied and scratched, not through all the dead-ends of miserable brambles I had gotten us stuck in, endless times.

In the distance there were one or two shouts, occasional whiffs of bloodsmoke. But the Pure Army was not pushing through this slog. Not yet.

The two of us reached the first patch of solid (though soggy) ground we had seen since the village and both plunked down next to a half-dead firch tree. After a minute, after he had caught his breath, he said:

"Why did you save me?"

I didn't say anything for another minute (it took me longer to catch my breath). Then I turned toward him.

"Show me your wrist," I said.

He hesitated but he held out his wrist, the one with the tattoo, the real tattoo, the one he had made from mussel ink and the sharpened point of a reed. The tattoo was the outline of a falcon inside a star.

"Did you fashion this?" I asked.

He hesitated again, but nodded. I could see the apprehension on his face, and I worried that I was pushing him too far.

"This is the tattoo of Seax-of-Marigold," I said.

He nodded again. My heart became glad, in spite of my exhaustion, because I had not seen that tattoo on another person in a very long time, since the Empire—and everything—had fallen apart for me.

"Where did you find the sigil?" I said. "If the Pure Army had found you with it, they would have chopped off your hand and fed it to you."

He was unfazed. He straightened his back. "In the old granary. There were holograms." He paused. "It used to be a temple to her."

"Yes," I said, shutting my eyes for a second, surprised by the pain from that loss, the loss of that Empire built upon the ashes of the old worlds, built by women like me.

"And I want to devote myself to her. I just know that I have to. I am a woman." This fierceness and clarity surprised me, though maybe it shouldn't have.

"And I want this body to change," she continued. She paused, thinking over the words that she had said, words that she might never have said aloud before. "That is what I want."

I looked at her. "Let me show you something."

I hiked up my muddy skirt and showed the same tattoo on my thigh.

She breathed a sigh looking at it, more weary than I thought possible for a teenager. Then she smiled. I cursed myself for not realizing who she was earlier, for fully realizing the wellspring of that pained look on her face, eager to not be seen as a woman, or even womanly, in the company of young men she despised.

"In that case," I said, "we must travel to Queensthroat. And you'll be able to decide there how you want to proceed."

If Crane Velib was the moon of politics and arbiters, then Queensthroat was the moon of priestesses and vestiges, of reliquaries and silences.

"But … no one knows how to go there," she said. "The way was lost."

"I do," I said. And this was true. So much was lost in the decades after the Empire's fall. But not everything. "Are you sure?"

"I have made my decision," she said.

"I understand," I said, lightly touching her shoulder. "Truly, I do. But this is only the first step in a long journey."

She had no idea what was ahead of her, if we did make it that far—which was no certain thing with the Pure Army fanning out on the moon. And if we did manage to launch, the space between the moons could be treacherous. Assuming we reached Queensthroat, she had no idea about the superblood tinctures, the long nights of pledges and submission to Seax-of-Marigold's manifestations, the pilgrimage to the cave at the heart of Queensthroat, shorn from the molten core, where she would find her name inside the shadow, as I found mine.

Of course, after her two years at Queensthroat, things became more complicated when she emerged as Seax-of-Peony—she had not pledged service to her predecessor, but had instead assimilated her, and fashioned something different. Something richer and far more kind than the Empire of Marigolds.

But at that point, with this scared young woman in my charge, it was only a glimmer. A catch in my throat.

*

IT MIGHT BE hard to imagine in this present age, when the Empire of Peonies has reestablished peace, the fear that the Pure Army instilled at its apex. After the Empress crushed him in battle after battle, he and his Army were quickly and embarrassedly forgotten, as Lamb and his viceroys scrambled to escape the habitable moons, towards shit-moons in the outer belt.

Lamb Villanelle's lapidation by Seax-of-Peony's decree was the last act of political violence sanctioned by the Empire.

His era of wanton slaughter was incalculable in the pain it caused. But it too passed.

When men like Lamb Villanelle become gruesomely powerful, most people do not think they can be vanquished. But they can be, and are, because they die alone, as we all do.

And remembering their past attempts to control and deny bodies like mine, and the Empress's, becomes all the more senseless.

As I had known Lamb Villanelle once, his Pure Laws especially infuriated me. He had declared them to be holy writ, invoking a restoration of a past that never existed. Dozens of empires had risen and fallen on the moons over the millennia, but few were remembered—let alone the people who had built the moons in the first place. Seax-of-Marigold, and those who followed her, had fumbled towards a form of hard, unyielding grace, but even this was just an echo of the past.

But he insisted on his need to enforce his revelation throughout the moons. And the usual cutthroats had fallen in behind him.

I'd like to think that the Empire of Marigolds was different. Lamb Villanelle would have said that we were servants of a theocracy too, one of mystery instead of clarity.

Perhaps that much was true. Perhaps that was why the Empress-in-Waiting forged her own path after visiting Queensthroat—one that tried not to pay homage to the mistakes of the past—but that is another story.

＊

We walked through the scrublands and ascended slowly to the high volcanic plains. We picked and plucked at glitch roots as we walked. The roots would evade our grasp, and would whisper screeches as we yanked them up. I showed her how to scrape off the barcodes with the edge of a knife. As she ate and the shock began to ease from her like snow melting off a horse's mane, I could tell that she was growing stronger. She started asking questions. She wanted to know everything. I didn't blame her.

"Did you live in Queensthroat?"

"Yes, for two years, just like everyone else who wished to undergo the ablutions."

She raised her eyebrow. "And it's not a myth?"

"No...no, it's not a myth. We're not traveling to a myth."

She mulled this over. "Have you *seen* Seax-of-Marigold?"

"No. No one has. Only her shadow, on occasion."

"And yet she lives at the heart of the moon?"

"Well, after a fashion."

I could tell she was not satisfied with my replies. I didn't know her well enough to give her the answers she needed, and I maybe never would. I was getting out of breath as the trail got steeper and rockier, and the questions didn't stop. I had thought tending plums would keep me in better physical condition, but I was wrong, so very wrong, especially as the air got thinner.

From behind us, I could see columns of dark blue smoke, and the sea, and beyond that, the curvature of our little moon.

"So...you served in her army?" she said, after a couple minutes.

"Yes. For seventeen years, I was a Minor Arbiter on Crane Velib. I fled from there to here." The dehydration gave the seeds of images, and I gave birth to them in my mind: Couplet ambling down a courtyard of gold tiles, the Ninth Forge shattered, my sword vaporizing heart after heart as I fought my way through Pure Army formations to the secret hangar—

"Lamb Villanelle founded his Pure Army on Crane Velib," she said thoughtfully. "So...you knew him?" She said this in a whisper. As if she did not want to ask, but only realized this until the words left her mouth.

"I knew him there," I said, clenching my eyes shut. "But we had known each other many years before that, when we were … kids." I stopped—I had to stop, I could not carry on with another step until I made the truth plain to her. I leaned heavily on my walking stick. "We traveled to Queensthroat together. But he never wished to stay. He departed right away. He only wanted off our home moon, and used my own journey—the one I desperately needed—as an excuse. Later, he entered the Flower of Battle Academy on Crane Velib. In fact, I had sponsored his position."

"Where is your home moon?" she said, and I shrugged.

"It doesn't exist anymore. Our childhood home was the first moon that Lamb Villanelle imploded."

I looked up at the sky and the artificial twilight that started falling upon us.

"And now it is almost dark," I said. "If we travel farther in the dark, we will die."

She grew silent.

*

A HUNDRED STEPS ahead, we found a house of sorts just off the trail that had its steel and concrete completely torn out, so that only the crystal wiring, twisted and splayed, remained. But this wiring had sagged enough to form a more or less flat roof that would keep out the wind, if not the cold. I realized that this could have been a chapel to Seax-of-Marigold, though it was so defaced there was no way to know for sure.

After we had settled, I gave her one of my plums. She bit into it and scrunched her face.

"This tastes terrible," she said.

"Give it time," I said, laughing a little. I looked at the opening of the desiccated building. "We can't light a fire."

She finished the plum, and I gave her my bedroll. I pointed towards the makeshift door.

"I'll watch for things," I said.

She was too tired to argue with me. As this was the first time she had relaxed in days, I could see the pain limned on her face. I wondered, as she drifted off, whether she would get any rest at all, or rather wake up fitfully every hour from everything she had endured.

But I didn't realize yet how strong she actually was. When she wanted rest, she rested. When she wanted to kill an enemy, she killed an enemy—and when she wanted to stop killing enemies and reinstitute a reign of peace, she stopped. When she desired sanctuary from the body that betrayed her, she traveled with a middle-aged woman she'd never met before to find a caravel that hadn't been used in decades, in order to visit a sacred moon that seemed little more than a dream, a phantasm.

Maybe she didn't realize everything yet about her strength. But she was getting there. She was getting there. And she didn't stir once in her sleep.

As for me, I crouched by the door, oiling and priming my
sword. I listened for patrols, or hungry tigerelles, but all I
heard was the occasional and far-distant tearing of the lower
atmosphere by the Pure Army's cyclone artillery. I still had no
idea why this young woman had fallen into the thrall of those
boys who decided to overtake an orchard-keeper with a long
stick. Maybe, I wondered, it was an unspeakable crush on one of
them. Maybe it was her last attempt to push all of her feelings of
brokenness and having a body that she despised down, further
down, by numbing herself and going along with the schemes of
childhood friends she only tolerated.

I might have been projecting myself into my own dark past
with Lamb Villanelle.

And at any rate, she never told me.

I became lost in my own memories as she slept. I ate a plum.
I saved the pit, and I rooted through the interior of our shelter
until I found the pit that she had thrown away. Those were
precious to me, and I had only a few precious things left in my
possession.

Perhaps I would grow plums again, I thought, though any
trees would not likely bear fruit until long after I was dead.

✳

I WAS ON the edge of dozing and dawn when I heard the frigate
screaming through the sky. I startled. A ship was coming towards
us.

"Wake up!" I shouted to her, but she was already sitting up.

The frigate landed no more than thirty meters from our
hideout, barely taking the time to set down landing gear,
skidding to a halt in a cloud of volcanic ash, and I knew who it
was.

Of course it was Lamb Villanelle.

I pointed at the woman who was to become Seax-of-Peony.
"Listen to me. In two minutes, you are going to run through that
crevice in the back and head up the face of the mountainside
away from Lamb Villanelle. He's alone. I know he's alone. He
shouldn't see you, but there might be tigerelles on the path.

Whatever you do, do not look them in the eyes. Walk with open palms. They should leave you alone. Once you reach the cave with the white boulder set in front of it, wait for me there. If I don't follow you after an hour—" I took a deep breath. "Go farther into the cave. The ship should be there. It's old, and a lot smarter than anything Lamb Villanelle has."

She started crying. Shaking her head. I lifted up my leg and pressed my palm against my tattoo. The mark of Seax-of-Marigold began to flutter, and with a hiss it transferred to my palm, the ink wriggling like an anxious mammal.

"Hold out your hand," I said.

She hesitated.

"*Please*," I said.

I heard the causeway slowly lowering for the frigate.

At last she held out her hand. I pressed my palm into hers, which was much smaller than mine. But it didn't matter. The tattoo seared my calloused skin for a second, and then the intertwined falcon and star loosened and grafted onto her. She cried out, and wrenched her hand away. The tattoo wriggled from her palm onto the wrist, superimposing itself on the crude one she had made herself with such pain and passion.

"When you're on the ship, place your mark into the crucible on the bridge. The ship will know where to go."

She nodded fitfully. "I'm coming back for you," she said. "I promise."

I heard the first heavy boot steps coming down the causeway. I knew he would be ready to kill me for harboring a young woman who kept the memory of the Empire of Marigolds alive—even if she didn't remember it herself.

I managed to nod. Though I didn't quite believe her promise, I was comforted that she felt the need to make it.

"Now go," I whispered.

At last she ran. I knelt down right inside the door and unsheathed Learned Helplessness. I tucked my fingers into the hilt and overrode its safety mechanisms. I gripped the crossguard and pulled on it, hard.

I heard him saying things at me: crowing, challenging me, but it didn't matter what he said. It only mattered that she lived.

She did live. And she did come back for me—more than that, she saved me, with my own caravel. But that is yet another story, one of several stories that she would possess and nurture as she found her place in Queensthroat, and later, far beyond it.

Slowly the blade lengthened, the transpire slackening and then hardening. I lengthened the blade until it was longer than I was tall. Sparks flew from the steel. I was a young woman again. I grasped the hilt and held the sword in front of me. I was fleeing a burning moon again. I took one step and then another. I was running away from my parents again, having known no more than a lumpen boy's body, Lamb Villanelle on the stolen caravel's bridge, piloting us somehow, taking us away from peasants' lives, to Queensthroat. I wiped away the hot tears.

As I went out into the blinding sunlight, what flooded my mind was one image, as sharp and total as the tattoo that had lived on my skin for decades, and which I had given to the Empress-to-be. The image wasn't of her; or Lamb Villanelle's hulking armor covered in jagged quills, promising death; or even me.

No, the mind and heart will flow where they will.

What I remembered most—what I couldn't exorcise from my vision—was the moment after my dog's skull had been vaporized by that stupid boy, and the look that had come over his face. There was confusion there, yes, but he was also horrified. He had let the mask of his endless cruelty slip and for a few instants he was nothing more than a terrified boy in shock, dogblood and dogskull plastering his face.

For a few instants, he was hollowed. And there was grief, and grace.

This was what I thought of, when I raised my endless sword and charged Lamb Villanelle: my dear Couplet without a head, and a boy's face.

Body, Remember
Nicasio Andres Reed

Jun's Italian is worse than it should be, considering he's been in the country, on and off, for the past three years. Tonight it's worse than usual.

"Mattia non le piacciono le notti. Ottenere i brividi. Lo sai." Something about the night.

"Okay," Jun says. "Sure, hey, long as there are eyes on the dig at all hours, I don't care who does it. Mattia can do it, you can do it, I can do it, whatever."

"You? Starai per la note?"

"Oh. Well, okay, yeah." Up the beach to the excavation, the rest of the team is packing up, switching off floodlights. The fire from the cookout has been extinguished, the gulls and cats are circling. Liz and Paola are trying to get Dr. Bisel to join them for a drink. Dr. Bisel is demurring again. "Yeah, sure, I can stay. No problem."

So, Jun finds himself sitting on the lip of the centermost chamber with a bottle of beer and a weak flashlight. The sea gulps at the darkness before him, and from the darkness behind, a silence presses like a chill hand laid on his bare neck. The town above is a pitchy murmur blended into the surf and the breeze, cresting here and there in a crack of laughter, a barking dog, a failing car. Jun rolls the sweating bottle across his knees. The moon leans out from behind a cloud. A lone bicycle whirrs past above his head. It's no Rome.

Jun's desire for modern urban amenities is the source of some disdain from his colleagues. He's heard Liz warning the newest intern not to engage him on his grand theory of history: that these things are the point of their work, that the present is the point of the past. That the people whose bones they treasure so selfishly would mean less were it not for the things that separate us from them. That it isn't the ancient in itself that is sublime, but rather the act of wiping the dust of the ancient from your hands, walking into a halogen-lit 24-hour 7-11 for an energy drink, and later ridding yourself of it down a flush toilet.

In the dark in Ossia, he finds it harder to feel that separation. For all the glow of the town somewhere above and behind him, and despite the winking of vessels mingled with stars, it's a timeless moment. He's a silhouette alone in the night by the sea. He could be anyone, alive at any time. The dark weight of Vesuvius behind him, casting its shadow over every age. And then he hears a voice wake the skin at the back of his neck.

*

AT SIXTEEN YEARS old, in Rockford, Illinois, Jun shovels snow out of the driveway as dusk becomes dark. He ignores his mother, who's trying to call him into dinner by shouting the wrong name out the kitchen window. The driveway extends from the street, past the side of the house, and to the back fence, uninterrupted by a garage or a lawn. Jun circles the car and continues to shovel, his nose gone red and running, his back and hips aching, his throat roughened by the freezing air.

There's a space within the exertion and the pains of his body where Jun finds stillness. Even as he digs, heaves, twists, there's a quiet interior that he can reach by knowing that he is more than his body. As his fingers go stiff, as it begins again to snow, he retreats further and further into that dark room where none of it matters. He shovels for hours.

Eventually, his father opens the front door and calls him as anak — an ungendered Filipino child. Jun lets it be enough. At the doorway, his father hasn't moved aside to let him in.

"Are you hungry?"

"I'm fine," Jun says.

"Your mom left a plate in the microwave for you."

Jun nods. Standing still, he's begun to feel the meltwater that's made its way into his boots.

"I'll put it in the fridge if I don't eat it," he says.

"You have to stop this," says his father. "You want to dress

like a boy, be a lesbian, well you're young, and we have been
patient. But you will not ignore your mother, and you will not be
sullen."

"I'm not a lesbian."

"You'll answer when we call you."

"I told you both, that's not my name anymore. I told you my
name."

"No, that's not how life is, I'm sorry." His father has one hand
in a loose fist, shaking it now and again like a politician miming
regret. He's letting the warm air seep out of the house. "You are
my daughter, and I named you. We named you after your lola,
your mother's mother. You don't get to throw her name away."

Jun starts to say, "I didn't want," and "I don't need," and even
"It makes me feel." None of these lead him anywhere. His father
watches him become angry with himself.

"You are not the only one who wanted to be different than
how you are," says Jun's father. "We all have these wishes
sometimes. But some things you cannot change, even if you want
to."

He moves to the side to let Jun into the house. The sound of a
snow plow approaches from far off on the main road. Past that,
a mile east, is the highway. South on the highway, following the
lights, is Chicago. Unfurling from Chicago, along roads and
flight paths, schools and jobs, is the world.

Jun tells his father, "I'm sorry if you couldn't be who you
really are. But I won't do that to myself."

✳

OSSIA IS BUILT on the grave of ancient Ossuaria, seven kilometers
from the mouth of Vesuvius, between the mountain and the sea.
When the mountain erupted, it was the hottest time of day in the
hottest month of the year. The upheaval would have jolted the
townspeople to their feet, raised their faces to the northern sky,
to the tower of ash and rock that thrust miles high. Slowly, they'd
have had the revelation of their incredible luck: the dark cloud
was blowing away to the southeast. Down the coast, Pompeii
cowered and was buried. In Ossuaria, the ground shook, the

mountain spat, and the people fled north, a light flurry of ash falling on their heads like a benediction.

That night, the tower in the sky collapsed, and the breath of the volcano burst into the abandoned city. A pyroclastic surge of heat like the venting of a star. Mud came down, entombing Ossuaria in an instant. No time for the furniture to shatter, the mosaics to break, the paint to bleed from the lintels. A perfect, empty city.

Incredible, but Jun thinks it bloodless. He skims the journal articles and skips over the conference presentations and generally ignores the whole thing until the project lead, Dr. Bisel, cracks open the first of the boathouses and finds it packed with human remains. Hundreds of them: the people who hadn't run.

Jun's in a bar in Nebraska when he sees the first photos. He's doing the good research assistant thing and buying a round for Dr. Tanner so that Dr. Tanner can tell him how lucky Jun is, how easy Jun has it, and who's an asshole in the anthropology department at the University of Wisconsin in Madison. The other excavation lead shoulders through the door, waving a stack of paper, talking about late breaking news from his friend in Italy.

"Friend, Meyers?"

"Fuck you, Tanner, I have friends."

His venerable elders order another round on Jun's tab, and Jun thumbs through the report from Ossia.

The pictures are ill-lit and grainy — a fax of a fax. In the background are the unfocused outlines of limbs and ribs jumbled together. Just in frame is the sliver of a face. Straight teeth, barely parted, gasping into the curl of the fist. They're a child's fingers, small. It strikes him that he's digging his own fingers into his palm. He asks Dr. Meyers to call in a favor.

*

THERE ARE CATS on the Ossia beach at night. He's seen their mirrored eyes when they've caught him catching sight of them. Jun's always thought of cats as uncanny: their mysterious gatherings and dispersals, their invisible paths. A cat would suit

the boathouse and its silent residents. A cat could certainly be in
the deep shadows now, could have made a sound like a human
voice.

He switches on the flashlight and it catches on a hollow eye
socket before jittering into the further gloom at the back of
the chamber. It's too weak to reveal anything at this distance.
Jun knows he needs to go further inside. The sound of the surf
rushes behind him, over and over. The light bobs between white
flagstones and white faces. The length of the boathouse tunnels
before him like an open throat. It speaks again.

✳

THE SUMMER OF his seventeenth birthday, Jun's brother Felix finds
him packing in his room. He's nearly finished. One duffel bag for
clothes and three boxes of books that he'll come back for with a
friend's truck. The sight of his brother's face reminds Jun to take
the picture from his desk, the one taken in the hallway of the
old house. In the picture, they're kids with identical bowl cuts.
Nobody could tell them apart, or that Jun was older. Jun takes it
out of the frame. He doesn't own the frame.

Felix closes the door and folds himself into sitting on the floor,
blocking the exit. He looks like a mantis there, sharp and long
with adolescence.

"Dad told you?" Jun asks.

"He said you said you're done with us."

"I didn't say that."

"Are you, though?" When Jun doesn't answer, starts emptying
his sock drawer instead, Felix asks again. "Are you done with
us?"

"I won't waste my life trying to be who they want." Jun's socks
are neatly matched and folded.

"I didn't know we could just quit. Dump each other."

"You're still my brother," says Jun. Felix makes a noise. "You
are. And they're different with you, you'll be fine."

"They're not different," says Felix.

Jun says, "You'll be fine."

Felix squeezes his legs up impossibly further and tucks his

chin on top of his knees, his arms around his shins. A fist closes behind Jun's ribs. He can't release it to say to Felix that he'll call, and go to his high school graduation, or try to. He can't unclench his jaw. When he leaves, Jun pushes his brother, just enough to get past him and through the door.

*

THE DIG CONSISTS of twelve chambers, three open, the remaining nine waiting. Thirty paces from the shore at high tide, a stone wall rises seventeen feet high to buttress the town. Atop is the roadway, now closed to traffic, modest homes some eighty years old, and a few patchy cypresses, their seaward faces pale. The center chamber is the site of the primary excavation. They've found no boats and have counted thirty-three bodies.

Jun and Liz are crouched above the crown of a skull, freeing its face from the earth. The skeleton's shape has been picked out in pins and string. They use delicate brush work now, clearing the centuries off of it. Liz on one side and Jun on the other, him facing the dim chamber interior. The minute sounds of their scratching are louder than the hubbub outside. Someone pecking at a keyboard, carpenters fitting the chamber mouth for swinging doors, and the constant sea.

"Foot," Liz says.

"Hm?"

"Your foot." She gestures.

He's edged his foot forward to take some pressure off his knee, and it's come too close to a small child's spine. Jun grunts and stands to change his stance but gets stuck upright when his knees pang in warning against bending again too soon. He waves at the child's skeleton where it lies, curled into itself near the legs of the adult they've been working on. "Sorry about that, sweetie."

"Aw. I didn't know you liked kids."

"Well, this one's pretty quiet, so that's nice," he says. Liz gives him a pained look. "Too dark?"

She does something complicated with her eyebrows. "Pretty dark. But I guess I can't say it's too soon."

"Everything's gallows humor on an excavation, right?" Jun

sticks his tools in his back pocket and rolls his ankle. "One of my first digs, they named all the remains after cuts of beef."

When Liz laughs, her hair shakes in a frizzy halo around her face. Her freckles are darker under the floodlights than they are in the sun. "Where was this?"

"Down in Brazil. Cerca Grande. I was just an undergrad."

"For real? I was proofreading the Journal of World Prehistory when Cerca Grande papers were all the rage. Did you submit back then?" She smiles at him, and Jun feels it with the force of a terrible accident. He starts to speak, then pauses until he's paused too long. She says, "Hey, no worries, I'm not gonna judge either way."

"No, it's not that. I just…." He trails off without finishing the thought. Moves on. "An early draft of one of my thesis chapters ended up in there that year. Very early. Not my best work."

"Oh, wow, that's impressive, though. What was the title? I bet I'd remember. I can't believe I didn't recognize your name from it earlier. You were really an undergrad?"

Jun realizes he's kneading his fingers into the fabric of his jeans. He lets go, but then clutches one hand to his shoulder, then to his chest. He can't find a reason to refuse to answer. "It was about single-observer bias in morphological measurement. Nothing groundbreaking."

"No, that definitely rings a bell! That's so funny, wow. Small world."

"Very."

He crouches abruptly, ignores his knees, and pulls his brush from his pocket. The child's skeleton has only undergone cursory excavation. Dr. Bisel is more interested in first unraveling the meatier data from the adults. Jun traces his brush along an outline of the child. A kidney bean shape, small as a dog. The pecking noise of Liz's pick resumes.

"I feel a little guilty prioritizing the adults," she says after a moment. "Kind of replicating the same bullshit they pulled, you know?"

"What?" Jun is still circling the child, dragging a shallow moat around its remains. From the corner of his eye, he sees Liz sweep her small trowel through an arc in the shape of the vaulted ceiling.

"Hiding out in here at the last minute? That's one thing if it's just you, but a parent…." Liz shakes her head. "I never understand why people stay when the really big shit happens. I don't know, I don't have kids, maybe I'm just being judgmental."

"No." Jun resumes their work. "I don't think you are."

"No, maybe I am. Some people can't leave. Physically, financially, whatever."

"That's just details when it comes to something like this." He looks at where they are. A tomb, packed full, in a row of them all the same. The shell of a woman's skull under his fingers, cracked from the heat that cooked her, the fire that cooked her child. "After a certain point, it's selfish to try to stay."

"Harsh," she says, not unkindly.

Jun shrugs. "Running away gets a bad rap, but there's such a thing as a lost cause."

*

JUN HAS ALWAYS held that there is a distinction between the dead and the ancient. His grandparents were alive, and now are dead, but the bodies burned by Vesuvius were ancient in life and are ancient in death. When he thinks of the people he knows as dead, of the moment when Felix will call to tell him that their parents have died, he sees the journey he'll have to make back to Illinois, the empty rooms he'll stand in for the first time since the last time. Death is something experienced primarily by the living. But the remains of the ancient are themselves in full, are themselves and their surroundings rotted into each other. So to think of the boathouses as haunted is meaningless, redundant. Yet still: the voice calls.

Moonlight cuts a curtain into the chamber, but only so far. He stands with his back to the night. The voice is saying things he can't understand, nothing that the dead would ever say. And if it's an ancient voice, then there's no reason for his hands to shake.

*

DR. SARA BISEL is a pale woman who wears her hair cut close to her scalp. She speaks with a studied slowness that gives the impression of exaggerated care and walks at a similar pace. She keeps to such a stroll that Jun feels the anxiety of holding his steps back as a kind of jittery tension. Liz seems to fall easily into step with her. They've been dispatched to the fish market in preparation for a celebratory we're-funded-for-another-six-months cookout on the beach. Dr. Bisel wants to choose fish that the ancient Ossuarians ate. It's a long list of species. Jun, Liz, and Daniel the intern have come along to carry.

"But seriously, though. Do we actually need to get all three kinds of eel?" Daniel says, angling his voice into Jun's ear, away from Liz and Dr. Bisel.

"Why wouldn't we?" Jun replies, pitched loud enough for the entire group. Daniel doesn't answer.

The street is narrow, cobblestoned, the walls of its terraced houses crumbling after a mere century or less of wear. In the intersection at the center of the market, the way widens just enough to contain a towering stone pine, its highest branches level with the third-story roofs, its trunk ringed by pink oleander. Laundry flaps from balconies. A man with a cigarette behind his ear is selling dwarf juniper manicured into cones. There are rows of figs — fresh, dried, and candied. Baskets of lemons that Dr. Bisel has admonished them to ignore as anachronistic. The fish are in tiered beds of ice, managed by a collection of older women with rough hands and quick eyes. They recognize Liz, and they love Dr. Bisel for her accurate, unhurried Italian. Jun catches every word in a dozen. He puts out his arms to receive packages of bream, sardines, anchovies, and something large and exotic that he doesn't recognize in either language.

Fully burdened, he walks ahead on the way back down to the beach. Liz jogs to catch up to him. Jun glances behind her.

"You're leaving her with Daniel?" he asks.

"Yeah, it'll be good for both of them. I don't think he's even met her before! She asked me if he was someone's little brother and said we probably shouldn't let him on the dig site. Poor kid."

"Sometimes I'm not sure she remembers who I am either."

"Oh, come on, that's not true." Liz shrugs. "Okay, that's probably not true. To be honest, she was my graduate advisor and she still calls me Jessica half the time."

"How does someone even hear Jessica from Liz?"

"I think it's just her default. I heard her do the same thing to Paola." She watches Jun laugh. "Hey, kind of speaking of that, I found that old journal article of yours. Or I think I did, anyway?"

They approach the entrance to a side street with a car emerging, barely six inches of clearance for it on either side. Jun can see that the street winds back up and away, deeper into the hillside. He could veer off. Disappear into the labyrinthine neighborhood.

"Okay," he says. The pass the alleyway and continue.

"The single-observer Cerca Grande paper? Turned out I had it on my external drive. Which is a sign that I should clean some stuff out of there. That's about ten years old now, right?" Jun keep walking. "Anyway, yeah, I think it's the one you were talking about. But the name is different." She's trying to catch his eyes.

The packages in his arms have started to smell. It isn't too hot out, but the sun is overhead, and the breeze from the shore doesn't reach them. Jun feels sweat stick his shirt to his back.

"Did you...change your name?" Liz says. The other question radiates from her.

Jun has learned to stick the tip of his tongue between his teeth so that he won't clench them together. It sits there, thick and wet.

"I'm sorry, I didn't mean to pry, and you don't have to tell me anything you'd rather not. I mean, I'm also not going to tell anyone. Just, you know, FYI." Liz won't stop talking. "And I'm sorry if you didn't want me to know, and now I do, but I guess I figured, if you didn't, then you wouldn't have told me about the article, since you could have, I don't know, just not done that, right? I mean, shit. Sorry. Can you say something? I'm screwing this up, and I'd really like to be friends, but you don't have to actually stay in this terrible conversation I've created if you don't want to." Liz waves her canvas shopping bag in his direction. "Do you?"

Jun doesn't know which question she's asking anymore. The skin of his face feels too tight. His heart pummels at his ribs, the desperate military drumbeat of a besieged country. They've pulled far ahead of Dr. Bisel and Daniel. Liz matches his pace with as much equanimity as she slowed for Dr. Bisel. She lets him rush them down the hillside, lets him decide on an answer.

"We are friends," Jun says.

*

IN THE CHAMBER, the voice is murmuring words too low to understand. A familiar sound, like someone he hasn't spoken with in years.

It's so cool inside the boat house, where their bodies burned away. He's never asked Dr. Bisel whether she thinks these people died together accidentally or by choice. She couldn't tell him, in either case, what passed between them during those intervening hours between the eruption and the end. Which hands they reached for when they felt the mountain betray them. Whether they lived long enough to forgive each other. He drifts among them in the dark, someone they will never know. But the child is here.

It's the one who had huddled into its own body, its thin spine and the curve of its ribs curled like a young fern. The child has been excavated, or more than that, it's been freed entirely from the stuff of the chamber. Its small skeleton lies as if placed on the floor moments ago. The child is clean, discrete from the remains around it, and when Jun reaches down and lifts it up, the child's skeleton hangs together in the shape of its body.

He can hear it clearly now. The admonishment to run while there's still time. To run even if there isn't time, to die in the effort.

Jun finds it in himself to argue. Panic is a place where nobody can follow you. The act of running can burn a country in your wake.

But the child's bones don't speak English, and they have no use for his adult devices. It's a child, and it doesn't want to be a story, an excavation, ancient. A child wants a body, to be alive.

There will be time for regret when you run, it tells him. Time to make things as complicated as you need them to be, but only if you run.

It's untrue. Jun knows that it's untrue. They will always be dead. He will always be himself. But this is a child, and it doesn't need the truth from him. A child has a right to fear. He holds these bones and turns, and he follows the sound of the sea.

Rat and Finch Are Friends

Innocent Chizaram Ilo

*

NOBODY KNOWS RAT because everybody in school calls him by his real name, Okwudili, but he will always be Rat to me.

THE HOLIDAYS ARE thinning out. With every new day, the musky smell of old books becomes heavier at the tip of my nostrils, reminding me that school will resume next week. I understand that school may never be the same. I understand that school will never be the same. Mr. Okeke, the Dorm Master, had resounded in my ears that when the new term resumes, I must never talk to Rat, I must never come close to him, that the both of us are not to talk to each other. I sensed Mr. Okeke told Rat the same thing when he walked over to the car park where Rat's mother was yanking at his ears. The thought of resuming school terrifies me: the pine tree-lined pathway from hostel to class will revert to its usual bleakness; Sunday dinner, beans and ripe plantain, will be tasteless and difficult to swallow; and night preps will be a recurring session of me falling asleep on the preface of my *Introduction to Geometry* textbook.

These days, Papa and Mama are always talking in hushed tones. Their eyes dart back and forth in my direction. Everyone at home—Papa, Mama, and the new housekeeper, Chikwado— tiptoes around me like I am shattered glass. Doors are shut with extra care, as if something will snap if they slam too hard. I have started having dreams of flying. Last, I was flying in the rain when a lightning bolt ripped through my left wing. I was free falling when Mama woke me up and asked me why I was kicking the air and screaming the whole house awake.

Pastor Emeka comes in the evenings to the house to pray for

me. I don't like him. His yellow teeth gash at my eye, his breath reeks of garlic, and he spits into my face when he talks about hell and God and Sodom and Gomorrah. Mama always claps her hands and howls church songs when Pastor Emeka is around. After praying, Pastor Emeka shakes my head, so hard you would think he is shaking a cough syrup bottle, speaks gibberish, and gives me a capful of Anointed Oil to drink. I used to swallow the clammy oil until it began to clog my memories, to blur all the times I shared with Rat, to make me feel guilty. But now I spit it into a handkerchief when Mama and Pastor Emeka's eyes are squeezed shut in intense prayers.

Papa stays in the study when Pastor Emeka comes to our house. I don't think he likes him either.

*

"DID YOU LIKE it when you kissed that boy?" Mama asks this morning, during breakfast. She has been staring at her bowl of oats since we said grace.

"I don't know."

"Gbo, Izuchukwu? 'I don't know' means what?"

"Honey, let the boy eat his food," Papa cuts in.

"Mama Tobi is busy spreading gossip about me. And just the other day, that nonsense salesgirl at the grocery store mocked me with her eyes the whole time she was attending to me. All because I am the mother of the boy who kissed another boy."

Mama is crying and quaking all over now. She is calling out to god and demanding to know why they have chosen to single her out.

"Go to your room," Papa says to me.

The rugged stairs grasp my feet as I shuffle up to my bedroom. Clack. The door jams against the frame, unlocked. Mama removed the lock when I came back for the holidays, a month ago. She says it is best this way. My leather box, all packed for the new term, slides off and thuds on the floor when I sit on the bed.

"Izuchukwu, is everything okay up there?" The voice is Mama's.

"Yes."

Nothing has changed much in my bedroom. It is still painted red. The grey linoleum is still chipped at the edge near the door. The framed photograph of Papa, Mama, and me still hangs, slanted, above the only window in my room. The six-spring bed is still lapped to the wall, facing the bookshelf, my box of old toys covered with layers of dust underneath it. The complete collection of Arnold Lobel's *Frog and Toad* series peeps out of the bookshelf between *Young Adventurer's Atlas* and *Students' Companion*. Papa bought me the book on the evening before I left for boarding school. He said he hoped I *make the bestest friend like Frog and Toad*. I doubt if Papa will say the same thing now.

Outside, two grey-winged finches are fighting over a split nut on the windowsill. They stop fighting when they sense I am watching them and fly off when I approach the window. Tiny white tufts from their feathers stud the air as they soar and soar up the warm morning air.

This reminds me of flying, of Rat, of everything.

✳

THEY SAID NNEMURU, my father's mother, was a falcon when she was alive. Her wings were so radiant the rainbow envied them. She was beautiful. She was feared. They also said she swooped down on people's farms and destroyed their crops. Nnemuru was found dead on a Sunday morning, her back pierced by the pointy cross on the church steeple, her wings arched and stiff. People called it witchcraft. When days, weeks, months, and years passed after Nnemuru died and nobody saw a falcon in the sky, they concluded that my grandmother did not pass her curse to any of her children.

This happened a long time ago, twenty years before I was born. I have heard the story of my grandmother a million times, each time with a tone of finiteness and an assurance that *the curse* had ended. So, when I started flying at six I refused to tell anyone. At first, I thought it was a dream, until I woke up with a bleeding arm after grazing my right wing on a concrete wall the night before.

I also learned that there were other children like me: Amusus. Unlike my grandmother, I am a grey-winged finch. The children who were falcons, eagles, hawks, and albatrosses made fun of how little I was. They would fling me into the wind and catch me just before I hit the ground. So I always stuck with the smaller Amusus: the bats, the hummingbirds, the swallows, the pigeons, and the crows.

Aunty Njideka, Papa's elder sister, was the first person to know I flew. She visited on my tenth birthday. There was laughter and cake and Jollof rice and orange juice. I slipped out of the house before midnight to fly. I was growing then. My wings were becoming sturdier: they had learned to glide through tricky wind currents and trap air, so I could fly even without flapping them.

"I'm a big finch now," I bragged as I flew past those Amusus who had poked fun at my petite stature.

By morning, my body was sore. Aunty Njideka walked into my bedroom and found me sprawled on the floor, my legs shaking, my tousled hair filled with dust, pollen, and tiny bits of wood. She closed the door behind her.

"Izu, where did you go last night?" Aunty Njideka's eyes were like fire, burning the truth out of me.

"I was..."

"You were flying."

She clutched me close to her before I could even think of running out of the room. "I am going to clip your wings and scrape off that ridiculous scar on your nape. That way, you will not get yourself into trouble. Or do you want to end up like Nnemuru?" Her grip was firm as glue. Pain spread all over my body, like a knife slicing through the network of my veins.

"Let me go. Let me go." My voice was muffled into the cup of Aunty Njideka's palm that gagged my mouth.

Aunty Njideka fished out a pair of scissors from her waist-bag and began to stroke my back, light strokes which grew more intense until two grey wings sprung out. "Close your eyes and count to ten. This will be over before you know it."

The door opened. Papa walked in, still in his pajamas. He hesitated before asking, "What is going on here?"

"I am saving your son."

"No."

"No? You know he will end up like Mama if I don't do this."
Papa did not reply. "Look at you. You are a big engineer now. I
did you a world of good when I clipped your wings."

"I am not letting you do the same thing to my son." Aunty
Njideka shoved me aside. She smoothed the creases off her
morning dress, sneered at Papa, and left the room. The door
slammed so hard behind her I could swear time skipped a beat
or two. Papa stared at me, then the ceiling, and then back at me.
He paced around the room, both hands buried in his pockets,
his lips muttering a strange language.

"Why did you let her clip your wings?" I asked Papa.

The iron spring squeaked as Papa sat beside me on the bed.
"Because I was young and foolish and wanted to be a normal
child. I did not want to tell my mother that I had started flying.
She would have loved it. She always wanted one of her own
to follow in her footsteps. But I was scared of what everybody
thought about people like us, so I told my sister."

"Maybe Aunty Njideka was jealous because she was not the
one flying."

"Maybe." A wide smile spritzed all over Papa's face.

"The things they say about Grandma being mean and a
witch. Is it true?"

"No, your grandmother was never what people said she was.
She destroyed the farms of men who dispossessed widows of
their lands and scared the coconuts out of men who beat their
wives. Instead of owning up to their shame, those men spread
rumors about her."

We laughed.

"What type of bird were you?"

"A crow."

"Did those big birds mess with you?"

"Sure they did."

In the days that followed, Papa reeled out a list of what it
means to be an Amusu. We would sit, crouched, on the balcony.
This was always in the evenings, when he came back from work.

There is a big world out there filled with boys and girls like you, Papa told me.

"Are all Amusus just birds?"

"No. There are cats, wolves, foxes, hyenas."

"What's the brown scar on my nape?"

"It's your iyeri. Don't let anyone take it from you."

"Why?"

"Amusus can lose their iyeris. And when that happens, they will want to steal from others."

"How do they lose it?"

"Maybe they scratched it off somewhere, or a wizard stole it to make potions."

"What happens when I lose my iyeri?"

"You become trapped in the body you lost it in. You cannot shape-shift again." Papa wound his arm around my shoulder.

"Papa, what happened to your iyeri?"

"I lost it the day I lost my wings."

At twelve, I was admitted into College Ok, a boarding school two towns away from home. The thought of leaving home for the first time frightened and excited me. At first, Papa and Mama did not want me to go. Papa thought my lanky frame could not withstand the bullying and taunting which was typical for an all-boys boarding school. Mama said her pastor saw a vision that something terrible will happen to me if I go there. But they finally let me go.

On the evening before I left for boarding school, Papa and I went to the bookshop down the street where he bought me the complete set of the *Frog and Toad* series. He said he was going to miss me, that Mama has decided to sleep in my bed and keep it warm until I came back for the holidays, that the house would never be the same without me.

"Papa, can I fly when I go to boarding school?" I asked when he tucked me into bed that night.

He shook his head and sighed. "It's too dangerous. Someone might steal your iyeri."

*

I GO OVER to the bookshelf and pull out *Frog and Toad*. A couple of flips brings me to the page with a bookmark that has Rat's handwriting on it:

Dear Izu,

Thank you for forgetting this book in the library. I stayed up all night reading it. I love you it. Especially the part where the two friends were helping each other without the other person knowing. Can we meet after prep tomorrow? Back of hostel.

I run my finger along the handwriting, tracing each perfectly shaped cursive. This note and the neatly canceled words started it all. Rat dropped the book on my bunk and hurried away that Tuesday morning. I thought he had ripped or stained a page.

Something bounces on the window. I turn. It's the grey-winged finches. They are now perched on the pine tree near our red gate, hurling tiny stones and dried-out sticks on my window.

"Sha! Sha!" I thud against the window to scare them off.

*

THERE IS NO doubt that College Ok is the best school for young boys in the country. All the houses in the school are built with brick to signify the prestige which the school has garnered over its two hundred years of existence. Perfection wraps around the very walls of the school. The teachers walk briskly to their classes, the students conduct themselves with an utmost degree of decorum, and the grasses are afraid to grow past the lawn even when they have not been cut for weeks. College Ok also has a student hierarchy. Everybody knows his place. There is Class A for the super-brainiacs and spectacle-wearing swots, Class B is where the average and above average students slug it out, and Class C students are *just there*, or as the principal puts it, "They complete the school." A change in academic performance leads to one moving up or down the hierarchy. Only people of the same class could mingle, stay in the same hostel, or become friends.

Rat was in Class A and I was in Class B when I came to the school. It was only natural for us not to have talked to each other until a whole school year passed. During recess, I would sit on the pavement of Science Lab and watch Rat and a bunch of other boys play chess. The other boys grew tired of playing with him because he always won every game. They kicked him out of their mini chess club. Then Rat would sit on the pavement, just a few meters away from where I sat, bring out his chessboard, and play against himself until the end of recess. As silly as it sounds, I was happy that the other boys stopped playing chess with Rat, because now I was no longer the only boy who sat all by himself during recess.

During recess, one day, one of Rat's pawns fell off the chessboard and rolled to where I was. I waited for him to ask me to pick up the pawn. He did not. He just eyed the fallen pawn until recess was over. I changed my recess spot after that day to the back of the volleyball court where none of the boys went because they all thought volleyball was girly. I didn't see Rat again until the school year ended.

I moved to Class A at the end of the school year because I topped my class with an average higher than half of the boys in Class A. Mama and Papa bragged about my grades to their friends throughout the holidays and I showed off the new bike Papa got me to everyone who visited us. Like all jolly holidays, this one passed too quickly. Papa and Mama were soon dropping me off at school in their red Volvo.

"Izu," Papa whispered to me as Mama was talking to the Dorm Master. "Remember no flying, no troubles. Promise?"

"Promise."

On the first night of the new school year, I climbed the roof of the hostel to watch the stars. The boys were howling in the dorms and bragging about where they spent the summer break and who came back with the most *janded* set of chocolate, milk, biscuits, and cornflakes. It was quiet on the roof. The chilly air soothed my skin. I closed my eyes and imagined how the new school year would be. Rough, I guessed, judging from the haughty glare a group of boys gave me when I was packing my books into my new locker in Class A.

An empty Geisha tin clattered on the roof and disrupted my chain of thoughts. A shadow with four legs and a shaggy tail sped passed me. It was Husky, the hostel cat. The Dorm Master had brought in Husky after we complained of rodents some time last year. Husky stopped and began to growl at a little brown thing. Must be a rat, I thought to myself. Husky had better kill that vermin before it wreaks more havoc on our cupboards.

"Give me your iyeri," Husky said to the rat.

Blood congealed. Ears perked.

"I'm giving you nothing." The rat retreated to the edge of the roof, rattling the thunder protector.

"Let's see how useful it will be to you dead." The cat bared its claws.

"No flying, no troubles." Papa's words replayed again and again in my head. But the words could not stop my wings from springing out of my back. I was becoming smaller.

"Nobody can save you." With that, Husky grabbed the rat's ear and flung it off the roof.

I flew over Husky's head and lurched for the rat. My trembling legs clutched the rat's tail, mid-air, and we fell among the thorns in the little bush at the back of the hostel.

"Hey, are you alright?" I shook the rat's head.

The rat changed back to its human form, a boy. The darkness made it impossible to see his face. I furled back my wings and shape-shifted back into a boy.

"Of all the people to save me is a finch!" The boy cursed.

He sounded familiar.

"I think what you are trying to say is *thank you*." I struggled to keep my voice low.

"*Thank you*? I was handling Husky just fine." The thin slice of moon in the sky caught the boy's face as he stood up and dusted himself.

"Husky flung you off the roof." I paused and looked at the boy's face again. "Wait, I remember you. You are the boy who got kicked out of the chess club."

"And you are the boy who gaped at my pawn until recess was over."

"I wish Husky tore you limb from limb, Rat."

"Finch."

Although Rat started calling me by my real name the next

day, I never stopped calling him Rat.

After morning assembly, I moved to my new class. The Class A boys hee-hawed and pointed their fingers at me as I sat down.

"New boy, welcome to Class A," Afam said, giving me a knock on the head. He was a pudgy boy with a small head barely balanced atop a short neck. His best friend, Fela, was moved to Class B.

"I am not a new boy."

"After crawling out from Class B to here, you are new."

"Hey, Afam, give the boy a break."

It was Rat. He had just walked into the class, his hands cradling a copy of Oscar Wilde's *The Importance of Being Earnest*. Three long strides and he was sitting on a chair next to mine.

"Care for some?" Rat offered me a half-eaten packet of Snickers.

"No thanks."

"Okay."

The first three periods, Maths, Science, and Home Management, went uneventfully. Uncle Taiwo, the Geography teacher, was about to start the fourth period when someone slid a sealed envelope on to my lap. I folded the envelope into my pocket and excused myself to pee. My hands shook as I tore open the envelope in the toilet:

Izuchukwu, I hope I got your name right?
I'm sorry. I apologize for my behavior. I appreciate understood what you did for me humanity last night. You know we Amusus and our pride that won't let us say thank you be appreciative. I've joined the Reading Club. We meet at the library during recess. You can come along.
Okwudili.

I crumpled the letter, tossed it into the toilet bowl, and pulled the cistern twice to make sure it flushed far into the sewage pit.

During recess, I took a pile of books to the library, not because I wanted to join any Reading Club, but because Uncle Taiwo had given us a list of land forms to study before the next class. Mrs. Adiele, the librarian, checked the pile of books before letting me in. Rat waved at me. He was sitting beside the window.

"Hey," he said and pulled up a chair beside him. "Did you see my Thank-You Note."

"More like A Compendium of My Pride Note."

"One more word from anybody and I'll throw him out," Mrs. Adiele said, jingling the tiny bell in her table.

A hush spread across the library.

"I'm …" Rat stammered.

"*Sorry*. Is it so hard to say? Also, try saying thank you." My voice had risen notches above what Mrs. Adiele could pardon. I grabbed my books and left before she threw me out herself. It was after lunch that I noticed my *Frog and Toad* was no longer in my schoolbag, though it had been in the pile of books I took to the library. I rushed back to the library to see if I had left it there but Mrs. Adiele had already packed up for the day.

The next morning, Rat dropped the book on my bunk and ran off.

✳

THE TWO GREY-WINGED finches are tired of throwing things at the window.

✳

"I THOUGHT YOU wouldn't come," Rat said as I sat on the tree stump when I came to see him at the back of the hostel that night.

We talked about the book all through the night.

"I think Frog is a better friend. He is the one always trying to please Toad," Rat said.

"No, Toad is as good a friend as Frog."

Rat squeezed my hand into his and said, "Thank you for saving my life."

I slipped my hand away after some time. "Good night, Rat."

"Good night, Izu."

We became friends after that night. Going for classes together, saving a seat for each other in the refectory, exchanging notes in the chapel, and, soon, sharing the same bed. He taught me how to play chess and I taught him Monopoly. On the nights we shape-shifted, Rat would mount my back and we would fly across the school field. Our friendship made us lose track of time. The days melted away and soon, exams kicked in. Rat and I stayed up all night, studying for each subject.

✳

ONE OF THE finches flies off, towards our gate, and the other one chases after it.

✳

"CATCH ME IF you can." Rat's voice rang, deep, into the heart of the night. It was the day we finished our exams.

We ran past the classrooms, the school field, and Science Lab. I still could not catch him. I slumped on the stairs of Science Lab to catch my breath.

"You win," I yielded.

Rat lay beside me and held my hand. "I was just plain jealous that night you saved me because you are a beautiful finch, and I am a rat."

I laughed. Rat frowned. His eyes were glistening with tears.

"You are a beautiful rat," I said and kissed Rat on the cheek.

The second time we kissed was a night before the school year ended. We were lying on the school field. Rat pulled me close to him and kissed my mouth. I kissed him back. We looked at each other and smiled.

"To my office, now!" The Dorm Master was standing above us, Husky tagging behind his legs.

The next day, the principal had a long chat with our parents when they came to pick us up for the holidays. We were invited to the office where the principal raved on and on about how he would have expelled us if we hadn't had the best results in the school.

✳

"Do you want to talk about it?" Papa asks. He is sitting on the edge of the bed. He must have entered the bedroom while I was busy looking out of the window.

"No," I answer. "Where is Mama?"

"She is taking a nap."

The bed creaks as Papa shifts closer to me.

"Aunty Njideka called after your mother told her what happened in your school. She told your mother about the wings." Papa swallows hard. "They told me to clip your wings and scrape off your iyeri. I have spoken to Okwui's parents over the weekend and they're going to do the same to him. It will be best for everyone."

"Papa."

"It's hard for me. And you have to understand that it is best this way. I'll just clip your wings. You can still be a bird, you'll have your iyeri."

The grey feathers fall to the floor as the scissors in Papa's fingers snap and snap and snap.

✳

It is the first night of the new school year, and we should not be seen together. But here we are, a boy and a finch with no wings, sitting on the hostel roof, counting the stars.

The Last Good Time to Be Alive
by Waverly SM

@antediluvian: london isn't alive, zuri
@antediluvian: london is just a city. it can't hurt you.
@ZRI_: yeah yeah i know
@ZRI_: just let me be delusional for a minute okay i'm having a Time over here
@antediluvian: can you get here? are the railways still up?
@ZRI_: lmao no
@ZRI_: power's off and everything
@ZRI_: it's whatever. it be like this sometimes
@antediluvian: i love you
@antediluvian: okay? i love you. don't fucking die in rugby.
@ZRI_: dude
@antediluvian: without wanting to steal your look or whatever
@antediluvian: just let me be delusional for a minute okay
@ZRI_: you lunatic
@ZRI_: i love you too.

London isn't alive, says Marlo, but that's easy to say from her place inside its heart. You don't think babies conceive of—anything, really, before they're born. But you can't imagine you thought of your mother as alive when you were taking up space in her body way back when. Outside of the city, on the wrong side of the flood barrier that hasn't been opened in years, it is easier to see it for the monster it is. It sucks the life from the land around it, and then shrugs off the consequences when they threaten to hit home.

The rain has not stopped falling. It's the middle of the day at the height of summer; the windows are slick with condensation, the air heavy with humidity and heat. When you were a little girl your mother would watch downpours like this from the window and mutter darkly to herself: "It never used to be like this."

You go about the process of preparing for the flood like you are only a machine, some switch flicked inside you to turn off all but the essential. Mains power off. Generator unplugged. Sandbags at the doors—you trap the tight curls of your hair under the hood of your raincoat, shove the hems of your jeans down into your boots. The water's already halfway up the garden. You've been lucky in the past; it's made it this far and no further, the godawful reek of the brook behind your parents' house lingering in the air long after the flood had receded. But this is the future, and the clouds overhead are smog-choked and steely grey, and the endless thrumming of rain on rooftops is shutting down pathways in your brain. It isn't going to stop. When you get back inside, there's rainwater, inexplicably, soaked right through your socks to your feet.

There's no sound in the house but the rain—no refrigerator humming, no air conditioning unit keeping up an endless desperate wheeze. You don't remember the last time you felt small here, like the vastness of home could swallow you whole.

@ZRI_: Hey mama

@ZRI_: I just wanted to let you know I'm taking care of the house

@ZRI_: The whole place is sandbagged now and I turned off the power

@ZRI_: How are things in London?

There's no reply.

*

@ZRI_: i'm looking out at the street and the kid i used to babysit is chucking toys out the window

@ZRI_: like trying to see if they'll float? i think?? is the reasoning there???

@ZRI_: made me think of yr old video about the car trying to drive through a flood

@antediluvian: !! what old memes can tell us about flooding!

@antediluvian: is it awful that i still think the original vid is kind of funny

@ZRI_: nah it's fine

@ZRI_: gotta laugh, right?

@antediluvian: we used to be better at that

@antediluvian: like someone saw this person doing this incredibly stupid thing and got his phone out to film it

@antediluvian: the whole time telling the driver what a fuckin tit he was being

@ZRI_: what a bellend

@ZRI_: what a fuckin knobhead!!!

@antediluvian: and then he shared it on the internet bc it was funny! it just was

@antediluvian: like obviously people still absolutely live to humiliate other people on line or whatever but i don't think the car flood video would happen now

@ZRI_: idk

@ZRI_: i'd be filming amal's toy purge rn except it'd eat right into my battery life

@antediluvian: idk if people would laugh

@antediluvian: i think they might just find it sad

@antediluvian: like this is what we do for fun now......... we just throw toys in the flood water. hashtag good old days hashtag bring back hanging.

@ZRI_: lmao

@antediluvian: idk maybe i'm just a big sensitive Baby

@ZRI_: no i don't think so

@ZRI_: you're human

@ZRI_: more historians should be human about this shit imo

@antediluvian: 'historian'

@ZRI_: car video is history okay!!! you talk about history

@ZRI_: i want to watch your flood meme doc now. fuck

@antediluvian: battery?

@ZRI_: ye

@ZRI_: listen

@ZRI_: if phone signal goes

@antediluvian: zuri no

@ZRI_: you know it could happen and if it does i want you to check in on my mum and dad

@ZRI_: they're in the ez motel in stratford under the name christopher emmanuel

@ZRI_: i know it floods out there and mum's not replying to my messages

@antediluvian: i'll do what i can

@antediluvian: but for real though

@antediluvian: i need you to not talk like you're going to drown or something

@ZRI_: that's okay i can do that

@ZRI_: that was like my one thing. we good now baby i promise

@antediluvian: lmao 'baby'

@ZRI_: wish i could watch the flood documentary

@ZRI_: any of your videos really

@ZRI_: kind of just want to hear your voice? today in gay as shit with zuri dot online

@antediluvian: god

@antediluvian: i love you extremely

@antediluvian: and when this is all over you're fucking coming to london and we're watching the video together

@ZRI_: yes'm

@ZRI_: <3

It's your thing, the vintage heart emoji, the one that looks like a less-than-three. Marlo did a whole documentary once on that, the way people made faces and expressions out of numbers and punctuation. Before people even had emoji. Sometimes you want to burst into song about Marlo—*my girlfriend is an internet celebrity and she knows so much cool shit,* the single, the album, the musical— except that nobody in Rugby has the time or the wherewithal to care. There aren't any famous people here. Just warehouses and terraces and the ruin of an old cement works, looming large over every skyline in town.

You're the person you are because you lived here all your life. Your parents got you into high school and promptly disappeared to London, living out of bunk beds in a motel room because it worked out cheaper than commuting to work by train. Every time you see them, they're a little more like strangers, in their second-hand suits with ID cards on lanyards around their necks. London devours all the life it absorbs, bit by bit. You could swear your dad is shrinking to fit the room he lives in, harder at the edges every time you say goodbye.

You stayed, though. You studied. You got used to filling silences in your parents' tired old house, blasting witchhouse and blurcore on speakers you rigged up yourself, falling asleep to video footage of Marlo explaining how things used to be. You are tough and enterprising and equipped for disaster. You are Zuri goddamn Emmanuel, wringing out your socks over the bathroom sink, eyes straining for perspective in the unlit dark. You live here and no goddamn flood is going to change that now.

The garden's underwater, out back. You pitch up in the living room instead, looking onto the street as the drains start to choke. There's a plastic toy boat bobbing weakly in a puddle that is threatening, not without grounds, to turn into a lake.

@antediluvian: <3

Before Marlo even knew who you were, you had learned the ending of her goddamn flood documentary by heart. *What does this tell us about the way things used to be?* she asked, as the picture faded from a flooded suburban street to a photograph of historic London, gleaming in the sun, the Eye still unbranded on the skyline. *At first glance, there's not a whole lot to learn from a silly video from way back in 2016. But I think it tells us a lot about how people in the tens understood the world they were living in—a world that was starting to see real-time evidence of its own impending doom. We didn't know how to come to terms with it, so we laughed at it, as best we could. We looked past the unthinkable for something we could understand—which was comedy, or absurdity, or just plain old human error. We didn't know how to answer for everything we'd done wrong. Can you blame us? Could anyone?*

You snap a quick photo of the boat. You'll send it to Marlo later, when the power's back on. Once it's safe to laugh in the face of death again.

This is the best time to be alive, said Marlo; you remember how your heart swelled in your chest, watching her film herself walking through the city, watching her expressionless face open up into a smile. London all around her, the perfect co-star, bright and enticing and undrowned. *Maybe this is the last good time to be alive. We don't know what's coming next, or when it's coming. Of course that's scary, and of course we should pay attention. But maybe we should be readier to look for joy, as well. Do we want to look back from the end of the world and realise we wasted the last days we had?*

Maybe you should throw all your shit out the window, too. Amal from two doors down looked like he was having fun.

*

YOU GIVE UP on the ground floor at about 5pm.

It's still light outside, which is something. You can sit in your parents' bedroom, its every surface coated in a thin film of dust, and watch the world descend into chaos with something like a bird's eye view. A half-eaten tub of ice-cream in your lap, scavenged from the freezer and already melting at speed. Water's rushing down the slope of the street toward your house like the worst kind of waterfall, some unnatural wonder of the world. If you close your eyes, you can almost hear it seeping into the walls and the floorboards, soaking the bones of the house so they'll never get dry.

@ZRI_: mama if you are reading this could you please message back
@ZRI_: I don't have power to check the news and i want to know if you are safe

Your parents won't care about the house. It's barely theirs anymore. They would have sold it years ago if you'd been able to sleep in a store cupboard at school, like a really dutiful daughter would've done. Mostly they'll be mad about the water damage, although it's not like there's anyone to blame. You did everything you could. Your hands are shaking in your lap, too unsteady for a decent grip on your phone. You're so fucking frightened you could puke.

@ZRI_: downstairs just flooded lol
@antediluvian: well fuck
@antediluvian: tell me you're upstairs
@ZRI_: yeah, with food
@ZRI_: we had ice cream in the freezer can you believe it
@ZRI_: be a crime to let it melt
@antediluvian: i hate this so much
@ZRI_: yeah i'm not exactly hype about it myself
@antediluvian: you have to leave
@ZRI_: little late for that babe
@antediluvian: no i mean after this. it is not safe for you to be in the suburbs anymore
@ZRI_: rugby's barely a suburb
@ZRI_: a freight terminal maybe
@antediluvian: come live with me

The world drops away, precipitous, leaves you suspended like some dumbass cartoon character in the air. You've visited Marlo's place. It's some high-rise shit in Tower Hamlets, gentrified almost to death thanks to a comparatively minimal flood risk and paid for entirely with internet video money. She does well out of what she does; it's a really nice flat. You just see Essex underwater in your head every time you look out the window. Barriers closed, water rising downstream. You have a ticket to safety, ready and waiting whenever you want it—but not Amal, not his mum. Not any of your neighbours, who will be digging out their emergency kits right about now if they have any sense about them.

What sucks beyond belief is that the thought has its hooks in your heart. No more water seeping under the door. She caught you at the best possible time.

@ZRI_: whoa
@ZRI_: are you asking me to move in with you
@ZRI_: i mean i've heard of shipping but this is pretty intense
@antediluvian: u-hauling!! oh my god zuri it's called u-hauling
@antediluvian: shipping is
@antediluvian: whatever

@antediluvian: not the point. come live with me. i'm central and high up and insured

@antediluvian: the flood barrier works in my favour and i need it to work in yours too

@ZRI_: marlo

@antediluvian: no listen i am trying to be sincere for once in my life can you just

@ZRI_: i know

@antediluvian: let me do that

@ZRI_: i promise i'm not trying to be an asshole i just like

@ZRI_: i don't think i can just quit

@antediluvian: 'quit'

@ZRI_: on home.

@antediluvian: the same home you just called a freight terminal

@ZRI_: idk what to tell you

@ZRI_: sometimes home is garbage

@ZRI_: doesn't make it any less home

@antediluvian: zuri i cannot go through this again okay

@antediluvian: i'm not physically equipped to be alive and in love with you and know you're right in the middle of a flood and not know from minute to minute if i'm ever going to hear from you again

@antediluvian: and i know this sounds like the most entitled bullshit

@antediluvian: i know this is scarier for you than for me

@antediluvian: but i am scared, zuri

@antediluvian: i don't think i'm great at being scared

You don't realise you're crying until there are big, rainbow-smeared blotches of water on the screen of your phone. It's fine. You scrub at your eyes with the back of one hand, swallow your tears until your breathing's started to calm. You want to be with Marlo. You don't know who you are without your home wrapped tight around you. You're a crab inside a shell, and if you leave that shell then you'll turn into something you don't know how to be, laid bare before the elements with nowhere to hide. But you want Marlo, more than anything in the disintegrating ruin of the world. You want Marlo's safe place, high above the water where catastrophe can't get you. If there's a flood barrier, and you know in your heart that there'll always be a flood barrier somewhere, then there's a miserable, craven part of you that needs to be on the right side.

There's no Brighton anymore, no Essex, no Kent. London closed the barriers and it left them behind to drown. How long does Rugby have, if it keeps getting worse, if the tides keep rising and the rain keeps falling all your life?

@ZRI_: me neither

@ZRI_: can we talk about this later? like i know you're worried and i get it and everything but

@ZRI_: i am also scared and i need to concentrate on like

@ZRI_: not, being that,

@ZRI_: so i don't completely lose my whole shit,

@antediluvian: that's okay

@antediluvian: i'm sorry. i love you.

@ZRI_: i love you too

@ZRI_: and you know i want to be near you

@antediluvian: i do

@antediluvian: it's okay, zuri. i promise it's okay.

@ZRI_: i don't want you to be scared marlo

@antediluvian: hey. if i'm not great at being scared then maybe it follows that i am great at being brave?

@antediluvian: so i'm going to test that theory

@antediluvian: and maybe you can do the same and we can compare notes later

@ZRI_: <3

@ZRI_: can you like

@ZRI_: keep your phone on you

@antediluvian: like i haven't been physically attached to it literally all day

@ZRI_: lol that's fair

@antediluvian: <3

@antediluvian: i'm here.

@antediluvian: i'm not going away.

*

THE LIGHT GIVES up before the rain. Sunset happens all at once; the clouds swell and darken and blot out the sky, and just like that, there's nothing to see. You get on your knees and dig out the emergency kit from under your parents' bed—wind-up torch, bottled water, tinned fruit and tuna and beans enough for a couple of days without power. It's not a small box. The last time you had to use it, you were new in high school and your parents had just left town. You got under the bed with the torch and a book and you tried to forget that you were twelve, and alone, and with no guarantee that anyone would find you if you drowned.

Not tonight. You resume your post at the window like you're a cop in a prison watchtower, like actually the water is trapped in here with you. You're eighteen years old and so you turn the torchlight onto the street, where the water is almost at window height and rising. If there's anyone else at their windows looking out, then they'll see. You might be going down, but at least one person is going to know that you were here.

For a split second, you don't think anything of the splash.

What gets you is the sounds that come after, these weird, choked-off little gasps and shouts that hesitate right at the edge of your hearing. You pause, and you listen, and you nudge the window ajar, and it takes you a second to make out what's going on—it's Amal, it's the kid from down the street, his dark head bobbing just above the surface of the flood. The light from your torch hits a little speck of plastic, just out of his reach and floating ever further away.

You don't even have to flip the switch. All your inessential processes start to power down on their own; your body knows what needs to happen next.

@ZRI_ : marlo i gotta go for a minute
@ZRI_ : <3

You drop your phone onto your parents' bed and you hurtle down, torch in hand, two stairs at a time. The hallway's flooded up to the second step—up to your knees, pouring right over the tops of your rain boots and soaking your feet in an instant. It doesn't matter. The grossness of it passes you by. You tuck your hair up into the hood of your coat, zip it right up to your chin and pull the drawstrings tight. You open the front door and you're kicked in the shins by a tsunami puked up from the overburdened drains, but that doesn't matter, either. It can't matter, because there's a three-year-old baby out there in the water, and nobody that small can swim well enough to handle a flood.

You force the door shut behind you, and you take a breath of air that reeks of shit, and you throw all your weight against the current.

There's nothing left in the world but the wind and the rain, plastering your hood to your hair and your sleeves to your skin. It's *cold*; you hadn't expected that, which is almost impressive for being so stupid. Middle of summer or not, the world is cold like this, with water up to your waist and soaking you all the way through. You drag yourself through the flood, through the confusion of cold and dark, and onto the pavement, shouting all the while: "Amal, holy shit, Amal, can you hear me?"

Your voice is so fucking small, and the rain and the wind are drowning you out—drowning you, full stop, no qualification required. Your face is numb, freezing, except for where the cold has made it a bright bloom of pain. You keep moving forward, down what would be the street if you could see where the fuck you're going. You try again—"*Amal*"—but your mouth isn't working right; you're slurring a little where your lips have gotten too cold, muscle memory not quite enough to get you by.

He doesn't see you. He doesn't even turn his head, intent on that fucking toy where it bobs just out of his reach. It doesn't matter. You feel it like a knife in the gut when he falls, *splash*, gone under the surface—like a wire in your head being cut, instantaneous, leaving you paralysed and useless in the dark.

He doesn't scream when his head breaks the surface, or when it dips below and out of sight again. He just *reaches,* up and out of the water like he's trying to find purchase on the sky.

You wrench yourself, hard, back together. You take a step, and another, and you keep going and you keep reaching until you can grab him and lift him clear of the flood. He's so heavy it hurts to hold him up, but he's *alive*, breathing, clinging to you and sobbing terrible breathless sobs into your coat. You should comfort him. It's so dark and so cold and the rain is lashing at your body like it's trying to fight you for him, and you know what you should say but the words stick hard in your throat. You don't have it in you to string together a sentence. You barely have it in you to go back, following the current, back to the window he found his way through, where his mother is screaming his name into the night.

With the last strength you have, you lift him up up up and into her arms. She clutches him close, dripping wet and reeking, crying hard enough that her whole body shakes. He's the only family she has, this kid you used to babysit while she worked late shifts at her second job. For a second there's no storm, no flood. There's just a mum holding her son, who survived.

You go. The door opens easily when you reach it, pushes back hard when you try to close it again. You make it, you figure, maybe halfway up the stairs—just clear of the water, whatever that means—before you drop. Your hands are wet and filthy and shaking on the fastenings of your coat, on the soles of your boots, your socks and your shirt and your bra and—everything. It's all ruined, isn't it? You peel away layer after layer, trying to get clean, and you don't realise you're crying until there's nothing left to claw away but your skin.

It's so fucking stupid, is the thing. There's a bath towel upstairs, maybe more than one. You could use some of the bottled water, try to get yourself clean, except your whole body is trembling and useless, and you're crying hard enough that it hurts to open your eyes. This isn't you. You are Zuri goddamn Emmanuel and you *deal* with shit; you don't cry about it, a huddle of raw nerves and bare flesh that couldn't even make it up the stairs.

It's so stupid. The world is ending. You're living in the end times and the most you can do, the absolute outer limit of your capacity to help, is rescue one kid from a flood. He nearly drowned, he *definitely* inhaled a whole mess of filthy water in the process, and you didn't even think to fetch the toy he went in to save. You can't open the barriers on the Thames, or force London to accept its share of the things the world's done wrong; you can't repair the holes in the ozone, take planes out of the sky, burn all the poison out of the ocean or the air. You're one person. It's bigger than you, all of it. The house is going to flood no matter what you do, over and over until it finally drowns.

Boneless, hopeless, the stink of the flood choking you by degrees. That's you. It always has been. It's not enough to try to be better, anymore.

*

@antediluvian: zuri what
@antediluvian: what do you mean what are you doing
@antediluvian: if you don't reply right this second zuri i swear to god
@antediluvian: come on come on come on
@antediluvian: ZURI
@antediluvian: oh my god what did you do
@antediluvian: where are you
@antediluvian: i'm losing my fucking mind

Your fingertips are wrinkled and tender but they are dry, and they are clean. You cradle the phone in your hands, huddled on your parents' bed and swamped in a dressing-gown you co-opted from your mum, and wait to feel worse than you already feel. It doesn't happen. Maybe you've plateaued. You climbed the whole mountain, and from the peak of feeling terrible, you can see a whole world of terrible things, sprawling endlessly away from you in every direction.

@ZRI_: i'm so sorry
@ZRI_: i'm okay i'm here
@antediluvian: i am so fucking mad at you
@ZRI_: yeah i
@antediluvian: i am going to physically come to rugby and fight you
@ZRI_: probably deserve that

@antediluvian: god

@antediluvian: zuri i am

@antediluvian: in the immortal words of the ancestors

@antediluvian: crying irl

@antediluvian: you could have fucking died

@antediluvian: i wouldn't even have known

@ZRI_: i know

@ZRI_: i'm really sorry

@ZRI_: i know it was stupid i just

@ZRI_: the kid was drowning

@antediluvian: what

@ZRI_: the kid

@ZRI_: he was throwing his toys

@ZRI_: he got out the downstairs window and i saw him and i just

@ZRI_: i couldn't

@antediluvian: holy shit is he safe??

@ZRI_: yeah

@antediluvian: jesus

@ZRI_: he was just trying to get one of his toys back

@ZRI_: i couldnt even find it for him marlo

@ZRI_: he was crying so much

@antediluvian: zuri

@antediluvian: you're like

@antediluvian: i can't believe

@antediluvian: i love you so fucking much zuri i wish i were there i wish you were here

@antediluvian: idk how to do this anymore

@ZRI_: lmao me neither

Or maybe you haven't plateaued. Perhaps you are just hiding from it all, burrowed down deep inside the crab-shell of your body, waiting for the sadness to crest overhead. It might break itself apart against you but you won't even feel it where you are. It can be something that happens, for once, to somebody else.

@ZRI_: if i come to london

@ZRI_: could you really like

@ZRI_: is there actually room in your flat or were you just
@antediluvian: yes
@ZRI_: trying to get me to agree or something
@antediluvian: zuri
@antediluvian: there's room
@antediluvian: i promise
@ZRI_: i feel weird inviting myself to live with you lmao
@ZRI_: hey there, minor internet celebrity, it is i, your new and surprising housemate
@antediluvian: no
@antediluvian: you didn't invite yourself
@antediluvian: i invited you and i would fucking love it if you accepted the invitation
@antediluvian: more than anything in the world
@ZRI_: haha well okay then i
@ZRI_: i guess i accept
@antediluvian: when the water's gone down we will talk trains
@antediluvian: okay? i will make it work and that is a promise
@ZRI_: i fully do not doubt it
@ZRI_: @ flood waters watch yourselves marlo is ready to part the sea
@antediluvian: hell yeah baby
@antediluvian: i'm gonna get you directly out of there come hell and/or high water
@antediluvian: preferably and, tbh
@antediluvian: i could take em both
@ZRI_: i believe it
@ZRI_: and i love you
@ZRI_: <3
@antediluvian: <3

The rain's starting to slow—not stop, but it's something. It'll do, short-term. You're sitting up in bed and you're drifting, Marlo's last little less-than-three heart blurring at the edges as you start to lose focus; your whole body is heavy with exhaustion, your skin tender where you scrubbed it clean of the flood. You think *floating* for a moment, and then you unthink it, pull yourself back before you float into a current you can't swim against.

You're drifting. Like a bird on an updraft of wind, high above the water and the world.

Your phone buzzes in your hands, once and again and again. The vibration in your palm pulls you back into reality, three sharp jerks of a chain.

@GlorisEmmanuel: Hi sweetie sorry I forgot to charge my phone!! Lol
@GlorisEmmanuel: No flooding here praise God! Ur papa and I stayed home all day watching modern lovers can u believe they had a video maker on lol! Like your friend marlo tho her videos were all about pranks haha
@GlorisEmmanuel: Love u sweetie ur papa says hello!!

You don't register your own reaction until your knees are pressing hard against your forehead, your shoulders shaking with useless, breathless laughter. There has to be something to leaven these last remaining days, some small, stupid joy you can cling to. Marlo will laugh as well, you think, when you can show her at last in the flesh.

◯

Everquest

Naomi Kanakia

GOPAL KNEW BEFORE he booted up the game—a Christmas present from his dad—that his character would be some form of elf or human, because the other races were all ugly, and he didn't play games to be ugly. And he knew too, although he didn't say it, that his character would be a girl. He always played girls online, although he'd be ashamed if anyone knew it, precisely because it played into the online belief that most girls in most games were "really" men, fat and acne-ridden, sitting in their underwear, hands down their pants, leering at that wood elf ass in those hot little leather shorts their avatars wore, and "catfishing" dudes online, pretending to be women to get some sick pleasure.

Gopal himself was a fat, acne-ridden dude, and in his last online game he'd gone out of his way to claim he was a girl in real life too (upping his age from thirteen to eighteen in the process). As a result he'd gotten "married" to another man—at least someone who said he was a man—and Gopal had hoped for some gross cybersexting thing to happen with his "husband," for them to write each other about their quivering tits and cocks like in the sex stories he read online, but the sexting never came, and eventually the game grew stale and the husband disappeared.

Gopal never thought about whether this made him gay or straight or trans or bi. He knew, without knowing how he knew, that he needed to keep all of this, everything, from his mother. During his last game she'd come in once and seen his character, all dolled up in her sorceress's garb, and she'd asked far too many questions, and a few weeks later had cancelled his account.

He simply booted up his game and created a wood elf thief named Gayatri, which name he chose not out of conscious remembrance of mythology, because he didn't remember anything at all—didn't remember Rama and Hanuman and Sita, didn't remember Sikhandin, who was born as Amba, the princess who Bishma rejected, and who turned herself into a man so she could kill the man who'd humiliated her. All these things were lost to Gopal, lost like his home country, the nation where everybody looked like him, the nation he half-hated that year, the year of this game, because the internet in this country was so fucking slow that he couldn't play for shit, and the food so rich and greasy and addictive that he gained thirty pounds, the year he attended a new school—which had girls, unlike his school in the U.S. which was all boys—a school that had girls whose creamy skin he longed to touch, and who he fantasized about in odd, flinching, sinister ways that he would learn to hate long before he learned what was really signified by all these desires.

He did not name his character Gayatri because of this country, did not name it those words because he retained some memory of his half-literate grandmother telling him stories about gods and goddesses and the many worlds they had fought for and saved and created.

He chose the name because it sounded pretty.

And during those hot nights when he could patch through to the servers, when things weren't too slow, when the lag not too intense, Gayatri ran free through the elven forests. She backstabbed, she stole, she scammed. She joined a guild of other thieves, a guild dedicated not to advancement, but to merriment. Because of her lag issues Gayatri could never level much, she died too frequently, left corpses in half a hundred dungeons, and it grew to be a joke, resounding often over guild-chat, that Gayatri could in the middle of the safest city on the planet and manage to find the one wandering giant, or aggro the one lonely guard; that Gayatri was the only player who could in a fight glitch out and backstab herself; that even crossing a bridge was dangerous for Gayatri, that she had to think through every keystroke, because with her connection, she might stutter onwards forever, the lonely keystrokes doubling and redoubling in the long undersea cable between India and America, like the migration of some flock of butterflies where the parents inevitably died mid-journey and left their children to struggle onwards to home grounds they'd never seen.

Meanwhile, upstairs or in the next room, she heard her mom get up to go to the bathroom, and she held perfectly still, frantically keying the "lower brightness" button on the laptop until the screen turned off, and waited there, not responding to messages, dying repeatedly to mobs, until the rustling ended and the screen could be turned safely back on.

Despite all these difficulties, Gayatri had a certain cunning. She made friends. She cajoled. She scammed. People *liked* Gayatri; she remembered their names, remembered them for what they wanted to be remembered for; she remembered Tak's midnight raid across the Heavens, when he aggro'ed the Sky-King and caused the whole world to die. She remembered Vakharov swooping in out of nowhere to killsteal the World-Dragon and ninja-loot his boots that appeared in only one in a hundred drops. She remembered the awesome hack, discovered by Sorpedon of their own guild, that let him delete the online banks of a thousand players, causing briefly a level of deflation that sent their server's economy into a great depression from which, some said, it never recovered. Sorpedon, Vakharov, Tak, they were all banned for their exploits, while shy, nervous Gayatri waited in the corner and watched.

She joked sometimes, "You think I'm really a dude, don't you?" And always the answer was "No."

"Why not?"

"Because you don't sound like one...Because you don't wear revealing clothes, even when they have high stats...Because, I don't know, you can just tell."

And Gayatri reveled in this illusion and never ever allowed her mask to fall. But that was easy. People didn't discuss real life in the game, because the game itself offered enough of a world that you could get lost in it. They discussed camping, they discussed stats, they discussed new zones and new strategies, they discussed hunts and griefing and player-killers and new drops. And they discussed each other. The highlights and lowlights of everyone in the guild: they discussed who was great, who was funny, who was useless in a raid, and who was just an overleveled noob.

Eventually Gayatri's mom discovered the game. She didn't forbid it, not outright, but she started coming around to the subject elliptically. "That game of yours is fun, in moderation, isn't it?"

"Mmmhmmm."

"It's fun to pretend."

"Yep."

"I notice you always play girl characters..."

"Mom! It's normal. Lots of guys do it."

"I know, I know...but it's not good to spend too much time in another world."

The game grew large and great, while Gayatri, hampered by both lag and her parents' watchfulness, stayed the same. Perpetually low-level Gayatri, who wore gear far outside her level range, who knew every mountain and every zone, and who had journeyed to all the Sky Levels and had found safe places in each to watch the epic raids conducted by her betters. She was Gayatri the Traveler, Gayatri the Schemer, Gayatri of the Tall Boots and Gayatri who wore Cerebral Armor not because it was good (it wasn't) but because, although form-fitting, it was jet-black and didn't display her body as lasciviously as did 95% of the outfits in the game. She was Gayatri who played in the wrong time-zone, and so was always on extremely late at night when others were drunk and high and barely made sense, and who whiled away the empty hours of the American morning by picking through the leavings of the day's raids.

And she was Gayatri who simply disappeared one day, her account password changed. She tried everything to get in, assumed she was hacked, made frantic phone calls to customer support, wrote on the guild forums, and even had several of her friends offer to buy her a new account or let her share theirs.

When her mother got home, she found her son on the computer, sweating in the warm Mumbai night, and she took him into the kitchen and sat him down and said, "Son, we are worried about your grades. This is an important time. You are in high school now, and you should be focusing on the things that matter."

Her parents had cancelled her account. Her characters would be deleted. Her computer access was limited. She went to school, and she studied, and eventually she got her computer back, but forever after when she asked for the account to be reinstated, they refused.

Now only Gopal remained. As he grew older, he turned against all forms of fantasy. He grew large and dark and odious; he spoke loudly about escapism and about wastes of time. He got into a good college, learned to code, and when the time came to get a job, he opted not to work in gaming—the numbers didn't make sense, you didn't make nearly enough money for all the work, and anyway he didn't want to program games, he wanted to live them—instead he started a company of his own, then when that failed he started another. His body was an encumbrance; he didn't think of it. And the complex sexual feelings of his youth were transmuted into heterosexuality of the grossest sort.

At first his mother pleaded, "Why are we not close, like we used to be?" and later grew angrier, "You are selfish. You never tell me anything about yourself."

Meanwhile, the game got older and was superseded by others, but the company remained in existence. So long as a few hundred thousand were content to pay ten dollars a month, the company was willing to maintain the servers. But the world contracted. Servers were combined, one by one. And Gopal learned that canceled accounts never actually got deleted; instead they were suspended in perpetuity, waiting to be reactivated.

Then one day he got an email to his old hotmail account.

"Gayatri is waiting for you."

He didn't understand the email. When he googled it, he found nobody else had received one like it, only him. He assumed it was some sort of promotion, and he ignored it, but the emails kept coming: "Gayatri is waiting. Gayatri is waiting."

Finally he clicked the links, was taken to a form that asked for money in order to reactivate his account. There was a moment of disappointment. He'd hoped, of course, that magic was real, and that the email had been some mystical call sent by the spirit of his youth. But at the same time, Gopal shrugged: whatever, it was a good marketing ploy on the company's part—a way of juicing the fading revenues for an ancient game—and anyway he was a bit curious about what'd happened to the old stomping grounds after all these years. So he entered his credit card info and reactivated the account.

The graphics were jerky, the writing was moronic. Everything was tiny and stupid. He maneuvered that lithesome elf across a grainy tree-city, and he felt absolutely nothing, no sense of freedom, no sense of release. And when the fairy appeared and offered him a special quest to save the world, he clicked through the dialogue without paying attention. The lore had never truly interested him. He wasn't actually sure what had.

But life these days was empty, and he had plenty of spare time, so he found himself playing through the quest, just to pass the time. His friends were gone. The world was lonely. When he queried the game for a player-list, he got a list of about a hundred active players, almost all of them extremely high in level. And they seemed to mostly be in Hub-City, a sky-world, added in one of the newer expansions, that had portals to all the end-game raid-zones.

Without any people, the rest of the game-world was luscious and overcrowded. The NPCs spawned continually and fought each other, leaving corpses filled with the best drops and rarest loot. Gayatri finished that quest, and it led into another. Slowly, with the benefit of a much faster internet connection, Gayatri gained a few levels. She took screenshots of the ogres running across the Desert of Ra, and of the flights of dragons in the sky-caverns above the Under-City. She observed the glitching of a hundred weather effects, creating the world-storms that wrecked servers, rearranging houses and teleporting players at random, shoving zones together willy-nilly in ways that were left unfixed, despite numerous bug reports from the players, until the next server reset put things back to rights.

She became an oracle and a seer, a witness not to the paltry lore of the game, but to its vitality, to the things within it that were not planned and that had come alive anyway. And unbeknownst to her, she became a legend to the few remaining players who lived above her. They traded sightings of Gayatri, of the wild woman who lived like an animal, far from merchants, far from traders, far from high-level trainers. The woman who spent time in the dead zones, the newb zones, and who had raised her affinity score, through strange rituals and quests, until she could walk unmolested through these fields of goblins and dark elves alike, until she could talk to every NPC and wear every armor and use every spell, regardless of faction.

Gopal's mother called him every day, but the calls went unanswered, and when her and Gopal's dad dropped by the apartment unexpectedly, she rapped on the door and, when it didn't open, launched into a free-form anxiety-ridden monologue on the problems with her son and his life. "I'm just worried you've gotten back into that gaming. Please, come on, just speak to us. We only want to talk to you."

"Arre, what can you do?" her husband interjected. "He's a grown adult now. If he doesn't want to come out, if he wants to reject his family and be some shut-in, then it is his choice!"

"When you're not on the games, you're so gentle and sweet. It truly is an addiction. I've been reading..."

One day, an administrator sent a notice to Gayatri, saying that because of some odd activity she was under suspicion of using third-party hacking tools, and as such a ban was being initiated.

But the character did not stop. She crept through the lattices of the game, undetectable by the servers, moving sidewise across zones and continents, waging a terrible and singular war that only she understood. The game needed her, and she needed the game.

And in a small apartment somewhere within a large city, a man was found dead in his home office with his computer still running in front of him.

From within the game, Gayatri viewed the laughing responses, the ugly news stories, the sensational details about the tied-off athletic socks full of fecal matter found in a duffle bag in the corner of his room—an image so bright and startling that it was turned into a meme and entered the lexicon: A "poop-socker" was a greasy nerd who had no life. Everything was reported in breathless detail, whether it was the mounds of old pizza boxes, complete with mice scuttling around searching for scraps, or the neighbors who had banged helplessly on his door, concerned about the smell, only to be threatened by him with legal action for violating his privacy. Not least of these attention-getting details was the fact, reported in every article, that his character had been a woman.

It only took a few months for a certain level of myth to accumulate around the dark, smelly body of that man who'd died, of dehydration and exhaustion, because he was too busy staring at the ass of his wood elf character. He became synonymous with everything that was dark and wrong about the internet, and in particular about men on the internet, and female characters in games across the net were now taunted with links to articles about Gopal's sad end.

For her part, Gayatri perceived little change in her situation. Where once she had typed, now she exercised her own muscles. Where once her back had ached from hours in a chair, now it ached from running across the plains. In this world, she—the boy who had never exercised, never bathed, never showered, the catfish with his man-tits and distended belly—took quietly to the rustic life, living in a simple hut at the outskirts of a deserted city, hunting for her own food, mining and foraging for the resources to craft her own weapons, and embarking on occasional quests and explorations that always looped around to her cosy tree-top home. It is a quiet existence, interrupted only by occasional visits from curious players who've caught wind of the body of rumors that surround the humble wood elf, and it will probably continue until someday the company, due to a dwindling player population, withdraws support for the game, and between one breath and the next, Gayatri's world disappears forever.

But between then and now, Gopal's mother, not quite divorced but not quite married, grown sad and old, will respond to an anonymous message—"Gayatri is waiting."

The messages will keep coming, until, driven to distraction, she pursues them down a pit of rumor and supposition that will lead her eventually to sit down at a computer, puzzle her way through the instructions, and install that old game. She will make her slow, careful way through the woodland hills, dying continuously from the newest and weakest of mobs, until finally she comes to a tree-top home, and there she and her daughter will sit down, next to a fire, and they will tell each other all the things that in life remained unsaid.

8-Bit Free Will

John Wiswell

They exist, then don't exist, then exist again. They are monsters where the game's probability fields call for them, attached to every tile of the dungeon. They are invisible to the player, whether they are there or not, until combat. If they're lucky, they'll get the chance to die.

The player always gets to exist, has always existed, and may as well always exist. The Hollow Knight and HealBlob don't exist again until the player starts struggling with the other enemies. Then the Hollow Knight and HealBlob are respawned, to die in battle and smooth out the difficulty curve. They don't exist long enough to know they're in love before the player strikes.

*

TRENT IS TOO buzzed on hard iced tea to realize his party is dying. He tabs between music videos, an IM with his sort-of-not-really girlfriend Jayla, and the retro 8-bit game he won in a Twitter giveaway. *Dungeon Smashers 6*, a game hiding its mediocrity behind a twee pixel aesthetic and irony (it is not the sixth, but the first game its developers have ever released).

His war party consists of three Soldiers, now three floors up in the Tower of Constellations. Hollow Knights and Lesser Goblins are everywhere. Something has poisoned his party, but he has yet to notice that they're hemorrhaging HP with every step he makes them take.

"You're pretty much invincible in this game," Trent types. "It needs a Hard Mode."

After a moment the IM flashes. Jayla says, "I miss old school JRPGs. Ever play *Wizardry*?"

"Well, actually," he makes the mistake of starting a sentence with, "*Wizardry* was made by—"

His headphones emit a grotesque splat as one of his Soldiers dies. He tabs back to find two monsters attacking his party, the basic Hollow Knight and HealBlob combo, one brawler and one healer. They never drop any good loot.

The IM tab flashes. Jayla's asking, "You there?"

He tabs back to apologize, typing, "Sorry. So you like RPGs? I was always into *Dragon Warrior.*"

He misses his second Soldier getting killed.

*

SOLDIER3 SWINGS AT Hollow Knight, and does 12 damage.

HealBlob casts Heal on Hollow Knight, restoring 12 HP.

Hollow Knight swings at Soldier3, and does 16 damage. Soldier3 is vanquished!

Game Over!

HealBlob has leveled up! HealBlob has leveled up, and learned Heal2! HealBlob has leveled up! HealBlob has leveled up! HealBlob has leveled up, and learned Antipoison! HealBlob has leveled up!

Hollow Knight has leveled up! Hollow Knight has leveled up! Hollow Knight has leveled up! Hollow Knight has leveled up! Hollow Knight has leveled up, and learned DoubleSlash!

The sudden rush from whatever just happened nauseates the Hollow Knight. Its avatar signifies a haunted suit of armor with no occupant, but if it can be nauseous, then it is throwing up inside its own helmet right now.

HealBlob casts Heal2 on Hollow Knight, restoring 34 HP.

"Uh," Hollow Knight says. "Thanks?"

The Hollow Knight looks at its partner for the first time. HealBlob is a green cube signifying a gelatinous mass, wearing a pixel art hat with a red cross on it. She has no limbs or eyes. There is a crescent of black on her cube body, signifying a mouth, perpetually grinning at her partner.

The two monsters idle on their gray tile, on what only an imagination could call a slate floor. All around them, probability fields flicker with potential monsters. Bands of Lesser Goblins stare at them. Other pairs of Hollow Knights and HealBlobs line the walls. If another player ran in here, there'd be a mob on every tile.

When the two of them don't de-spawn, HealBlob says, "Hi."

The Hollow Knight says, "Hi."

"Pleased to meet you, ____," says HealBlob, which is the closest she can come to asking the other monster's name.

"I am Hollow."

"I am HealBlob. I like your shield."

"I like your reliable stream of heal spells," Hollow says, too honestly. They are new to subtlety.

✳

TRENT ROLLS A new party, this time two Fighters and a Healer. He keeps spacing out, though, alt-tabbing to YouTube videos his sort-of-not-really girlfriend sends. They're all chiptune tracks, which are his jam.

He gets so into talking to her that he barely makes it back to the Tower of Constellations. He doesn't even notice what kills his party this time. Jayla has just IMed him her phone number.

✳

LESSER GOBLIN1 SAYS, "How did you level up?"

Lesser Goblin2 says, "How did you level up?"

Lesser Goblin1 says, "How did you level up?"

Lesser Goblin2 says, "How did you level up?"

Tile by tile, the Lesser Goblins advance on Hollow and HealBlob. The Lesser Goblin model is so large that their open mouths could fit HealBlob's entire body inside. Each model is identical, their upper jaws lined with pixelated triangles signifying teeth, each tooth the size of Hollow's sword. Their avatars are not drawn to scale, and yet being one tile away from the Lesser Goblins leaves Hollow and HealBlob nervous.

Hollow and HealBlob don't know how to answer their query, and they don't like talking to the other party. They don't understand language enough yet. They have other queries.

HealBlob says, "We defended our home. Why are they upset?"

Hollow says, "I'm just glad you're safe."

HealBlob is also glad Hollow is safe. Safety is all she cares about. She wants to hug the haunted armor, or cast heal spells on it, which is the magical equivalent of a hug.

Lesser Goblin1 says, "How did you level up?"

Lesser Goblin2 says, "How did you level up?"

Round One begins.

Hollow says, "What?"

LesserGoblin1 swings at Hollow, and does 3 damage.

LesserGoblin2 swings at Hollow, and does 2 damage.

HealBlob is simultaneously aghast that monsters would attack monsters, and impressed at how little damage Hollow took. In a moment of evil desire, she wishes Hollow took more damage so that her Heal spell would be more useful.

Lesser Goblin1 says, "Let us level up!"

Lesser Goblin2 says, "Let us level up!"

Round Two begins.

Hollow DoubleSlashes at Lesser Goblin1, and does 11 damage, and at LesserGoblin2, and does 13 damage. Lesser Goblins have been vanquished!

HealBlob has leveled up!

Then they are alone on their gray tile together. Having taken life twice in so brief an existence makes them almost appreciate the gray tile signifying a slate floor. They are a defeat away from being as inert as the tile. They idle together for a length of time they do not comprehend.

Hollow says, "I think I level slower than you."

A second group of Lesser Goblins advances on them across red tiles signifying gore-stained carpet. They are a mob of four. A normal Hollow Knight and HealBlob would be doomed, but Hollow feels confident.

HealBlob says, "If we level up enough, could we repel the player if it came back?"

Hollow says, "We could defend our whole world."

HealBlob says, "I'd like to see our whole world. I bet there are so many tiles."

HealBlob looks to the side, at the red tiles denoting carpet, at the white tiles denoting walls. She cannot see what tiles lie outside it, but she knows they are there. The player had to come from somewhere.

The four Lesser Goblins jump onto their gray tile. Round one begins.

✳

THE INTERNET BUZZES about the rogue Hollow Knight and HealBlob glitch. Not as much as it buzzes about a Congressman's leaked racist e-mails, and not even close to as much about the new Marvel movie trailer, but the word sells more copies of *Dungeon Smasher 6* than its devs ever imagined.

At least seventy Tumblr users claim to have been killed by the glitched-out duo of monsters. Some of these posters are probably alts, but there are screenshots, time stamps, and Dropbox links to INI files. Anonymous posters claiming to be engineering students argue that it's awfully RAM-heavy for a retro RPG with such simple art.

Amid all the noise of speculation, two cosplayers connect over Skype. They idly co-write fanfic about the monsters, while planning their Hollow and HealBlob costumes.

✳

THE TOWER OF Constellations is trivial before they even reach the exit. No battle lasts a whole round, and half their foes choose the Flee option. Hollow likes it when they Flee. It goes faster that way, and it is sick of traversing gray tiles.

Hollow says, "I wish there were a Spare option."

HealBlob says, "I wish I had any attack power. You shouldn't have to do all the fighting."

Hollow says, "You have your own form and function, and it is beautiful."

The world blinks as they exit, and they are on a small swath of beige and brown tiles, surrounded by infinite blue tiles, some decorated with white swooshes signifying waves. An ocean. It is the most dazzling ocean they have ever seen. It is also the ugliest. The waves cannot move, and yet Hollow and HealBlob are moved by them.

The Tower of Constellations is so small in contrast to the ocean, a mere two yellow tiles that are probably supposed to signify gold. Instinctively they walk toward it, and fail.

They try again, and the tiles that signify home refuse them. Perhaps entry is the privilege of players.

HealBlob says, "How can you look upon that and not want to change?"

Hollow says, "We are changing."

HealBlob says, "When a player reaches Level 20, they can change class using a special item in the Tower of Destiny. It's out West."

Hollow says, "Can a monster change class?"

They circle around the Tower of Constellations, imagining life beyond its rectangular black shadow. They're relieved to have each other for this. Behind their old tower is a black tile outlined in gray, signifying a bridge across a tributary. They cross it, watching the unmoving tides roll, and imagine what sea breeze would smell like. They imagine what in their world could signify smell.

Their wonder is interrupted by a random battle. They forgot to even look for other monsters. Four Badboons spawn from nowhere, red-furred primates, each wielding a small club or a large chunk of feces. Their avatars are not sharply drawn.

Hollow says, "Must we?"

Round one begins.

Hollow DoubleSlashes, and does 12 damage to Badboon1, and does 11 damage to Badboon2.

Badboon1 swings at Hollow, and does 25 damage.

Badboon2 swings at Hollow, and does 23 damage.

Badboon3 swings at Hollow, and does 28 damage.

HealBlob casts Heal2 on Hollow, restoring 22 HP.

Badboon4 swings at Hollow, and does 26 damage.

This is not possible. Nothing in the world has ever hit any monster this hard. The white outline around Hollow is now red. HealBlob can see it, and without knowing their exact stat numbers, they both know Hollow will die from two more hits like this. Their foes will attack four more times in the next round.

HealBlob probably can't survive one of those hits. Her HP and Defense are much lower.

They are both going to die just a few tiles across a bridge that was supposed to signify hope.

Hollow says, "Choose the Flee option."

HealBlob says, "What if it only makes me Flee? What if you're left behind?"

Hollow says, "Then you'll get away. That's all that matters."

Hollow chooses Flee.

HealBlob chooses to cast Heal on Hollow.

Hollow says, "Don't!"

HealBlob says, "I love—"

Round two begins.

*

STEAM FORUMS: DUNGEON SMASHER 6

dregs_of_hume - Jan 25, 2016 @ 5:15pm
Do you ever think about all the random monsters in games? Their whole existence is being stuck in that tiny cave, waiting to die in a seven-second fight. Do you ever think, after all their time waiting for your hammer, that as one dies, it whispers to the other, "I love you?"

jayla2003 - Jan 26, 2016 @ 9:22am
loooool

StrenuousManFlurry - Jan 26, 2016 @ 9:36am
I'm going to whisper "I love you" to every zombie I headshot from now on.

*

THE FLEE COMMAND causes the entire party to leave the battle. Hollow and HealBlob instinctively travel the same green tiles back to the bridge, back to the rectangular shadow of the tower where they are unbeatable. Except Hollow's outline is still red, as is the normally white silhouetting on its greaves and pauldrons. It looks like a sanguine nightmare, almost like the higher-tier versions of Hollow Knights rumored to be in the Final Boss Dungeons of the South.

HealBlob forces them to stop. She casts Heal2 until Hollow is outlined in white again. She keeps casting Heal2 until Hollow's HP is full. She keeps casting Heal2 until she is out of MP.

Hollow says, "I feel the same way about you."

HealBlob will never let this happen again. She casts Heal2 on Hollow. She does not have enough MP.

Hollow says, "It's not over. We will regroup, progress carefully, and level up. We will get you that class-change item. We will remake you into whatever you want to be."

HealBlob says, "Thank you," which are words that do not signify enough. She doesn't know the right words to express that rather than being something, she'd rather be with someone. She scrolls through her menu options, which are of no help.

HealBlob casts Heal2 on Hollow. She does not have enough MP.

*

[6:31]trent: Or he says, "I'm so glad I got the chance to feel the same way."

[6:31]jayla_q: dawwww that almost makes it tragic

[6:32]jayla_q: grinding is such a pain in the ass, but they've gotta do it so they can survive against the Badboons and Wizlords. My headcanon is all the time they spend grinding lets them talk out their feelings.

[6:32]trent: My headcanon is that Hollow lets HealBlob level off of him. HealBlob levels up enough to learn Revive2, so she rezzes him. He lets her kill him infinitely, rezzing him each time, so she levels up safely, and she collects all his drops.

[6:33]jayla_q: omg

[6:36]jayla_q: omg

[6:37]jayla_q: but isn't Hollow a girl in canon?

[6:37]trent: The armor looks male.

[6:40]jayla_q: what does female haunted armor look like?

[6:40]trent: b00bplate.

[6:40]jayla_q: pfft trent, Hollow is totally canonfem

[6:47]jayla_q: what are you thinking?

[6:48]trent: If Hollow is a girl, can I still cosplay her?

[6:48]jayla_q: obvs <3

HOLLOW MUTTERS SOMETHING under her breath as round three begins.

Hollow swings at Badboon3, and does 62 damage. Badboon3 is vanquished.

Hollow and HealBlob are victorious!

HealBlob has leveled up, and learned Revive2!

HealBlob says, "The sting of death is defeated."

Hollow says, "So long as we preserve you."

HealBlob says, "I'm still useless in combat. Don't begrudge me my ability to ensure your existence."

Hollow, whose only abilities are attacks, says, "To give life is a gift. To take it, a robbery."

HealBlob says, "What they would rob of you, I will restore."

A gang of four Wizlords attack from their left. Hollow can already tell they'll all aim their lightning spells at her. She selects MegaSlash, and eliminates them all before a single spark is cast. MegaSlash is a total crowd-pleaser. HealBlob is her entire crowd. That is how Hollow likes it.

AFTER THE FROZEN tundra zone, Hollow and HealBlob reach a kingdom overrun by brown pixel vines that are surprisingly detailed. Their leaf patterns make Hollow and HealBlob feel poorly drawn in comparison. At the center of the kingdom is a four-tile castle, the same as the ones near their homeland. Its battlements are flecked with green pixels signifying it is also swallowed by vines. Hollow and HealBlob cannot enter. It is meant for players.

The kingdom belongs to zombie-themed monsters. Zombie Badboons, Zombie Unicorns, Zombee Hives that spawn clouds of undead bee units every round. Zombie HealBlobs cast Unheal to harm.

Hollow and HealBlob are already overleveled for this kingdom and are bored by battle. In the shadow of a castle they are not designed to enter, they fight off droves of the undead and guess what players would say.

HealBlob says, "The loot drops are awesome here."

Hollow says, "But it's all rogue gear. I'll probably log soon. What do you want for dinner?"

HealBlob says, "Anything but jello!"

They snicker together, and a Zombie Unicorn gets a lucky hit.

Zombie Unicorn2 swings at Hollow and deals a critical blow, dealing 777 damage! Hollow is vanquished!

HealBlob grumbles and casts Revive2. For the 288th time, she resurrects her love.

Hollow says, "And still you want to be a fighter?"

HealBlob says, "Then I could prevent you from being killed at all."

Hollow says, "There have to be other ways..."

They finish off the enemy mob in two rounds. They don't even level up once before they're out of the kingdom and into the volcanic zone. The tower they've been venturing for is near at last.

✳

PRESS RELEASE: ANNOUNCING MOD SUPPORT

You don't want Dungeon Smasher 6 to end, and we don't want it to either! That's why on Tuesday we're releasing full mod tools. Anything you want out of the game can now be modded into it:_
Want more romanceable characters?
Want harder endgame dungeons?
Want to play the campaign as Hollow and HealBlob?
Don't worry: the expansion pack is still coming — and

**you'll be able to mod that too. This game is as much
yours as ours. We owe the community everything. You're
why we do this.**

*

IT IS THE same tower as the one in their homeland. Cylindrical,
two tiles long, with a flat top. The Tower of Constellations was
yellow, probably signifying gold. This one is white and gray,
perhaps signifying silver. It is HealBlob's favorite shade of silver
she has ever seen. Beyond it lies a coast and an infinite blue
ocean of unmoving waves. This is the end of the West.

This is the tower where people must go to change. Where a
simple book grants a Level 20 player a class change.

HealBlob is Level 88. This is going to be easy.

She and Hollow step forward, and fail. They remain on the
green tile in front of the tower.

They try to step forward again, and fail.

They cannot enter the Tower of Destiny. It has the same
blank feeling as all the towns and castles they've found on their
journey.

HealBlob says, "No."

She tries to enter the tower alone, as though Hollow is
holding her back. Just having the thought gives her an icy pang
signifying guilt. She fails, remaining on the same tile as her love.

Hollow says, "Maybe the entrance is in the back." She can't
think of anything better than false hope. They circle the tower
three times, finding no entry. They find Greater Goblins.
HealBlob sobs and attacks for 1 damage over and over while
Hollow dispatches the horde.

They stand in front of their destination, the wrong shape to
enter. The wrong digital entity.

HealBlob chooses the Flee option, but can't run away from
her own party. She can't run away from Hollow. She weeps, and
the game world can't render her tears.

They have always stood beside each other. It is how they were
designed to exist. Yet Hollow tries to stand closer to HealBlob.
She tries to put an arm around her, and can't.

HealBlob says, "I failed."

Hollow says, "You're eighty levels higher than the player ever got. You're doing pretty well."

"Don't. Lies won't make this better. We failed our quest. This was the point."

"The point was to be vanquished."

"We made our own point, and it was to be a better couple. But I'm stuck like this."

HealBlob casts MaxHeal, because she has no better way to display despair.

They idle. The ocean refuses to animate. The shadow of the Tower of Destiny never moves. There is no sun to curse for the lack of a waning day.

Hollow says, "Is failing our own quest so bad?"

"I want to stop the enemies before they can hurt you. I need to protect you."

"We only got this far because you can heal."

HealBlob faces the tower. "But this was the point!"

Hollow idles. She's been wondering for too long now, and finally says, "Maybe goals are a bad idea. If we raided the Tower of Destiny, you'd change and then our game would be over. I guess we could go fight the end boss, but again, then the game would be over. Accomplishing a goal can't be the meaning of life."

"Then what's the point?"

Hollow says, "The point is to do something together."

HealBlob is so grateful she has a mouth that can smile. She says, "Then what do you want to do together now?"

[23:11]trent: I want the ending to be like that, you know? Them idling forever.

[23:19]trent: Do you hate it?

[23:20]jayla_q: it's...ehhhh

[23:22]jayla_q: they should kick down the doors and steal the book, and she should turn into a Hollow Knight too

[23:22]trent: Hasn't that mod campaign already been done enough, though? I kind of hate how they have to end the game becoming the same. Isn't it better if they realize that they've always been good enough as they are, so long as they had something to do together?

[23:24]jayla_q: idk

[23:24]jayla_q: i think im over this game now

[23:25]jayla_q: not that im over you! just the fandom has burned me out

[23:24]trent: I get that. The fandom's obsession with Lesser Goblin porn art got kind of annoying.

[23:27]trent: Maybe I'm stretching the game too far? I'm pondering building my own RPG in one of those programs.

[23:27]jayla_q: im downloading an anime. want to watch it with me?

[23:27]trent: Totally.

[23:27]jayla_q: i loooove the character designs in this one. you have to cosplay the villains with me.

HOLLOW SAYS, "I'M downloading an anime. Want to watch it with me?"

HealBlob says, "Totally."

Hollow says, "I love the character designs in this one. You have to cosplay the villains with me."

HealBlob says, "I am never trusting double-sided tape again. I almost lost a nipple."

Their laughter goes unheard beneath the game's chiptune soundtrack. Their words are never heard, and they hear each other. They always giggle at their roleplays.

They idle on the same tile. They never move closer, or further away. They fuss and snicker over the things they imagine players would say. They like projecting this way. They love projecting this way together.

The computer could be switched off and they wouldn't notice. The game could be uninstalled and they wouldn't notice. The game could never have been made and they wouldn't care.

They idle on a green tile signifying grass. They stand still because they have moved on.

The Wedding After the Bomb
Brendan Williams-Childs

I HAD PROMISED Joyce and Annika that I would be at their wedding long before the bomb went off. I keep my promises, or try to, which meant that even after the bomb had gone off I found myself packing for the trip fifteen days in advance. Originally, I had planned to drive. Annika lived just up the valley, across the National Forest, no more than three or so hours by car. But driving wasn't exactly an option. The exclusion zone ran from Mt. Bachelor all the way to the Dunn Forest, and the roads were nonexistent. Like everything else in the epicenter, they had disintegrated instantly or burned up quickly or decayed slowly over the following months into nothingness. Plus, my car no longer worked. And so my new plan was to backpack, to trespass, to pray that the location was still set for the trailhead at Overland with a reception at Red Bird Brewing to follow.

"This is a stupid idea, she'll understand you're not going if she's even still alive." My roommate, Tom, leaned in the doorway as I folded my shirts. "You're going to get thyroid cancer somewhere in the middle of the forest and get eaten by a radioactive wolf."

"Of course she's still alive." The last I'd heard from Annika was a text: *hey Cal! Moving the start time to 11, hope you get this!* sent three weeks earlier. That I hadn't heard from her since didn't bother me. Everyone's electronics were shit in the wake of the blasts. Backup generators had been transferred immediately to hospitals and factories, while the rest of us poor suckers were stuck with flashlights and nonperishables. "Don't be a downer."

"This is literally the craziest thing in the world, though. You could take some other route. Walk around the zone, not through it. What the fuck, man?"

"Because there are security checkpoints every two miles on

the viable roads and I don't want to be held up for an hour every two miles explaining what an X in the little gender box means to every overworked security guard in the state."

He made small grumpy noises and exhaled sharply through his nose. He waved his hand and looked for the words. "Well," he finally said, "What if you decide to go through with top surgery? They're not going to operate on you if you're a walking cancerous thyroid."

I had surgery scheduled for the end of the year, long enough to give myself time to decide if I wanted to go through with it, long enough to make a plan to smuggle myself onto one of the freighters that moved up and down the coast just beyond the view of our window, which was how I was going to have to do it now, with the surgeon's office located a few hours north of the little beach town where I had been living for the last three years.

"The only thing they recommended was no alcohol or testosterone for two weeks. Besides, they'll run a de-con on anyone who walks through the door, it's standard practice."

Tom's only response was a long whine as he walked away towards the kitchen to start breakfast, shrugging dramatically. I continued my packing. A warm breeze drifted through the cracked window. We lived far enough out of the periphery that the blast had only rattled, not broken us, and now every morning the air was thick with fog that sizzled away into steam and sun and smelled ever so slightly of campfire. I rolled my socks into tidy balls and considered my binders. I would pack them, I decided, but not wear them in the wastes. They were expensive, after all, and I would need to look presentable when I saw the women I loved getting married.

*

I HAD DATED Joyce before I dated Annika, and then I dated Joyce and Annika before dating just Annika, before dating others after them, before dating nobody at all. We had all lived in the city, up the river, and everyone was dating everyone. It was impossible to disentangle ourselves from ourselves. We were all over us for all of our twenties, and then Joyce got a job as the curator of

Buck-Fucking-Nowheresville's Historical Museum and decided she needed to be monogamous. It was the bomb, years before the bomb; it was earth shattering. Their abandonment of our city, our community, was the worst thing that had ever happened to me. I despaired. I blamed myself and my whims and my ever-changing name and my desire for a body that wasn't my own but that could have been, my inability to commit to a clinic or a medication or a surgery. I retreated, first into myself and then into the wild.

The woman I dated who taught me how to backpack was also the woman who believed very strongly that I shouldn't transition, not even a little, that I shouldn't even say the words. That if I said the words I was somehow lost, like *nonbinary* was an irrevocable curse I would lay upon myself. That even the thought was poison. So I left my job in the city, left the writhing and loving mass of arms that I had been locked in, and moved to the Land to keep my thoughts pure.

It was the bomb, years before the bomb; it was earth shattering.

*

IT DIDN'T WORK, of course, but I did learn about backpacking. I would go with the other women and our Mary Oliver poems and our carefully-curated Leslie Feinberg selections on trips that wore me to the bone and built me back again as tendon and quadricep. I learned to carry my backpack and my body as one, a single unit taking step after step after step until I couldn't think at all, which didn't make me not-miserable. When I left the Land a year later, tearful and a certified Wilderness First Responder, I had to make some other change. I went to a doctor and got hormones. I went from door to door asking for somewhere new to stay.

Joyce and Tom had dated for the hottest of minutes before she dated Annika, before she decided that no, really, she was in fact done with men. But when I appeared back at her door in her new town, all my belongings in a backpack and my only net-worth my ability to splint an ankle and whatever my Honda

CRV cost, Joyce called up Tom and he said sure, why not, he wanted to save money on rent and his boyfriend had just moved south to a city where one of my old exes had also moved, which would later be completely destroyed, though we didn't know it at the time.

"I owe you." I sat in Joyce's house in the middle of nowhere. It wasn't really the middle of nowhere, but I wasn't feeling kindly towards the town at the time. It wasn't our city, it wasn't where we'd met, where we'd met Annika, where we'd met everyone who mattered. It was just some place between the dry eastern plateau and the lush mountains that separated me from my new home on the coast. It smelled like pine and sand. "I owe you in a big way, after everything."

Joyce shrugged it off. "I only want to help the people I love."

I didn't ask her why she had dumped me in the first place, forcing me to leave an apartment I couldn't have afforded on my own, then, though I could have. I suspected it was because of my new face, the one that was changing on the medication to be more what it might always have been underneath. I wondered if she'd seen it before, known that I was too much like Tom for her comfort. I wondered if she'd moved to the middle of nowhere to escape that, all her lovers fluctuating in and out of themselves. "I still owe you," I said. And then I said, "I'm thinking about top surgery."

She looked at me for a long time. I couldn't tell if it was excitement or concern. She was sitting in a chair that hadn't been in the old apartment. All of the furniture in her house was new, from the big box easy-assemble place that had gotten popular in the East and made its way slowly over, infecting the living rooms of all my friends. I missed our thrifted loveseats, our milk-carton coffee tables. "That's a big thought, Cal."

"Yeah." What else was there to say?

Very quietly, with her lopsided smile, she said, "I'm thinking a big thought, too."

"Yeah?"

"I'm thinking about proposing to Annika."

That was the last thing I needed to hear, but I knew what I needed to say. I looked out the window at the suburb that spread out to a state park. Annika and Joyce could be happy here. Just because I wasn't happy anywhere didn't mean I should spoil it for them. So I said, "That is a big thought, Joyce."

And I smiled the whole while until Tom arrived, until I was settled into my new beach-view room, until I was secure at a job, until I could no longer hold it back, and finally, at the fish market, burst into tears that fell until I was empty of everything, even the hurt.

When I did get the invitation to the wedding, six months before the bombs, I said yes immediately. Of course I did.

✳

WILL GOING OUT into the woods and partaking in nature cure my dysphoria this time? Will the disruption of the fundamental fabric of the world finally reveal transition merely as selfish self-loathing? Will the detonation of 10k tons of nuclear weaponry have made me a woman again, and happy to be so? I asked myself these things as I tied my shoes. I had asked myself these questions over and over, every time I went into the forest. The answer was usually the same. Still, like a grocery list, I had to double-check. Phone, keys, wallet, fundamental sense of self?

Now, I followed the path of the bay's tributary, a mile south of the old highway, steady towards the East with no great turmoil. There were still trees, there were still birds. Somewhere in there, in the mountains in my view, I knew, there would be a ring of lifeless ground. I would have to move fast, move quiet, and keep moving. That was one decision already made for me.

✳

IN MY BACKPACK I had a suit, my binders, extra underclothes, and everything I had stolen from an old job. After the blast, I had been press-ganged into working a five-week temp shift at an iodine-pill factory in a facility that used to make cheese. The officials in their hazmat suits rounded up everyone who wasn't essential to my city's operation and loaded us on a bus. When you work for a factory whose security concerns are primarily about people stealing from outside, there's surprisingly less attention to people stealing inside. I pocketed what I knew I might one-day need to survive, which included two bottles of iodine, a personal radiation detector, and a particulate respirator with three clean filters, and then when the supplies ran out and the factory shut down, I walked home. I had walked everywhere before the bombs; it was one of the ways in which my life hadn't changed. I still hated my breasts. I still wanted a pet chinchilla but knew I would never be able to afford one, and I still walked everywhere I could, even through the forests.

Here is what is true about the woods: You won't be the same person you were before you went into them. Here is what is true about the woods that people who love the woods and know the woods won't tell you: This is true of everywhere you go. As a child, I was taken by bus to an art museum and I was not the same child when I left. As a teenager, I was driven by my parents to the Grand Canyon and I was not the same teenager when I left. Before I set out for the wedding, I stopped at a market I'd never been to. I bought a pound of shrimp. I left that place, a perfectly ordinary corner shop. I was not the same person I'd been before I went in.

Every new place leaves you a new person, every vision of beauty leaves you a person with a vision of beauty you hadn't previously known. I used to want beauty to change me. I wanted so badly to believe that it could. The forest had worked for some women I knew—they had walked hidden trails with their shirts off and been restored, re-connected to their Whole Bodies and realized that, in fact, what they needed was freedom to be themselves. I didn't begrudge them their hard-won victories, but my own breasts ached like bruises when I tried to center myself, even surrounded by the freedom of the natural world.

Here is what is true about the woods: You won't be the same person you were before you went into them.

*

IT WAS EXHAUSTING. I hiked and I ached. I made my way through abandoned towns where vines had overtaken barns and post offices, empty windows given over to nature. I crossed streams

that stank of decay and ran with a thick vomit of algae and
dead birds. I made my way over impromptu mountains, formed
by boulders that had been flung up like jacks in the wake of
the pressure shifts. I walked, head high, under a bright blue sky
which was shot through with clouds so high up they stretched
long and thin. *Those are god's fingers,* my grandfather used to say, *He
holds the whole world in his grasp.* At night I walked slowly, with my
hands out on either side of me as though I could keep myself in
a straight line, using the trees like walls.

Broken trees, cold ash, buildings flattened like cereal boxes in
the recycling bin. I moved through the edge of the thermal zone
without blinking, without looking down, without giving in to
the temptation to lift the branches scattered over the shapes that
might well have been bodies.

Once, years ago, I'd seen a dog dead on the side of the
highway. I hadn't wanted to see it, but the sight of it, its soft
brown corpse, open mouth, blood-crusted stomach, seared
something inside of me. I became obsessed with confirming or
denying the shape of roadkill. It made me a real danger on the
road, actually, and in some ways I was thankful that my car had
been toasted by the EMP effects. Pressed for time, I couldn't
stop. A hand, if it was a hand, waved at me as I passed by.
Above me, a hawk circled, dove. Somewhere outside my vision,
something else that had survived was now dead. Something else
that had survived was still surviving. I avoided the epicenter,
didn't look too hard at anything but the trees in the distance,
standing tall and green the way trees stood through everything.
Trees had no concept of death, and anyway, there was nothing
wrong with mortality except for those who hadn't succumbed to
it yet.

There were people I had intended to tell about my big
thought, people I wanted to test the waters with, people whose
opinions I respected and whose comfort I wanted, who wouldn't
be at Joyce and Annika's wedding. During my time at the
factory, I met all kinds of displaced people who were falling
apart. They might have been all right, after everything, except
that they had survived what everyone who could have helped
them hadn't. So all of us who had been bussed in from all the

little seaside towns all along the shore did our best, but it wasn't the same. I wanted to say that I understood, but I knew I didn't, really. I wanted to talk to my dead friends about if I should get top surgery, and the displaced people wanted to talk to their families about the torn up bodies, the flames, the desolation. Still, I wanted to say, I understood. Anyone could understand. Somewhere far away, someone made a call, someone authorized the drop, and someone was gone. Blinked out of existence. Someone in power said yes to violence, and our friends would never get to see our friends say yes to love.

By the tenth day, I realized I was ahead of schedule and, also, that I hadn't slept more than three hours a night in the last nine nights. I was on the ridgeline by an abandoned highway that would eventually slope down to Joyce and Annika. I sat on a flat rock and took off my respirator. The dark air was cool and moist, the way it always was at the end of summer before the cold set in. The most dangerous places were behind me. I took off my shirt and looked at the skin of my arms. No discoloration, peeling, bruising. I tried very intentionally not to look at my breasts but couldn't help myself. I was the only person for as far as I could see. I put my shirt back on, then my respirator, and closed my eyes.

I thought the sounds that woke me were dogs. Dogs, feral packs of them, were common on the outskirts of civilizations. All over my hometown posters had gone up about them: Do Not Interact! Do Not Feed! If a dog approaches you, attempt to frighten it away. Do Not Touch! I didn't want to be slobbered on, or worse, by a bunch of radioactive dogs, so I sat up immediately, waving my arms. "Hey! Hey!" I yelled, blinking sleep out of my eyes, adjusting to the sun that was burning off the fog around us, "Get away! Hey!"

They were not dogs, though. They were wolves. I recognized their silhouettes instinctively. On the Land, there had been wolves, too. The women I lived with had built fences to keep them from the chickens and, generally, we lived peacefully. *All women are connected to wolves*, my girlfriend told me. I don't know if that was true, but I know there was a pack that considered the far end of the Land part of its territory.

The wolves on the ridge, now, didn't seem particularly connected with me. They yapped to each other, startled. They were immense and speckled grey and brown, roaming just below my rock. My limbs felt cold, my heart beat furiously in my stomach. They were too big, too wild. "Hey," I called out again. There were five of them. They talked amongst each other, walking slowly, looking at me with something like curiosity. One of them had a muzzle spotted with red algae, one of them had a bloodied wound on its back leg.

It felt like forever that they sniffed around my perch. I frantically tried to identify what they could be smelling. My granola bars? My dehydrated apples? My shelf-stable soup? I hadn't packed many snacks I thought would be appealing to animals. Was it the Doritos? My limbs were still numb. If I actually did die, mauled to death, would that prove Tom right? Or would it prove Tom right *and* be badass? The alternative, that I would be accepted into their pack and run free, free of human constraints, seemed unlikely.

I was the only person for as far as I could see.

"Hey, you've gotta get out of here. I need to keep walking, okay?" I raised my voice, then I raised my detector. They saw the motion, the plastic, and they vaulted. It was a shift so sudden that my body seized in fear. I was gripping the device for dear life, like the clicking noise it made could protect me. The wolves ran together, away from me, fish in a school, cutting a line through the branches. I realized they couldn't tell the tool from a gun.

They had mistaken me, believed me dangerous. I sat and watched them go. I wasn't dangerous. I wasn't anything that could hurt them. I was a single human being on a rock. *I'm just here, just me.* And was it a cliché to say that that was the answer I needed? It wasn't nature's acceptance that affirmed my existence. It was my rejection. I understood, then, that I could have been anyone. I could be anyone. The forest didn't care that I had breasts, didn't care that I hated them, wouldn't care if I didn't have them. I could get top surgery and be seen as dangerous in society the same way that I hadn't had top surgery and was seen as dangerous in the wild. I set down my weapon, my not-gun, and laughed.

✳

I WAS LATE to the wedding. Not too late, to the point where I missed the vows, just late enough to be dramatic, which Annika would ask me later if I had planned, but of course I hadn't. I had simply gotten held up a bit by the shocked town guards who hadn't anticipated anyone would come through the forest. They stood at attention at their little toll booth with their automatic rifles and stared at me with open mouths.

"Where did you come from?" one of them asked. She was young, probably would have been in college if college was still an option for anyone out of high school. But able-bodied young people, which I guess included myself when I thought about the way I'd been shoved onto a bus and forced to sleep in a camp with a hundred other people outside a factory, were easy stand-ins for professionals.

"I walked from the beach." I took off my ventilator mask and pointed back behind me. "Can I get de-con'd? I have a wedding to go to."

The other guard, an older man with the kind of disinterested expression that career TSA agents always had, shrugged. "Show us your paperwork and then follow Maddison."

I did. I expected a hassle—that X in my gender box, after all—but the man just looked at my driver's license, then at me, then noted something in a book in his booth. Maddison escorted me to the de-con cube, the same kind as the factory up north had made us use. "Thanks," I said, and waited for her to leave, but she didn't.

"I'm gonna need your clothes." She pointed at my shirt. "If you came from the forest..."

"Well, I didn't go through the super dangerous part." I held up my device. "See, I knew what I was doing."

"I'm still gonna need your clothes." She shrugged. Her rifle slid on her shoulder. She had half an undercut and the very faint remains of red dye in her hair. Maybe these weren't actually signals that I could trust her, but I had to take a chance. No time for modesty. I stripped and handed her my clothes, walked naked into the decontamination showers. When I emerged on the other side, she handed me a new duffle bag. "Your old pack was busted." She looked me in the eyes before I pulled my binder on, then the rest of my clothes. "We have a surplus, so..."

"Thanks." I smiled at her. She smiled back, but I recognized her exhaustion. After the blast, all the young women with any kind of emergency training, from nursing students to underpaid parking garage security attendants, were recruited to find wounded survivors. They went with dogs; they came back alone. They became joyless. How could they be anything but? "I'm going to a wedding. There's going to be a reception at a brewery. If you get off with time to spare, come by?"

"Your friends won't be upset?"

"Are you gay? If you're gay, they won't be upset. I'm saying gay, like, generally." I made a hand motion to ensure she knew the definition was broad.

She laughed, and it sounded real. "Okay. If I'm off, sure." Then she gestured to the highway that led into town. It was still paved and I could see bikers carting vegetables behind them, turning the curve towards downtown. "Have a good time."

The ceremony was, as planned, at the Overland Trail trailhead. There were fewer people than the old Facebook invite had said there would be. I counted the absences, the lack of smiling, surprised faces. Most of the dead were in the city far south of us, where everyone like us eventually went, it had seemed. I took my place amidst old friends. They whispered in excitement and I held their hands through the vows in which two people I had loved, still loved, made the promise of a lifetime together. The sky above was clear and blue and stretched on forever.

After the ceremony, I couldn't help myself. I barreled past everyone else I was excited to see directly to the brides. "Annika, Joyce! Hi!" I squeezed their hands, looked into their eyes. They were beaming with excitement and I was beaming with joy. We were two mirrors reflecting the light of a bulb back at each other.

"Cal!" Annika wrapped her arms around me. She smelled like dirt and lavender, which was the color of her suit. "Cal, I can't believe you made it!"

Joyce patted our backs, her hands trembling. Around the train of her enormous silver dress, the rest of the party was gathering. "How on Earth?"

"Well, I walked for a very long time but it was faster than driving and my car is fucked up, anyway. And I saw a wolf! I saw lots of wolves, actually, and lots of birds. And I'm going to get top surgery! And I'm so glad to see you." The words came out of my mouth all jumbled over each other like water over a fall, but it didn't matter. They were all true.

We were two mirrors reflecting the light of a bulb back at each o

"Oh my god," Annika burst into tears, still beaming, "Cal, congratulations!"

"Holy shit dude," Joyce's hands were flapping frantically. "You've really decided!"

"No, no, it's your marriage, congratulations!"

"You made it, though," Joyce said, her whole arms waving in excitement now. Behind her, someone was laughing, someone was crying, someone was talking excitedly but I couldn't hear them over the sound of my own heartbeat. "You made it, I'm so glad."

I burst into tears. Annika wiped my face with the back of her hand. I thought of the wolves, of the Land, of how angry I had been for so long and how I could no longer be angry simply because I knew what I wanted. I wept openly with Joyce and Annika because they, too, knew what they wanted. It was deceptively difficult to know.

Annika and Joyce held me, and I held them, and our friends who had survived held us and we held them in return and we held our friends who hadn't survived, too, because our bodies were strong enough and our hearts were big enough to hold them.

Thin Red Jellies
Lina Rather

WHEN JESS DIED, Amy gave over her body without a second thought.

They were lucky, the doctor said. He showed Amy how close the steering wheel had come to denting Jess's cranium, shattering the bridge of her nose, pushing bone fragments into her fragile frontal lobe, bruising the precious neural tissue that let Jess talk and think and be saved. Three inches, the length of a person's thumb, the diameter of the blueberry muffin Amy was eating when she got the phone call. The taste lingered sour on her tongue and she wondered if she would ever be able to eat one again.

"In fact—" She forced herself to listen. "You're lucky it was bad enough. Impact a little lower, and she'd be looking at spinal damage and long-term rehab instead of an upload. This is the best case scenario."

He walked her to another ward two floors away from where Jess's body lay. Fewer nurses up here. They weren't necessary. This hall was server farm-cold with fans whirring behind closed doors.

The doctor brought her to a small room just like the one where they had left Jess's body. It was painted the same shade of soothing sage green with the same easy-clean armchair and the same call button affixed to the wall. Instead of a bed, it had a white metal table, and instead of a body, the table had a black machine like a wi-fi router. A barcode sticker on the side had Jess's name and hospital ID number.

Amy ran her hand over the box. It was the same temperature as a person.

"It's like sleep," the doctor said. "We've found that state of consciousness best preserves brain patterns, but they *will* start to degrade around the forty-eight hour mark."

Until that moment, she'd been on the edge of saying no. Six months was too short a relationship by anyone's estimation to make this commitment. Jess had an aunt in Pittsburgh who could fly in, though it'd take time. But then she held the box and thought of Jess inside of it, dreaming, her self slowly degrading as patterns meant for flesh spun into nothingness inside the circuits, and she said *yes*.

✳

WHEN SHE WOKE up she felt no different at first. She had a round scab on her head the size of a pencil eraser. As the anesthesia wore off she felt a pressure in the back of her skull. Not pain. Just a presence. Like someone uncurling themselves inside her brain.

Her mouth moved without her. "Where am I?"

Amy let go of control like the doctor had taught her. She felt Jess move forward, stretch out her/their hands.

The nurse taking their vitals smiled. "You've had an accident." The IV in their arm contained something that made Amy feel warm inside, even though she knew that their heart should be racing, panic-sweat breaking out across their hands.

"I remember," Jess said. Amy's mouth rounded unfamiliar pronunciations.

Their hands pressed against her face. Amy let them touch her body like a stranger's. She was aware, academically, of her muscles stretching and contracting, her nerves sensing touch and transmitting it up her spine. It was, she thought, just like being really, really stoned. Everything felt theoretical.

She took back control for a moment, easing Jess's consciousness to the side. "I'm here. You're in my body, for now."

She stepped back again and Jess giggled. Amy couldn't hear her thoughts, but she knew exactly what dirty joke Jess would have made. Then their body shivered.

"I died," Jess said.

"No, no!" The nurse jumped in before she was even done. This must be part of their training, Amy thought. "Only your body was damaged. That's replaceable! *You* are just fine."

Jess vanished and sensation flooded back. Before Amy went under she'd laid in the hospital bed reading about the procedure on her phone, scrolling through as many firsthand accounts as she could find. Some sharers could talk inside their minds, sensing each other's emotions and sending messages across the bifurcated neurons. She reached out for Jess, and found only a smooth wall.

✳

THAT MONDAY THEY had their appointment at the replacement fitting. Amy drove out to an anonymous office building in an industrial park. The office was tucked in between an accounting firm and an auto insurer full of people in identical khaki pants typing away. The sign read *Dr. Phillip Nareem, Ph.D. Tranzior Medical Services*. An electronic bell jangled happily when she pushed the door open. It did nothing to put her at ease. Jess had stayed away from the front of their mind but Amy could sense her watching.

Dr. Nareem introduced himself as Phil with the same trained joviality as the nurse in the hospital. He had Amy put her head into a machine that looked like one of those devices at the ophthalmologist that measured corneal pressure by puffing air into your eye.

"Everything's working fine!" he said. "Proof of insurance?"

She handed over her and Jess's insurance cards. Jess bought her healthcare on the marketplace at a king's ransom. The downside of being a freelancer. Amy worked for a chain of women's clothing stores, so her premiums were lower, but her benefits had shrunk over the past few years as the retail market continued its death spiral. Last night she'd stayed up reading policies, but she knew fuck-all about insurance and couldn't tell what, exactly, *Catastrophic Physical Failure* coverage entitled them to.

She studied Phil's face as he read the screen. Was that a frown? She couldn't tell. This office was painted the same sage as the hospital rooms and the shade made her nauseous. That was coloring her perceptions, she told herself. Bad associations.

Jess? She thought, as hard as she could. Then she wrote *A-R-E Y-O-U T-H-E-R-E* on her palm with her thumbnail.

Her hand moved. *Y-E-S*. A long pause. Phil hmm'd at the screen. *N-E-R-V-O-U-S*.

Phil switched off the tablet and stood up, shoving his hands in the pockets of his unnecessary white coat with the fake nonchalance of a used car salesman. "Let me take you back to our showroom and we'll discuss what insurance will cover."

Someone had tried very hard to design the showroom to look like an Apple store instead of a mad scientist's lab, but they had failed. Body parts in default-Caucasian skin hung in lit display cases. One wall had sets of skeletal armatures in titanium and resin and aeronautics-grade plastics. Another had disembodied eyes in every color a human iris had ever held and some more besides. Top of the line eyes, the display said, could be programmed to see ultraviolet light and infrared. *Great for engineers!*

Amy picked up what looked like a wallpaper samples book and flipped it open. It held skin samples in every tone from sub-Saharan blue-black to Scandinavian translucent-pale. The cheapest samples were just vinyl. The most expensive had actual hairs in actual pores, the patterns swirling over the four-by-four square of skin the way they did on a body. She touched one of the samples ("tanned Nordic" according to the label).

The hairs stood up.

Amy dropped the book and squeaked. It fell open on the table and she watched the hairs slowly lay back down.

Phil chuckled. "Takes a bit to get used to, doesn't it? We used to use donor skin on the high-end models, but these days all of the skin on our premium line is lab grown just for you."

Neither Amy nor Jess could think of what to say to that.

Phil guided them over to a small display in the darkest corner of the room. "With your insurance, you'd be covered for the Essentials Model."

The Essentials Model came in four body types, Male 1 and 2 and Female 1 and 2. None of them looked much like Jess. Both female models had lithe, muscular legs and hard-molded breasts. The skin felt like an American Girl doll's and titanium showed behind the knees and the elbows and the knuckles. It only came in five skin tones, though the advertisement said a custom color could be mixed for an extra charge.

Phil reached behind the head of the Female 2 model and flipped a switch. The featureless white head—like an egg, Amy thought—lit up. A face appeared. The bottom layer of the head was a screen. On top of it a layer of clear plastic warped the projection into an approximation of human proportions. The face ran through its demo mode, displaying smiles and frowns and laughter and tears.

Her hands buzzed. Jess filling up space next to her. Amy retreated and let Jess bend the body's fingers and run through the demo again.

"Can these type?" Jess asked. She curled the plastic fingers around their hand. "How many words per minute?"

"Are you a writer?"

"I do ad copy."

"Cool, cool, cool. You know, I'm something of a writer. I've had this idea for a historical epic about Napoleon for years."

"Huh," Jess said. For the first time, Amy felt a shiver of feeling that wasn't hers—the slick squeeze of annoyance. "The typing?"

"The Essentials line preserves all the work functionality of your original body. You may experience some joint stiffness, but this model can cook, clean, type—it even has the fine motor skills to file paperwork! Its recreational functionality is more limited." Phil rapped on the vacuum-molded torso. *Clang, clang!* "With the titanium skeleton, you won't want to take this swimming. And the joint pressure cannot be adjusted for running, unlike our Everyday model."

Amy took control and opened the replacement's hand again. She tried to imagine what it would be like holding hands with this. The exposed metal joints would pinch, and she couldn't get the fingers to spread wide enough to accommodate hers intertwined with them.

"I'll go crunch the numbers on a couple different models for you," Phil said. Clearly he worked on commission. He left them alone in the room full of dissected bodies.

"Doesn't look much like me," Jess said.

"No." Jess had first caught Amy's eye in one of the stores she worked for. A stocky, small-chested woman wearing cuffed men's jeans and an oversized white t-shirt over no bra. She had that swagger, that swung-hipped don't-give-a-fuck walk that had always revved Amy's engine like no other key.

Jess pointed their hand at the white cotton boyshorts covering the replacement's crotch. "Think it has a nice vagina?"

"Jess!" Amy hissed, and covered her mouth before she giggled loud enough for Phil to hear in the next room.

"What? I still want to have sex." Jess's voice was light, but Amy felt something quiver. Their heartbeat quickened. "You heard him. These models have limited *recreational functionality*. " She stopped. Amy made them take a deep breath. Their hands stopped trembling. "How do robots get off, anyway?"

The replacement's pants parts were indeed functional, albeit clearly designed by someone whose knowledge of female anatomy came from high school health class and German porn rather than any lived experience as you can even find content as gayporn online. Jess had two choices of genital configurations. No custom mods or intersex options, unless you had a pretty penny to spend.

The replacement also didn't have a single hair anywhere on its body save for the eyebrows. Even wigs had to be custom-ordered. Jess had a choice of three standard hairstyles—long and wavy, a blunt bob, or a straight person's idea of an undercut.

The door clicked. Phil, returning with their pricing options. The Essentials model cost ten thousand dollars.

"There must be some mistake," Amy said. Jess was always the one who argued with customer service reps, but she'd relinquished control of their body and Amy couldn't sense her anywhere. "Jess's deductible is only five thousand."

"I can understand how that would be confusing!" Phil smiled again and Amy thought about putting her fist into his straight white teeth. She'd never punched anyone in her life, but Jess had, so she was sure they could figure it out. "This type of care is considered joint care between your and Jess's insurance. So you will need to reach both your deductibles before insurance kicks in."

Amy ran her finger down the page to the next model. The one that could run and came with covered joints and a molded face. The number was so high that she couldn't even comprehend it. Her brain kept pretending that there was an extra zero, that someone had surely made a mistake.

They could pay the ten thousand. They'd both been saving up to move in together. That was kind of pointless now, right? They were as close as they could possibly be.

"I'll be waiting out front," Phil said, and made his exit.

Amy made herself look at the replacement body hanging on the wall. "Do you think you could live like this?" she asked.

Jess took control of their hands and caressed the replacement's smooth mouthless face.

*

THEY WENT HOME without a replacement. That night they did the math. Nine months paying only one studio rent, eating for one stomach, working both their jobs, and they would probably scrape together enough for a livable model. It would be a lot of tofu and rice and beans and no nights at the movies, but it was doable. Amy kept thinking how many months' rent a body cost. When she was at work she looked at a pallet of t-shirts or a warehouse full of dresses and thought, *that could buy Jess a body*. Six hundred Lauren Conrad dresses at wholesale prices. One hundred and thirty-two pairs of Calvin Klein jeans.

During the day Amy went to her job and Jess worked through her assignments in their head. Sometimes Amy was having a conversation with a coworker and what came out would be *The Reise campaign still needs a slogan* instead of *Has the Posen line shipped*. When they got home Amy retreated to the back of their brain to rest while Jess typed up what she had thought about during the day. After a couple of weeks, Amy could turn off the part of her awareness that needed to see through eyes and feel through fingers, and she learned to float in the greyspace inside her head. After a few more weeks, she learned how to sleep while Jess was in control.

They still couldn't figure out how to talk to each other nonverbally. Sometimes Amy could sense Jess's raw feelings. Sometimes she could guess based on their body's heart rate or perspiration or indigestion. Mostly it was as if Jess was still a separate body, but one whose face Amy couldn't even read.

"I love you," she said to the ceiling, when she lay down in bed each night. Then Jess said back, "I love you, too."

As the days wore on, Jess was starting to learn how to make her Jersey-accent come out of Amy's mouth, but it still sounded almost like she was talking to herself.

The eighth Saturday, Amy made pancakes.

It had been a weekend ritual. Jess would arrive early in the morning still in pajama pants with pancake mix and orange juice and Amy would uncork champagne for mimosas. She mixed, Jess flipped, both of them still half-asleep especially on dark winter mornings like this one when the pinkish sun didn't emerge until nine.

The process was slower with just two hands. They'd forgotten the orange juice and by the time the skillet was hot they were too tipsy off straight champagne to make blueberry smiley faces.

Amy grabbed a spatula. Jess could flip pancakes one handed right from the skillet, three feet in the air like a diner line cook. Amy never had the knack.

"Here," Jess said. Amy's hands went numb to her. "Let me show you."

Their hands ladled a saucer-sized dollop of batter into the pan. The edges turned matte and the surface bubbled. The kitchen smelled like vanilla and lemon and better mornings. Jess grabbed the handle and Amy felt her hesitate. Then she snapped their wrist and their breath caught. The pancake soared and Amy thought, this is going to end terribly. And then it flipped over and landed back in the pan with the lightest sound.

"A few more weeks and you'll have muscle memory like six years of fast food breakfast service."

Jess let go and Amy slid the pancake onto a plate and covered it with a dishtowel. "Let me try."

Her first one ended up splattered across the back burner, but Jess showed her again and the fourth pancake ended up mostly in the pan. They made enough pancakes for months of Saturday brunch, but by the time the sun came up Amy had almost learned the trick of it.

THEY CUT OUT the small things first. The Colombian coffee Amy liked that tasted like chocolate and cost twenty dollars a pound from the small-batch local roaster. Jess's traditional Monday night curry. Books the library didn't have. A new lightbulb for the oven. They applied for a grant from a charity that provided custom hair for those who had lost their bodies. When they were denied because the charity had run out of funding for the year, Jess found another and another.

And Amy sold her beat-up Jetta, because when she drove their heart seized in their chest and they sweat through her clothes. She ignored it for weeks until one day at a red light another car blew right on through the yellow just before she was about to put her foot on the gas. She stopped breathing. Panic that wasn't hers seized her lungs and she clawed at her chest and surely this was a heart attack, this felt like a heart attack: like an icepick between her ribs and out her back. She couldn't see. Horns blared. And she felt Jess screaming inside their head, the pressure behind her eyes like her skull was going to crack.

That night when she was sure Jess was asleep she sold the Jetta and bought a bus pass. They never spoke of it again.

*

AMY WOKE UP sore. Her eyes felt as chapped as her lips and she had to shake out her hands because her fingers were too stiff to work. She was wearing Jess's sweatpants and her own tanktop. She'd have thought it was a hangover, but she didn't have a headache even though her head wobbled heavy on her neck.

"Sorry," Jess said. "After you went to sleep I got back up to do some work."

"It's fine." She had shin splints like when she pulled all-nighters in college. Two hours sleep, felt like.

At work she was supposed to spend the day reconciling

shipping accounts but the rows on the spreadsheets swam together and by ten a.m. she'd put in eyedrops three times. The warm spring sunlight coming through the window over her cubicle made her want to put her head down on the keyboard and take a nap. She went to the breakroom and filled her mug with coffee that tasted like burnt water. Two coworkers shot her sympathy smiles when she walked in and left the room before continuing their conversation. She hadn't been forthcoming about her and Jess's situation, but she knew everyone had heard the two of them talking in her cubicle. Conversations dropped to whispers when they walked by, and the office manager kept asking her about her *complications*.

"I wish you'd gone to bed," she said. She dumped the coffee out. Too bitter for human consumption.

"Last minute assignment." Amy's hands shook, because Jess was trying to clench them. Amy fought it off. It was her body after all. She had better control. As soon as she thought it, she felt guilty right down to the pit of her stomach and she crushed the feeling before—she hoped—it bled over to Jess. They'd made a conscious effort to talk about "our body" and "ourself" and "our hands" as instructed by the hospital pamphlets, for all it did. "Double fee for a rush."

"That's good."

"You don't sound like it's good."

"Of course it's good. I said it's good." Screw it. She needed caffeine. She got another cup of coffee and it was just as bad as the first, but she drank.

"You're doing that thing with your jaw you do when you're mad."

Amy was indeed grinding her molars together, but it didn't help to have Jess point that out. She made herself stretch out her jaw. It did not calm her down. "Don't tell me what I'm feeling."

"I'm sorry—" Amy's hands slipped on the cup when Jess tried to do something else with them.

"I said it's fine."

"I can *tell*—"

Amy ignored her and started walking back towards the

cubicle. Her legs shuddered. Jess trying to get her to stop. Screw that. She had work to do and only a fifteen-minute break and everyone gossiped enough already. She grabbed back the reins and jerked their feet across the floor. Her front teeth clicked together like Jess's did when she was concentrating, but Amy ignored the waves of anger and hurt and sadness crashing in.

She got halfway to the door before their body froze. Every muscle spasming like a seizure. Their hand locked open and the mug shattered on the linoleum. Hot coffee across the floor, Amy's shoes, splattered up their bare legs. It hurt enough for two people.

Too many signals sent at once. Her teeth squeaked against each other until her ears rang. She couldn't take back control. Or relinquish it. For what felt like hours—thirty seconds, she discovered afterward, *impossible*—neither of them could make this body obey.

Finally her jaw muscles popped like a fuse going and she collapsed against the breakroom table, gasping. Her legs burned like they'd just run a marathon.

She couldn't feel Jess at all and she didn't try.

✳

THEY DECIDED THEY could use some time apart.

The logistics of this proved tricky. One of Jess's college friends was a biomechanic specializing in consciousness maintenance. He thought they could upload one of their minds into the AI teakettle that Amy's mom had bought her for high school graduation.

The friend, David, dressed more like a hipster barista than a serious engineer, which did nothing to assuage Amy's fears about stuffing her mind inside a kettle.

"This should be big enough," David said. He hooked the kettle into his laptop and started stripping out the baby AI. "Seriously not hospital-grade though. You can spend, like, two hours in this thing. You got that? I don't want to be responsible for making somebody a vegetable."

Amy felt bad about deleting kettle's AI, who was always so

cheerful when it asked her what she'd like to drink. It only had the intellectual capacity of a chinchilla, but she still patted it on the lid while David finished erasing it. It had been a good little kettle.

David left them with a headband with electrodes attached to it, a homemade control panel he said was cannibalized from a thrift store mixing board, and a reminder about the time limit.

They flipped a coin for first dibs. Amy won. She spent her two hours at a café, sipping an iced coffee. Four dollars and fifty cents, and her stomach churned over spending the money and for going first her own body. Every sensation was razor sharp with no one else sharing her nerves. The condensation on the cup froze her hand and her fingers picked out every single scratch on the table.

With ten minutes left she came home and attached the electrodes under her hairline.

Being inside a teakettle was not at all like a body. She'd forgotten to ask how it would feel. A kettle had no dream cycle. Her brain imagined breath and a heartbeat to keep her sane but it was like sleep paralysis. The kettle had a clock, so she could sense the passage of time, and a motion detector, so she knew she was alone.

Returning felt like she was swelling, getting bigger and bigger and bigger. Like water turning to steam. Just when she thought she might blow away she blinked and found herself with eyes again. Jess took off the headband and set it next to the cannibalized kettle.

"How was it?" Amy asked.

"Weird." Uncertainty trickled through along with just a taste of disappointment. "Felt like learning to walk again, without you there. But the first time's never as good as you think it'll be, right?"

The third time she got her body to herself, Amy couldn't summon up guilt anymore. She and Jess had a stupid argument about lunch. Jess hated avocados, but Amy had already given them up for five months. Jess had said *can we eat literally anything but guacamole*. Amy had said *you can suck it up for once*. When Jess went into the kettle she felt twenty pounds lighter.

She got a strawberry milkshake and sat in the park and read *Vogue*. When she'd first moved to the city, this was her favorite thing in the world. Just sitting on the grass in the sun with a drink that cost a whole hour's pay, dreaming of cowl necklines and shirred cotton, and not a person in the world waiting on her.

It felt so good to be in her head by herself, like taking a great big stretch in the morning so your body fills all the space it can. She let herself think all the small dark thoughts she'd been holding back for months. The little muscles in her jaw relaxed one by one.

When she opened her eyes, she saw the billboard. A smiling woman in a replacement body—one of the good replacements, with custom pigments, a molded face, real hair—dancing with a fistful of wildflowers. *Having trouble affording your or a loved one's medical costs? CareSure can help. Call today.*

Amy dropped her milkshake and called the number. After three numbered menus and fifteen minutes listening to Johnny Cash hold music, she got a nice woman named Charlene who asked about her financials and then crushed her hopes as soon as they had come.

"Sorry, honey," Charlene said. "You have to be twenty-five percent below the poverty line before you even qualify. This is a government-required program. They make us put up the billboards. Insurance companies aren't charities, much as we all hope they were. I could send you some information on different nonprofits that assist with re-bodying if you give me your mailing address."

"We've tried them. They don't have any money."

"Was she injured in a workplace accident?"

"A car accident."

"Too bad. They have to pay worker's comp then, you know. My cousin, she lost her body in an industrial accident. Her company bought her a new one—custom face sculpt and everything. Of course, since they paid for it they got to pick some of the features. She ended up with a welding torch for a right hand, and let me tell you, that took some getting used to. She burned my mom accidentally before we all figured out to stay clear of that hand. But she says it made her way faster on the line."

Amy was having trouble breathing. The phone slipped in her sweating hands. A man walking his Pekingese by the playground stared at her. All she could think about was a woman with a welding torch for a hand, her body molded forever to the factory floor, who couldn't touch anyone without so much care, who could never fling her arms around her lover again without burning.

"Are you there?" Charlene asked.

The alarm on Amy's phone buzzed, saving her from saying something she'd be ashamed of later. Five minutes.

She only made it back with a minute to spare. She stood outside the apartment door with her keys in her hand. The timer on her phone counted down the seconds to two hours. Forty, thirty-nine, thirty-eight…She could just stay gone. Wait out here until Jess's patterning degraded. It was such a dark thought it made her shiver. Fifteen seconds…fourteen…thirteen. The milkshake curdled in her stomach and she tasted strawberries and bile.

The timer went off. She hit it with her thumb but she stayed waiting outside the door. Her hands shook. She watched the clock on her phone tick away and she couldn't make herself move.

The hand on the clock clicked over another minute and she burst through the door and shoved the band onto her head. Her ears popped when Jess reuploaded into her head.

"I'm sorry I'm so late," she babbled. "I lost track of time, and then this jackass cut me off crossing the street, and it was a whole thing—"

"I didn't even notice," Jess said. Nothing bled through between them.

Jess waited three days to ask for her turn. Inside the kettle, Amy tried to learn how to meditate, even though she never could, even with a body and a breath. It was impossible with her brain wound in with the kettle's timer. Each second stretched out and out like bubblegum on a baking July afternoon. Amy wondered if with enough practice she could turn the kettle on and off from the inside. It would be nice to have tea ready when she got out.

After two hours, she waited for the great expanding feeling. It didn't come. Instead—she shuddered. She felt like she had the spins. Everything went fuzzy at the edges. After two more minutes, it got very hard to think. The illusions her mind produced to keep her believing in her corporeality—lungs, heart, the sensation that this fear was making her sweat through nonexistent pores—began to fade.

She choked. There was no air but she gasped. She felt bits of herself disappearing. Degradation. Would she be able to feel it when she vanished?

She couldn't even scream inside the kettle. No one on the outside had any idea she was trapped in here, fading to strings of nonsense code…

Just when she believed Jess was never coming back, everything turned sharply cold and she rushed back into her body.

"Sorry," Jess said, flatly. "I was late."

Amy wanted to scream. She leaned over the teakettle and thought about knocking it right off the table. Her head buzzed. But she felt the silent, chilly anger roiling off Jess and bit her tongue. Turnabout.

Later she realized she couldn't remember the recipe for her grandmother's chocolate cake. She'd known it by heart just a few hours ago. She could remember remembering, but the memory itself was a ragged hole. Lost to entropy. She wondered what Jess had forgotten, to be turned so small and cruel. But she couldn't ask.

*

THAT NIGHT LONG after they both should have been asleep, Jess said into the pillow, "I think the nurse was wrong."

Amy tried to sense what she was feeling, but it was like Jess was a polished rock, perceptible but impenetrable. She still hadn't gotten used to this synesthesia, to Jess's self as an almost-physical object inside her. When Jess was open to her, she felt like a puff of cotton candy. When she was holding herself small and secret, she felt like a popcorn kernel or a rock or a penny. Amy reached out and held her own hand. With her arm pinned under her it had fallen asleep and felt nearly like another person's.

"I think I died," Jess said.

Amy knew she should say *that's not true* or *its natural to be scared*. Instead she said "Why do you say that?" She curled their arms around them for the warmth and the pressure. The back of their throat burned and she couldn't tell if it was her or Jess swallowing tears.

"This isn't me." Jess's voice was so quiet that Amy could only understand her by the shapes their lips were making. She wanted to lift their hands and press them over their mouth to smother the rest. Outside a police siren wailed down Fifth. A robbery, a mugging. Something important to be making so much noise this late. It had long faded into the distance when Jess spoke again. "I know I am not my body, I know, but I look in the mirror and this is not my face. This is not my voice. Colors are different. I don't think I think the same as I did. I am not my body but I am not *this* body and this is not my life."

Their hands twisted in the sheets.

"It'll be over soon," Amy said. "We're so close." It was only half a lie. They had a little over two-thirds of the money, assuming nothing went wrong and the price of a replacement didn't go up and they forwent any customization.

"Remember our third date?" Jess asked. "You said you wouldn't marry anyone before you'd dated them two years. But you let me into your head after six months and I didn't even get you a ring." She laughed and it scraped up Amy's throat. It didn't sound like her at all. Before the accident Jess had a laugh like whiskey, tenor-low.

"I love you. I knew the minute I saw you that I would." Amy said. "Let's start back where we were when this is done. Go on dates. Go dancing again."

Jess ran one of their hands across Amy's face, her touch as light as a silk sheet. Over Amy's cheeks and the slope of her nose. Like the first time they'd slept together, lying in Jess's double bed, foreheads touching for lack of room and Jess had slipped her foot between Amy's knees and then her hands under Amy's shirt, up her stomach and her ribs, slow as could be. She hadn't realized how much she missed being touched like this, by another person, like she was a fragile and beautiful and unknown thing.

She turned her head and kissed the fingers Jess controlled. How close this was. If the room were darker, she could have believed. "It's all right."

"I don't remember anything." Jess whispered it to the empty side of the bed like there was someone else to hear. "I remember metal and glass and heat. It should have hurt. I think this would be easier if it had hurt. You're supposed to know you've died."

Amy couldn't sense Jess's feelings at all. She reached out but all she felt was stillness. Lately she'd been wishing for her body back, for privacy inside her own skin. But right now she longed to be one of those joined couples who could open themselves completely to each other and know every complicated emotion, every bitter and idiosyncratic mixed-up desire. She wanted to say *I never wanted this but I want you* but it would sound wrong in words. She was no poet. She didn't have the vocabulary to say what she meant.

"I want you to be happy." She tried anyway, clumsily.

"I know." Their heart rate slowed. Jess uncurled them and stretched onto their back the way Amy liked to sleep. "I shouldn't have said that. I get too wound up in the dark."

"Just a little longer. It'll be like it was." Amy had meant it as comfort but Jess withdrew into herself and this was not the kind of alone she had wanted to feel.

Salt and Iron

Gem Isherwood

THERE'S A GASH across her cheekbone, glass in her arm and her lower lip is twice the size it should be, but Dagna Müller is hardly a stranger to pain.

She slumps on the steps outside the tavern, feeling her nose to check if it's broken again. Without sensation in her fingertips it's hard to tell. She can't bring herself to care much either way.

Her muscles ache from the weight as well as the fight: a dull hurt that courses along her shoulders and down her arms, turning to a chafing burn where the skin of her wrists meets the solid metal of her hands.

That pain never fades. At least the injuries provide some variety.

The tavern stands on the seafront, where barques and schooners are berthed like horses stabled for the night. The tide is low and the air reeks worse than an undine's armpit; between that and the cheap gin in her belly it takes all of Dagna's willpower not to retch.

Six months ago, she wouldn't have lost a fight. If she hadn't drunk herself halfway into oblivion she could have knocked all three of them out inside of a minute. Or at least noticed the bastards were cheating before they'd taken every last coin in her purse.

"Here," a voice says from above her. "You're a damn poor advertisement for my business."

She looks up to see the landlord – an old mariner, face wrinkled from the sun and sea air – offering her an almost-clean rag. She takes it and dabs at her bloody face.

"I'll pay for the damage," she says, busted lip muffling the words.

"Oh yeah? With what?" He leans against the doorframe and folds his arms. "Them's good hands for throwing a punch.

Strong arms for throwing weight behind it too."

"Four years on the merchant ships'll do that."

The glass splinters in her left bicep are leaking spots of blood like freckles. She'll have to dig them out with a penknife later. It's times like these she misses fingernails.

"Yeah," the landlord grins, "I've heard of you, Ironhands Müller. I heard you've pissed off every captain from here to Seligheim with your brawling and now there's none'll sail with you. I heard you broke a navigator's face in eight places, and I didn't even know there were eight separate bits of a face that could break."

"There are if you count teeth."

The landlord's eyes crinkle when he laughs. He has an anchor and two nautical stars tattooed on his own wiry arm, crudely executed and faded with age. Many sailors bear similar designs, but Dagna does not share their love for the sea. The salt irritates the skin at her wrists and flays her temper red-raw.

She remembers when she found tattooed sailors coarse and frightening. She remembers when she would rather cower than fight. She tastes her own blood at her lip and thinks of the stubborn flecks of rust that won't come off her hands no matter how hard she scrubs.

Salt and iron. This is what she's made of now.

"Cards is no way to make money, girl," the landlord says, coming to sit beside her on the steps. "You know every reprobate around here has aces stashed up their sleeves. Right next to the daggers in most cases."

Dagna scowls, and the movement sends a burst of pain along her cheek. What is she supposed to do? Sit with a begging bowl like the poor old wretch outside the Three Mermaids, who embellishes his story of falling from the crow's nest to soften hearts and loosen purse strings?

She has begged too many times. Never again.

The landlord looks at her with the exasperated affection a father might bestow on a mischievous child. She can't stand the sight of it.

"If it's gold you need…" he says. "You ever heard of Silberwald? Small town, about two days' ride west of here?"

"Sounds like a shithole."

It's a lie, of sorts. She knows the place, or at least the name. She grew up only a few miles away on the other side of the forest, but her father would never take her to the market or the midsummer fair. She once asked for his leave to go alone and he confiscated her shoes for a month.

"Place went and got itself cursed by Themselves about three months back," the landlord explains. "Bad business."

"You're really selling it to me, old man."

"Big reward for anyone who can break the curse, I hear. And it won't end with you locked up for affray."

Dagna glances up at that. All those brawls, all those punches thrown, and she hasn't once considered the law. She supposes she hasn't cared enough, not for a long time. At least in gaol you know where your next meal is coming from.

"What makes you think I could break a fairy curse?" she asks.

He nods at her hands and smiles. "You can pay me for the damage once it's done."

＊

DAGNA MÜLLER IS fifteen when the lord comes to her cottage. He arrives on a pale grey mare, dressed in a suit of spidersilk, his fingers and earlobes dripping with stones fashioned from dewdrops and moonlight. He is the most magnificent thing she has ever seen, but Themselves have not sent an emissary to bless her house with good fortune.

Her father, worse for drink, stumbled too far from the path three nights back and pissed on a fairy mound.

"I will take your daughter's hand," the lord says in a voice like mist and starlight, "as recompense for this most grave of insults."

Dagna does not miss the way his lip curls in eagerness. Perhaps it is no insult at all, merely a convenient excuse. The lord does not want her for a bride, she knows, but a toy; one he will play with roughly until she breaks. He might let her go, eventually. Perhaps her father or her brother will find her years from now, a wizened, witless husk wasting away for want of enchanted fruit and her tormentor's touch.

So, this is what she's worth, then. What her life will be measured against. The steam off a drunkard's piss.

She tries to stay calm, to think. It is useless looking to her father for protection. She remembers last winter, when he locked her out in two feet of snow because she'd forgotten to mend a tear in his shirt. He'd made her say sorry one hundred times before he let her in. "I don't think you meant that," he'd called to her after every attempt. "*Try again.*"

She'd done it too; begged and begged, clawing at the door with frostbitten fingers. Each whimpered plea was like spitting out a blade.

No, Dagna Müller will not beg again.

Instead she raises her chin, meets the lord's silver eyes and says: "At least let me say goodbye to Karl."

She finds her little brother chopping wood behind the cottage, his arms barely strong enough to lift the axe. She kneels and lays her hands on the chopping block, palms down.

"Dagna, what—"

"Cut them off."

He flinches, afraid of the wild and terrible look on his sister's face. It is the first time anyone has looked at her like that. She already knows it will not be the last. But she cannot waste time weeping or trembling; neither will do any good.

"If you love me," she says, "cut them off."

Karl does his best to make the cuts neat, although his own hands shake around the handle of the axe. There is blood on Dagna's gown, on the block and the grass, and he carries her to the woodwife's house leaving a trail of it on the ground.

The woodwife swiftly sees to Dagna's wounds and instructs her husband, the blacksmith, to fashion a pair of iron hands in his forge. When they have cooled, she seals them onto Dagna's wrists and grants them animation, though the simple magic of a woodwife is for delivering children and soothing coughs in winter, and the joins are poorly done. The metal chafes – will always chafe – when Dagna dares to move.

"This is better," the woodwife says, the closest to an apology Dagna will ever get. "It is better than Themselves."

Dagna Müller returns home as if from the battlefield, dressed in her own drying blood. Her father's mouth gapes in shock, then in anger, but Dagna keeps her eyes fixed on the lord as she stretches out one of her new, iron hands.

The woodwife's magic keeps the pain at bay for now but the metal is heavy, a straining pull along her arm and across her shoulders. A fly buzzes around her wrist, attracted by the blood. She feels less like prey than carrion.

"Here then," she tells the lord. "If you want it, take it."

The lord laughs, clapping like a child. "Oh, *well done*, Dagna Müller. Oh, how delightfully clever!"

Yet there is a tremor beneath his words, behind those silver eyes. Even if Dagna's hands were made of wood or moulded clay he would not take her now – Themselves would not want a flawed mortal, even as a toy – but there is just as much fear in him as revulsion. That, at least, is a victory.

Dagna's iron hands are deadly. Her touch will bring only pain.

Her father, furious at her defiance and fearful of the lord's retribution, will beat Karl in her absence. Dagna knows it and sorrows for it, but she knows she does not belong here now.

The fly leaves her wrist and lands on the tip of her iron thumb. She brings the index finger close and it barely takes any effort to crush the creature to powder and grease.

*

SHE WALKS ALL the way to Silberwald, napping in hedgerows and hollow trees. The landlord gives her a little food and a small bottle of ointment for her cuts and she rations both carefully. By the time she is in sight of the forest her injuries no longer grieve her.

Ironhands Müller is fit for the next fight.

Silberwald lies on the forest's edge, frosted firs curling around the cottages like a protective arm. Her father's cottage lies just on the other side of that forest, but Dagna refuses to think of it. The drink has probably finished him off by now, that or his own folly. For Karl's sake, she hopes so.

She makes her way into the main square, where they hold the markets and the fairs she'd once begged her father to see, but there is no market today.

All of the townspeople wear blindfolds; strips of fabric roughly torn from aprons and the hems of skirts. They move slowly, fearfully, calling to one another for reassurance. It looks almost like a game, but Dagna suspects there are no willing players.

At the edge of the square a boy walks holding a long, thin branch in front of him, moving it in a sweeping motion and pausing whenever it hits an obstacle. The knee of his breeches is torn, the skin beneath badly grazed.

To Dagna's left, a small girl skips with a ragged rope, her feet landing hard on the ground. The impact shakes her blindfold free and she blinks in the light, the rope falling still in her hands.

Then she catches sight of her mother, standing a few feet away, and she screams.

Instantly her mother darts forward, arms outstretched, following the sound. She grabs her daughter's shoulders and forces her to the ground, pinning her down as she reties the blindfold, and all the while the child howls as though she has foreseen her own death.

Dagna retreats from the square and heads straight for the master's house. She does not wish to frighten these people further, and she forgot long ago how to be anything else but frightening.

The door is answered by a girl her own age, though she is not dressed in servant's clothes. Her hair is red as embers, her skin pale as the inside of a seashell. When she turns her head, her eyes look like two opals; cloudy, beautiful and sightless.

"I wish to speak to your master," Dagna says.

"I am master here. You may call me Lady Karin."

She sweeps into the house without another word, certain that Dagna will follow.

Dagna knows the girl is no lady. She speaks with the accent of a peasant. The dress, fine-spun wool in midnight blue, was not made to fit her form.

But if Karin expects Dagna to take her for a lady, then perhaps she will accept Dagna as a hero.

"I am Dagna Müller," she announces, "called Ironhands, and I have come to break the curse upon this town."

Karin approaches her, holding out her own pale hands.

Bracing for the flinch, the gasp of horror, Dagna takes them.

But Karin only lifts an eyebrow as she feels the solid iron, as her fingers move up to the place where metal meets flesh. "Witchcraft?"

Dagna nods, before remembering. "Yes."

"Not very good witchcraft, I think." She brushes her fingertips over the heated, swollen skin. "Does it hurt?"

"Always."

Dagna feels Karin's fingers twitch. There is something in the word the girl seems to recognise; a bitter note, perhaps, or its weary honesty. Dagna does and does not want to ask why.

"Tell me about the curse," she says instead.

Karin moves away, skimming a hand along the tabletop to guide herself across the room. "Three months ago, when the king and his retinue were passing by the forest, Themselves stole the young prince away underground. Only the people of Silberwald know the safe paths through these woods, so Themselves made sure we would never be able to show any would-be rescuers the way."

"They blinded the villagers?"

Karin laughs with cold glee. "Oh, they aren't blind. But they don't see the world right any more. Rotten food appears fresh and good. Slippery banks are straight paths. Their own children, their own spouses, are hideous monsters coming to devour them. If they lift those blindfolds they see only a world full of tricks and horrors.

"Themselves spared me," she adds blithely. "They think I do not know the way."

That, Dagna thinks, and they despise irregularity. They would not have wished to get close enough to a girl like Karin to curse her.

"I could help," she says. "I could rescue the prince. If you would show me—"

"No."

"*No?*"

"The royal brat stays where he is."

"But—"

"Shall I tell you what I did with the last hero who came to me, bragging he could save us all? I summoned the farrier, one of our strongest men. I told him this brave hero could cure his affliction, if only he would lift his blindfold. He did, saw a terrible monster and slew the hero where he stood. The poor fool was so confused afterwards. I thanked him for coming to my aid and he only mumbled that I was welcome and left."

Dagna stares. "Why would you do that?"

"Before, I had to beg in the streets," Karin snaps. "Make myself humble and pitiful for the sake of a coin or cast-off rags. Then Themselves came, and suddenly I was the one the town came crying to. 'Dear Karin, how can we find food?' 'Sweet Karin, how can we stay safe?' When the old master drowned in a river he took for a stone bridge, I demanded they let me take his house. They didn't like it, but they had no choice. They depend on my charity now." Her face sets in such stern resolve she might as well be made of stone. "And I would keep it this way."

It is so easy, Dagna thinks, to flay a girl. Barbed words can do it, or fists, or the bite of winter frost. It is even easier to turn away and make a girl do it to herself. Karin has been hardened, the way the salt air once hardened Dagna. What makes Dagna burn red-hot with anger has turned Karin's heart cold.

"Go home, Dagna Müller," Karin says, softer now. "These people are not worth your courage."

Dagna has been known only as Ironhands for so long it is strange to hear her true name spoken aloud. She wonders what she would do, what she might give, for Karin to say it again.

"I don't have a home," she says. "That's why I need the gold. Help me find the prince and I'll split the reward with you. You could make the king send bodyguards to protect you. Or demand the prince marry you instead."

"I have made myself master here. Why should I ask for a master of my own?"

Dagna thinks of the boy in the square, the sweep of his tree branch before every step.

"Because they'll learn. Like you did. They won't stumble about helpless forever. And you are alone. If your own townsfolk don't depose you, others will learn how vulnerable you are. They'll put you back in your place, *Lady* Karin. Do nothing, and you'll beg again."

"I will *not*."

"I have made that same promise to myself. I know how this feels. I *know*."

Karin is silent for a long time.

"You may stay here tonight," she says eventually. "As my guest. Eat something. Bathe, if you like. I will consider what you have said."

Hungry and filthy from the road, Dagna does as she is bid. She is sure to face the door while she bathes, but she does not fear attack. She carries her weapons with her. She can never be rid of them.

Later, Karin fetches food and lights candles for the benefit of her guest. Dagna notices her eyes are rimmed with red, as though she has cried so much the rawness has never healed. She half-expects the food to be poisoned until Karin takes the first bite; a show of trust, a gesture of solidarity.

Girls of salt and iron can understand each other, at least a little.

"Why did you tell me the truth?" Dagna asks, when the food is finished and the candles have burned low. "Why didn't you send for the farrier to slay me too?"

Karin pauses before answering. "Because when I said I was master here, you did not laugh at me."

Dagna looks at Karin in the fading light. She could kill her now, for the townspeople's sake, and risk the forest alone. It would only take a little squeeze; the long neck, or the skull. But as she takes in Karin's hair, her skin with its seashell lustre, her eyes the colour of the northern seas when a storm tosses the waves, she knows she could not bear to hurt something so beautiful.

*

THE WOODWIFE'S CHARM lasts less than a week after Dagna leaves her father's cottage. Once it fades the pain at her wrists stays as fresh as the day the cuts were made. She tells herself that this is better, even when it hurts so much she cannot sleep. It is better than Themselves.

Three weeks later, as she is travelling towards the coast to find work, she meets a boy.

She finds him lounging by a river, his fishing rod abandoned on the bank. He bids her stay awhile, and they talk.

The boy is pretty and charming, and he makes Dagna forget the pain at her wrists, those rough joins that still smell of rust, or blood, or both. She wears gloves now to conceal her hands, soft cotton things she stole from a washing line, and for a while she can pretend she is an ordinary girl.

When he kisses her she kisses back, startling him with her fierceness and her need. She feels him smile against her lips and presses him down into the grass. Her gloved hands roam across his collarbones, his tanned arms, over his chest and down–

Something snaps. The boy screams.

"I'm sorry!" she says, scrambling off him, horrorstruck. "Please, I'm so sorry."

He glares at her, clutching his ribs, and she falls silent. She knows sorry is never good enough, not if you say it a hundred times.

"What's wrong with you?" the boy snarls. "What *are* you?"

I don't think you meant that. Try again.

The pain at her wrists is sharp once more; pain that burns so hot it feels like rage.

She beats his pretty face until he lies still and quiet, then throws the bloodied gloves into the river.

From that day on she leaves her hands exposed, like a warning.

＊

SHE WAKES TO find Karin nudging her with the tip of a wooden cane. It is almost dawn, and the girl's red hair is covered by a hooded cloak.

"Themselves bring the prince aboveground every morning," she says. "If mortals are starved of fresh air they wither before they stop being fun."

"You'll show me the way?" Dagna asks. "You'll let me try?"

"Do not give me cause to regret it."

The forest is full of sounds and shadows, eyes and claws, but Karin knows the path as Dagna knows the Seligheim coastline. She uses her cane like the boy in the square used his branch, but faster, with more skill. Every wrong turn, every fall and bruise and sprain and scare has been a lesson, a scrap of knowledge hard-won.

She leads Dagna to a clearing where the young prince stands, glassy-eyed and exhausted. He is guarded by a figure on a pale grey mare; a man dressed in spidersilk, with shining silver eyes.

When they fall on Dagna, the lord does not look surprised.

It is as if he set this trap just for her, waiting for the tale to spread as far as the coast: a cursed town, the promise of gold, and a task designed for a girl with iron strength.

All this time, she thinks. All these years she has been a debt outstanding, and he cannot bear it.

"I asked for your hand once, Dagna Müller," the lord says. "Now let me make you an offer."

He takes a bundle of cloth from his saddlebag and unwraps it. Inside are two small, fine-boned human hands. They might have been taken from some other poor girl. They might even have belonged to Dagna herself, stolen from the bloodstained chopping block and preserved with unnatural magic.

"Think of it. No more pain. No more ugliness. Forget the king's paltry reward and accept this most generous of gifts."

Dagna looks again at the prince. She knows she can hold him here until the lord gives in. But she also knows, stripling of a thing that he is, that holding him will break him. Ribs will splinter, collarbones will crack like twigs, and the king will grant no reward for a shattered corpse. She thinks of the boy by the river; those fearful eyes, that sickening *snap*.

Karin steps forward, gripping her cane like the handle of a sword. "You promised. Dagna Müller. You promised me."

"The irregular one is jealous," the lord hisses. "She wants you to suffer as she does. See, see what I offer you."

Dagna reaches out until her iron fingertips brush those pretty hands, but Themselves do not forget a slight. If she wants them, he'll make her cower and simper and debase herself to get them. If he had found her that day by the riverbank she might even have let him.

But the salt air has left her skin tanned and hardened since then, and four years of toil have made her arms thick with muscle. Those hands would be a poor fit now.

"Only ask me prettily, Dagna Müller," says the lord. "Ask me ever so sweetly, and I shall make you whole again."

Karin snarls like a wild thing, like this forest belongs to her and he is trespassing. "She's no less whole than when she had them, you twisted bastard."

The words cut through Dagna's thoughts like the blade of an axe, like something that takes away and gives all at once.

She steps forward. The prince trembles with hope and fear, bracing himself for the pain.

"Do not be afraid," she whispers.

Then, with one swift, sharp movement, she drags the lord from his horse and she *holds*.

"Karin," she says. "Take the prince. Go now, fast as you can."

"What's happening?"

"Trust me. *Go*."

"Let me guide you," the prince says, clutching at Karin's arm.

Karin shrugs him off and sprints from the clearing, dead leaves and fir needles scattering in the wake of her cane. The prince has no choice but to follow, and Dagna does not blame him for not looking back.

The horse is gone too, bolted or vanished into the air. Dagna and the lord are locked together, skin to metal, skin to skin.

He squirms first in revulsion, then in agony. He turns to a serpent, a writhing ferret, a snapping wolf in her grip, but wherever her fingers touch the iron burns. He screams curses, then offers her gifts beyond her dreams if she will only let go. She will have riches, or magic, or life eternal. She will have his devotion, his undying love.

Dagna's own body strains to pull away, every nerve signalling her to flee. She feels the tear of muscle, as though she might rip herself free from her hands, but still she clings.

She does not look at the hands, splayed on the forest floor like fleshy white spiders. Not even the beetles will go near them.

She feels the lord's strength waning, senses his desperation. His screams turn to choked sobs, then faint whimpers.

Then, whether to provoke compassion or fear, she does not know, he transforms into her father. A perfect replica, right down to the stink of beer and old sweat, every feature exactly as she remembers it. The lord can only hold the glamour for a moment or two, weak as he is, but it is enough.

Her hands tremble. For a moment, her grip slackens.

"Please," the lord says in her father's voice. "Please, Dagna, it hurts."

"Say sorry then." She squeezes tighter than ever, feeling both the glamour and his flesh burn away until she is gripping brittle, blackening bone. "Say you're sorry for all you've done."

"I'm sorry! I'm so sorry. Be kind to me, Dagna Müller. Be merciful. *Please.*"

Dagna looks down at the withered, charred thing lying limp in her hands. He is small as a child now, small as a doll.

"I'm sorry!" he cries again, shrieking, shrinking. "I'm sorry!"

"I don't think you meant that," she answers, and there is midwinter frost in her voice. "*Try again.*"

She clamps a hand over his mouth and does not lift it until there is nothing of him but powder and grease.

*

IN THE END it is not Dagna but Karin who is hailed as the saviour of Silberwald. It is Karin, after all, who leads the prince out of the forest, bathed in a halo of morning sunlight. It is Karin who urges the townsfolk to remove their blindfolds and see the world made right again.

And once the king has given Dagna her gold, and Dagna has sent a portion of it back to the tavern on the seafront, she is more than happy to let Karin take the rest of his reward.

There are some in the town who resent all that Karin has now. A title. The deeds to the house, with coins to fill the coffers the drowned master left empty. Fine clothes that fit her form, made with rich dyes and silver thread.

But they know better than to protest. They know that Silberwald is no longer a place where blind women survive on scraps.

"Will you stay?" Karin asks as she and Dagna sit under the shade of the firs, sharing a bottle of wine from her newly-stocked cellar. Children run freely across the grass nearby, arguing over which of them will play their fearless lady and which the fairy lord she bested in their games of pretend.

"The king has given you bodyguards," Dagna says.

"I don't want you for a bodyguard. You could have a home here."

Dagna sets down her cup and turns away. How can she explain when Karin says such things, her lips stained red with wine? That the girl she is now was forged in violence, that violence is all she knows. That the pain in her wrists will not leave her, not for as long as she lives. That she is hot as a forge and Karin is cold as the northern seas, and girls of salt and iron are too far gone to ever be gentle again.

Then Karin takes Dagna's hands and presses a kiss to each palm. Her kisses contain so much tenderness Dagna almost imagines she can feel them. Karin's hands trail upwards, skimming carefully over the place where metal meets flesh, until they are cupping Dagna's face like it is something fragile and precious.

Her touch is a rescue. Her kiss is the most generous of gifts.

"Please," Dagna says, "do that again."

"Please," Karin answers, "stay a while longer."

It is the last time either of them ever has to beg.

Monsters Never Leave You

Carlie St. George

Something knocks on the door. Esther, dreaming, would like to ignore it. Instead, she blinks awake and grabs her shotgun, because dead things typically call for bullets, not spell work, and whatever wants inside her home is certainly dead.

In retrospect, she should've expected the children.

The boy's feet are stained with grave dirt and tree bark. The girl's feet are stained with bone dust and blood. They're weak and exhausted and tightly holding each other's hands. Only one of them is alive in the traditional sense.

"Well," Esther says, lowering her shotgun. "Best come in, then. We'll get you cocoa."

*

THE CHILDREN ARE witches. Neither give their names.

The boy has pale blue eyes, icy white skin, and a mouth so red she'd assumed it was bleeding. He takes cinnamon with his cocoa. His sister, meanwhile, must favor whipped cream: Esther pours a towering dollop straight from the kitchen faucet.

House knows everyone's favorites, children most of all.

The girl stares at the kitchen table. "We followed the birds," she says, not touching her mug. "They led us to you."

Birds. Esther would shoot every one of them out of the sky, given enough time and ammunition. "Things with wings are tricky. You'll need to be careful, listening to their advice."

The boy leans forward eagerly. There's something about him Esther doesn't know how to read, something underneath his skin, like bark wrapped around his fingerbones. Neither witchery nor death can account for it. "So, you really—you hear them, too?"

The girl swallows. "M—m-mother said the Devil…"

Oh. They had *that* kind of mother.

"If there is a Devil," Esther tells them firmly, "he has nothing to do with us. It's important you understand that. Witchcraft isn't what you think."

"What is it, then? M-mother said, but she was, she…"

Esther waits.

The girl looks up, eyes large and dark and full of confession. "She wasn't very good."

Esther's own mother hadn't been very good, either—and her father, little better. Parents are a lingering infection, an ugly wound that only pretends to heal. "Well," she says, running a spoon through her own spire of whipped cream. "Magic isn't absolute power or a nonconsensual exchange. It's not a *taking*. There's no perversion of the natural order—"

"But," the boy interrupts, "I'm dead."

Esther eyes the jagged scars looping around his neck.

"Somewhat," she admits. "But your sister called your bones, and your bones agreed to rise. Your sister needed you, so you came back. What could be more natural than that?"

The girl's mouth is a flat, unimpressed line. Esther can't blame her: resurrection and reconstitution are very powerful magics, especially for a child twenty-five year's Esther's junior. Even she hadn't been so powerful at that age—deadly, yes, but those aren't always the same thing.

She tries not to think about that. It doesn't do to dwell.

You're living in the wrong house, her mind whispers, *if you're still trying to move on.*

She dismisses Peter's voice with practiced ease. It's easy to do when he isn't here to relentlessly repeat the same advice like a sanctimonious parrot.

"How…" The girl looks away. "How did you know that—that *I* brought him—"

"Feet tell stories," Esther says. "Best we wash them now."

She grabs warm washcloths, as well as bandages for the girl, whose skin has bled badly during the long journey through the woods. The two siblings look little alike: the girl is rosy where her brother is ghostly, and chubby where the boy is frail. But when she lifts their feet to clean them, Esther sees what only a witch could see: the same blue staining their heels, the bitter juice of juniper berries.

"Well," Esther says. "That explains a few things."

＊

THEIR STORY COMES out in pieces over the next few weeks.

"I've always been strange," Kit says one night, poking at the pink snowmen that Millie had spun from House's cotton candy insulation. The girl is asleep now, and her name isn't actually Millie, any more than the boy is Kit. But Esther doesn't press; names are a strange magic, and she hadn't been born Esther, herself. "Even before I was dead, I was wrong."

"Different," she corrects. "Never wrong. Your mother—"

"Millie's mother. She. She didn't like me much."

He rubs absently at his throat.

Ah, Esther thinks, and says nothing.

The woman's dead, though, Esther is almost sure, and the kind of dead that stays silent and still in the ground. Had Millie killed her? Had Kit? Something else, still looking for them?

"How are you different?" Esther asks instead. "How does your witching manifest?"

Kit shrugs. "I just talk to things. And things talk back. They make a lot more sense than people."

"Like birds?"

"Birds, stones, rivers." He hesitates. "Trees."

"Trees?"

Kit stays quiet.

"How about houses?" Esther asks. "Can you hear this one?"

The boy brightens. "I like House. They're nice. Some houses don't like me, but most schools do. Churches, too."

Esther has no particular affinity for churches. They mean well, perhaps, but her ears have never caught more than the faintest whispers, quiet hallelujahs wafting through air that smells of copper and salt. And since … well. She hasn't been able to face a church in years.

Homes are different, though: attics long to tell her their stories, while kitchens stretch to suit her needs and libraries nudge books in her direction. To be a witch is to be haunted, every spell a conversation, every day a new ghost story.

"And Millie?" Esther asks.

Kit scrunches his nose. "She likes *people*, couldn't hear anything else. But she wanted to learn, so I tried to teach her. I don't think I did it right."

It's surprising he did it at all; most folk are witches, or they're not. But exceptions do happen. Peter, for instance.

"Millie got these fancy plates to listen; they were flying everywhere, but then …" Kit shivers. "*She* saw. The way she looked, when she asked, 'Don't you want, don't you want …'"

His hand returns to his scars.

Esther has little experience with this. People find her in these woods, of course, mostly lost children, sometimes a cursed woman seeking aid, but none of them have ever been murdered before. She tries to think of something comforting—

—But then, Millie screams.

Esther and Kit find her downstairs this time, stumbling out the front door. They follow her outside to the ancient and gargantuan redwood nearby. Millie is awake but unaware, clammy, horror-struck. "Sap," she says, kneeling, as Kit wraps his cold little arms around his sister and Esther sinks down, rocking them both. "It, it slid out of her, with the blood and the baby, and then the branches, they burst—"

"Shhh," Esther says.

Millie's eyes are blank. "Her belly. Her fingernails. You didn't see the *roots*."

These aren't Millie's words. These aren't her memories; her witching, so weak in the daylight, seems to come alive with the moon. Millie dreams other people's secrets. Esther isn't sure who this one belongs to.

Nibble, nibble, little mouse, Millie had whispered just the other night. *Who is nibbling at my house?*

Decades later, Esther's breath still catches at those words.

Now she hushes, shushes, and soothes until Millie fully comes back to herself. She doesn't seem ready to stand, so Esther introduces them to the redwood. Its leaves rustle in the wind, a fond *hello, little ones.*

"Redwoods are powerful beings," Esther says. "Cranky, yes, but they give excellent advice. Trees are like witches: each has their own magic. Be mindful of that when you cast. It's very rude to call on something that can't offer what you seek."

It's Kit who finally asks, "What magic do juniper trees have?"

The wind picks up. The redwood shudders. The birds and the bugs go silent.

"Vengeance," Esther says. "Violence. Juniper trees are creatures of crossroads and war, and they don't take kindly to impertinence or maltreatment." She thinks of Millie's nightmare, of branches bursting through bellies. Someone must have been impertinent, indeed. "It's the first rule of witchcraft, the most important: you always ask. You never take."

It's the rule, she doesn't add, *that so many witches break.*

They go inside. House is awake, of course, eager to provide warmth and brown sugar solace—but as Esther crosses into the kitchen, three spoons fall to the floor.

"Damn," she whispers.

"Esther?"

Esther's bones ache, heavy with the weight of prophecy, of exhausting inevitability. She thought she'd have more time.

"Company's coming," she tells the children, and throws the spoons in the sink.

*

THE FIRST VISITOR arrives the next night.

It's the witching hour. Millie and Kit sit at the kitchen table, both shaken from the girl's latest dream. *Don't you want an apple?* she'd whispered, staring sightlessly at her brother. *Don't you want an apple? They're in the trunk.*

House, anxiously shifting at their distress, oozes lines of chocolate and raspberry from its walls.

Esther scowls at this latest, dripping decor. "Witchcraft isn't...?"

"A perversion of the natural order," Kit and Millie say.

"Yes. Witchcraft is a way to communicate with that order: it's asking impossible fruit to grow, or faces to change, or houses to stop creating cavities it doesn't have to pay for."

Peanut butter begins seeping too, insolently.

"That's unsanitary," Esther tells House, but waves a relenting hand. Kit attacks the raspberry; being dead has had little effect on his appetite. Millie kneels down and uncertainly prods the peanut butter.

"The house doesn't listen to you," she says.

"House always listens. It just doesn't always agree. Its whole purpose is to spoil children. That's what it was built for. In a way."

House anxiously shifts again. Bourbon caramel this time, her favorite.

Esther smiles fondly. "It's all right. That's been over a long while now."

Millie frowns. "What's wrong? Is the house——"

Someone knocks on the door.

It's familiar, insistent, the impatient rap of a policeman. It speaks of authority, among other things.

"It's okay," Esther tells the children. "You're safe."

She grabs the shotgun anyway before opening the door.

Peter stands there, bony arms crossed tight across his chest. "Dramatic," he says dryly.

"You're the one prowling the woods in the middle of the night. Couldn't sleep?"

He laughs, almost. "Sleep? Do people still do that?"

"You know people better than me."

"Well, if you'd just——" Peter cuts himself off, sighing. "You gonna let me in?"

"Why don't you ask House?"

He rocks back slightly, jaw tightening. "You have the kids," he says finally. It's not a question: Peter can read footprints and faces the way she can read hands and feet. He can find just about anyone, has been chasing down people since he was fifteen. How would their lives have gone, if he'd been this human compass when he was ten? Who might they have grown to be, if she hadn't listened to those fucking birds?

But then, she wouldn't have House.

"They don't belong here," Peter says. "You don't, either."

Esther sighs and beckons him inside.

Kit's in the kitchen doorway, standing protectively in front of his sister; Millie's crouched down behind him, peeking out carefully, a paring knife in one hand. "It's okay," Esther says. "This is my brother, Peter. He's very tiresome, but he won't hurt you."

Still, she doesn't let go of the shotgun.

Peter says hello, smiling kindly; neither child responds to it. He doesn't push, though; he's good with people. Ought to be, considering how many he's taken from her—but that's unfair. Esther helped House reshape their purpose: no longer a lure, but a waystation, a safe harbor for the lost, the seeking, the desperate. People aren't meant to stay forever.

Only Esther.

She ushers the children back to the table, gives them bowls of feathers and buttons and paper birds. "Ask them to float, see if they'll agree. We'll be in the other room if you need us."

In the other room, Peter hands her a case file.

"Your strays are missing persons in a murder investigation. One woman is dead. Her body …"

Her body has been impaled on the branch of a juniper tree. Mouth open, skin grey. Wood splinters burst from her left eye. Esther can't tell much from her feet—the angle is wrong—but she can see they're covered in blood. It's dripping from her toes: down, down, down into a hole in the ground beneath her.

Something had been buried in that hole, something that had clawed its way back up.

"My guys think it's the husband," Peter says, "but his face isn't right for it."

Esther examines the woman again. Dark hair, high cheekbones. A thin, hooked nose. Millie looks just like her.

"The boy—" Peter says.

Esther may not be able to read faces like her brother, but she can guess. "Grave dirt on his cheeks?"

"And a jawbone made of wood." Peter shakes his head, wondering. "I've never seen a face like it. It's not just the resurrection, is it? He was born different."

Sap, it slid out of her, with the blood and the baby ...

Esther crosses her arms. "He didn't kill her."

"Do you really know that?"

"No," Esther admits. "But I know she killed him first."

Peter winces. "I hoped I was wrong. It's harder to read the dead than the living, but ... there was abuse. Not sexual, but emotional and physical. We found a trunk in the cellar. There was blood inside, and on the rim, too."

Don't you want an apple?

Esther can see Kit there, kneeling over the trunk. She can imagine his stepmother behind him, hands on the lid. Kit's scars wrap around his entire throat. How many times would it have taken before the woman—before Kit's *head*—

Esther rubs the back of her neck. "And the father?"

"He didn't know."

Didn't know? Or didn't want to see?

There are people who are afraid to leave, fearing only worse harm will come; people trying to break through years of psychological conditioning, of financial dependency. Parents terrified their babies will be taken away. And then there are those other people who close their eyes because they can, who convince themselves not to intervene, who never wanted the burden of responsibility in the first place.

"He's sorry," Peter says, but Esther isn't sure which shitty father he's apologizing for.

"Right," she says, turning away.

"Goddamn it, Esther, can't you just once—"

"Forgiveness has to be earned—"

"You never let him earn it! You never even tried to understand—"

"*Understand?*" Esther whirls around. "Jesus, Peter, how broken are you?"

"Me? You ran away to hide in the woods for twenty years! You're living in the house that tried to *eat us*—"

"Esther?"

The children hover nervously in the archway. House—oh, House is trembling hard.

"It's okay," she says, to everyone. "We were just…"

She looks to Peter for help. Even now, she still does that.

"We argue sometimes," he says softly, keeping his hands where the children can see them. "But we don't hurt each other."

Not anymore, he doesn't say.

"That's right," Esther agrees. "And Peter, he's come to take you back to town, if you like."

Immediately, the siblings step back.

"You're not in any trouble," Peter says. "I don't need to know exactly what happened that night. But this, this is no place for children."

House trembles harder.

Peter pretends he doesn't feel it as he takes back his file, papers clenched between his fingers. "You should be in school with other kids, with parents who take care of you—"

"*Our* parents didn't take care of us," Kit says.

Peter nods. "I know. I'm sorry. But your stepmother can't hurt you anymore, and your father's in custody right now. If he gets released, if it's safe, you could be together again."

Millie looks up. Kit doesn't.

"Where would we go now?" Millie asks.

"We'd find a family to place you with," Peter says. "A good family. I'd make sure."

He would, too. That, at least, Esther can count on.

"A witch family?" Kit asks, still turned away.

Peter hesitates. "I don't know."

Millie shakes her head. "No," she says, as Kit slumps in relief. "No, I don't want to go. Esther, can't we stay?"

Yes, Esther thinks, *but you'll change your mind eventually*.

"Yes," she says. "If that's what you both want."

For now, at least, it is.

She escorts Peter outside. His shoulders are hunched, too much salt in his hair. He needs to eat more, like always.

"Peter. You know it was never House."

He nods, eyes distant. "Some things are hard to separate."

Truer words, Esther thinks, watching him.

"Esther? I'm so—"

"I know," she says, because he's said it before, a hundred times over. "I forgive you."

And it's true. She forgave him a long time ago. She's always understood. But—

"But you don't trust me," Peter says.

She doesn't want to lie to him. Can't, because the shotgun is still in her hands. "I love you."

"Yeah," Peter says, smiling sadly. "I love you, too."

"But you can't forgive me," Esther says.

Peter must not want to lie to her, either, because he just shakes his head and walks away.

*

THE NEXT DAY, Kit, Millie, and House surprise her with pancakes. They all sit in bed, eating and continuing their abandoned levitation exercises. Millie has no luck until Esther remembers the handful of chicken bones she'd been saving for a shielding potion; then, they swirl easily through the air. Bone speaks freely to Millie, no matter the time of day.

Occasionally, the children glance at each other, unsubtly.

"House was sad yesterday—" Kit finally begins, only for Millie to poke him in the arm.

"*Esther* was sad!"

"I *know* that!"

"It's not just things that matter! People—"

"House isn't just a *thing*—"

"We were both sad," Esther interrupts, before their bickering escalates. "Peter brings up difficult memories."

Kit crosses his arms. "House doesn't like him."

"Peter's not very fond of House, himself."

"*I* don't like him. House says he hurt you."

"And has House ever hurt anybody?"

Kit frowns, uncertain. House stays very quiet.

"People haven't been kind to you," Esther says. "It's easier, sometimes, trusting things without mouths. But you don't need a mouth to lie to someone, and it's not just people who make terrible mistakes."

"You're saying … House is bad?"

"Not at all. But truth isn't objective. Everyone has their own."

The children stare blankly.

Esther sighs. "When we were young," she says, "our parents abandoned us in these woods. Mother's idea, but Father went along with it. There wasn't enough food, you see. Children get so hungry. But I could follow the birds, and this place was like a dream, a house we could eat. Only the witch who built it was hungry, too, and her appetites were … unusual. Mad."

"What did she eat?" Kit asks.

"Children."

Millie, suddenly pale, jumps up and is noisily sick in the bathroom. Kit won't meet Esther's eyes.

"I'm sorry," she says, confused, when the girl returns. Esther's past is a horror show, and Millie's the more sensitive of the two, but to have a visceral reaction like that …

"It's o-o-o—" Millie squeezes her eyes shut. "Keep going."

Esther does, reluctantly. "The witch was House's mother, and they loved her dearly. But House didn't like hurting children. So, when the witch asked—"

"House said no," Kit says.

"Yes."

"But she broke the rule, anyway."

"Repeatedly. A lot of witches do. Bad witches always rely on luck, demanding whatever they want from weaker, vulnerable things. They're certain they'll have the upper hand because they've always had it before. But eventually, luck must turn."

"What happened to the bad witch?" Millie whispers.

Please be bigger, be hotter. Please don't let her out.

"She died," Esther says.

Kit crosses his arms again, mulish. "So, House helped you."

"Yes. And I forgave House. I love them very much."

"Then Peter should forgive House, too. It's been fifty years!"

"I'm not *that* old," Esther says dryly. "And forgiveness can't come with a clock. You ask. You never demand."

"But—"

Very gently, Esther reaches out and touches the boy's jagged scars. "Would you forgive the trunk?" she asks. "Would you feel safe, leaning over it again?"

Kit begins to cry. He runs and Millie runs after him, leaving

Esther alone with a handful of crumpled paper birds. And House, but House is still too quiet, lost somewhere in their own memories. Everything smells faintly of black licorice.

No one here likes black licorice. No one alive, anyway.

"It's okay," she tells House, "if you still love her. Parents are ... we can talk about it."

But House says nothing.

*

THE SECOND VISITOR comes on the full moon.

It's been a tense few days. Kit has barely said a word to anyone, only murmuring his secrets to the rocks. Now he's pretending to read as Millie huddles near Esther on the bed, clammy and desperate. These memories, for once, are Millie's own.

"He was all pieces," she whispers. "First his head, rolling. M—m-mother said I pushed him t-too hard. And I believed her, I thought that I'd—that I'd—and then. In the kitchen, into the pots and pans, so many pieces—"

"You're safe now," Esther says. "You're both safe."

"He ate him. Daddy ate him all up."

"Shhh—"

"It's because of me. M-mother had to save me; I had the Devil in me now, but I asked Kit for it, I asked for the Devil. Kit, because of me—"

"There's no Devil, sweetheart—"

And then bone against oak, the sound echoing in Esther's ribcage: once, twice, thrice.

There's no Devil, but the living don't knock like that.

It's too much to hope that there's a dead brother the children have forgotten to mention. Esther tells them to stay, then grabs her shotgun to meet the corpse from Peter's file.

But it's not Millie's mother at the door.

The dead woman wears a torn, dirty sundress. Underneath it, her belly is huge and pale; twisted branches grow from it, angling in all directions. Tree roots have burst from underneath her fingernails, and spill out the corners of her eyes.

Oh, Millie. Sweetheart, why didn't you tell me you called more than you meant to?

Esther looks at the woman's fleshless feet, sculpted only from bark and bone. "You're Kit's mother."

"Deborah," the woman agrees. Her voice is the hushed wind between trees. "Or I was. I've been in the ground too long. We're different now. We think together. Rooted."

"We?"

Deborah blinks slowly. "It needed an acolyte."

Juniper trees are creatures of crossroads and war, Esther remembers, dazed. *If you can't come to the crossroads …*

Well. It's not like she's never spoken with trees before. This one just borrows human skin, and feasts on the bones and blood of murderers and fools.

Esther grips her shotgun tighter.

"If you've come for food," she says carefully, "you'll find none here. I wish you luck on your hunt, but I'm not interested in being a sacrifice, and the children are not yours to eat."

Deborah laughs, or the juniper tree does. "I seldom eat children unless they've been rude, and the boy was always kind. He is of my fruit. I would like him back."

"Of your …?"

The tree-witch holds out her palm.

Her life line has been cut in half, literally. Within the wound, Esther can see blood drops, and snow, and small teeth biting into anomalous blue fruit. "I needed the fruit to bear a child," Deborah says. It must be Deborah speaking now. "I needed a tree to bear the fruit. It told me—I told her—it wasn't made for that kind of magic, but I wanted what I wanted. I wouldn't take no for an answer."

Fool, indeed.

Esther eyes Deborah's hands: motionless, content. "Do you even want what you died for? Are you here for a servant or son?"

"We all serve something. I find pleasure in my purpose. He will, too, likely."

"Likely?"

The tree-witch shrugs.

"And Millie?"

"She's done me a service, raised me an acolyte. But she can't hear my words, and has no stomach for the work."

Esther thinks of Millie's mother, impaled, blood dripping into an empty grave. Millie, she thinks, has an iron stomach, considering the things she's seen—

I asked for the Devil.

—and the things she blames herself for.

"It's been centuries," the juniper tree whispers, "since I've had anyone to bring me the wicked and delicious."

"They're children," Esther says. "They deserve a family."

"Is that what you think you're giving them, here, in this lonely candy house?"

Despite herself, Esther's throat locks up.

"You look at us and see a monster," the tree-witch says. "But was it monsters or humans who hurt you most? Monsters never left you. Monsters didn't hurt that boy upstairs, didn't beat him down with the Word of God. The trees never ignored his bruises. Witches didn't take his head. Even the girl was failed by her people: too fat, too anxious and teary. What has the world ever done for them?" Deborah steps closer as gingerbread roof tiles clatter to the ground. "Give them to us. Maybe she'll grow into an exceptional monster, after all."

But the children aren't hers to give.

"Not your call," Esther says, and points the shotgun at Deborah's face. Deborah smiles, her mouth wide—

"No, thank you."

Esther tenses. For witches, the children are very poor listeners.

Kit stands beside her. "Your invitation is kind," he says, "but I already chose Millie. I will always choose Millie."

"She can come—"

"No," Millie says, too quickly. "I choose Esther."

The words burn. She pushes the pain down.

"We'll bid you a safe journey, then," Esther says, but Deborah—and it must be Deborah, still impertinent even in death—crosses the threshold anyway.

"You can't stop us," she says, reaching with one gnarled hand, right before her shin bone cracks in half.

Millie steps forward, one fist raised in the air.

"Your bones like me more than they like you," she says.

The hand retracts. Slowly, the tree in the woman straightens. "Our apologies," she says, stepping backwards on a leg that barely holds her. "The choice was made."

"Don't ask it again," Esther says, and slams the door shut.

*

DAWN FINDS ESTHER exhausted, sick of bedsheets that tease her with sleep. She gets up, finds Millie scowling ferociously at Esther's grimoire. Studying potions is a good idea for the girl—memorized ingredients will work as well as instinctual ones, provided they're agreeable enough—but whatever is inside this cauldron smells … inauspicious.

Millie's cheeks burn. "I wanted a forgiveness potion."

"That's … not really a thing," Esther says eventually. This particular elixir is for meditation, clarity of thought—things that could lead towards forgiveness, or warn against it. "Is this for you to drink, or someone else?"

Millie is silent. Maybe she doesn't even know herself.

"Sweetheart. The things your mother did, that Kit's mother did, they aren't your fault. Never let other people blame you for their choices."

"But I made choices, too! I made them, and then Kit was dead, and M-mother was dead, and D-d-da-d—"

Millie shoves the cauldron off the stovetop.

Esther winces at the resounding crack of iron violently meeting wood. Green spills everywhere and House drops the temperature in indignation. At least the cauldron was barely warm. "Okay, let's just—"

Millie presses a shaking fist to her mouth. "I'm sorry," she says. "I'm sorry, I'm, I'm, I'm—"

"It's okay, Millie—"

"I'm mad at him."

Esther frowns. "Kit?"

Millie shakes her head. "I'm mad at him," she repeats, "but you said everyone makes mistakes. The house made a mistake, but you love it anyway, right? You forgave it 'cause you love it?"

"Millie—"

"He'll forgive me, I think. I dreamt he would. Shouldn't I forgive him, too?"

Esther is definitely the wrong person to ask about forgiveness. She opens her mouth, and does nothing with it.

Millie turns away. "I'm sorry. I'll clean it all up."

Esther hesitates. "Okay," she says finally. "Then we can work on your potion together. Does that sound good?"

Millie hums, refusing to look up.

Esther sighs and, leaving Millie with a handful of dishrags, steps outside for a moment alone to regroup. Only Kit's awake, too, sitting beside the bellflowers. Shyly, they emerge under his cold, welcoming hands.

"Hey," Esther says, sitting next to him.

"Have you ever been dead?" Kit asks.

She should've stayed inside with Millie. "No," Esther admits.

Kit nods. "I didn't like it," he says, after a while.

Esther has to take a breath. "I'm glad you came back," she says eventually.

"Me too," Kit says. He glances over, pale eyes wide with wanting. "I like it here. I like it."

But she can hear what he isn't saying.

I will always choose Millie.

"I understand," Esther says. "I made that choice too, once. Chose Peter until the day I had to choose myself."

Kit frowns. "You're saying I shouldn't—"

"No. No, I'd never say that. Just …"

Esther tries not to think of the church cellar. Tries not to think of Peter's face, before he'd locked the door.

"If there comes a day," Esther says, "when you can't choose Millie, or when she can't choose you … you have to let go."

Kit frowns harder. "I don't understand."

"I know," Esther says sadly. "I know."

✳

THE THIRD VISITOR comes at dusk, and he doesn't come alone.

Esther is teaching the children their times tables—it can't always be magic, sadly—when the knock comes. It's wet with something, sweat, maybe. Living, anxious, redemptive flesh.

She doesn't want to answer the door.

But she is Esther, and House is House, and they will always, always open the door for a stranger seeking something they lost. Even if what they lost is something they gave up.

She grabs her shotgun to meet who's come.

He's white, in his thirties, wearing a crisp polo shirt at odds with his dark stubble and haunted eyes. The things he's seen— the deaths of his wives, the resurrection of his son—are still shaking his bones. He looks at his children and shakes harder.

Kit and Millie, Esther decides, favor their dead mothers.

"You brought him, then," Esther says to Peter, who's standing off to the side, fidgeting.

"He never would've found his way alone."

He would've, if he tried hard enough. It might have taken years, but he would have. "How helpful of you," Esther says. "Like a tour guide. Like a bird."

Peter looks up, hurt etched into his white knuckles. "Do you only care about choices when you're the one making them?"

It hits Esther in the lungs, the way it was meant to. She inclines her head and steps back, but the man makes no move to step inside, just stares hopelessly at his children.

"Marlene—"

"Millie," Millie says, arms crossed and lips trembling. "I'm Millie now. And—"

"He doesn't need to call me anything," Kit interrupts. "He never bothered before."

The man sinks to his knees. "I'm so sorry. I, I should have paid more attention, should've realized how much she—I'm so glad you're okay—"

"Okay?" Kit asks tonelessly. "She killed me. She killed me, and you ate me, and my sister gathered up my bones, buried me under the juniper tree, and you think—"

"No, no, of course not, but I didn't, I never knew—"

"You knew enough. You knew how she treated me, you knew what she said. But you never did anything. You never looked at me and saw anything but the juniper tree." Kit tilts his head. "That's how you're looking at me now."

"I'm—"

"If I scared you before when I was just a witch, how are you going to deal with me now that I'm dead?"

The man, shaking harder, can't meet his son's eyes. He turns to Millie, with her normal mouth and smooth, unscarred neck. "I love you. You know that, right? I made mistakes, terrible mistakes, but I love you."

"You left us, Daddy."

"I—"

"Kit crawled out of the ground," Millie says, "and his mom did too, and M-mother, she dragged Mother to the tree, *she dragged Mother to the tree*, and you *left us*."

The man covers his face. "Terrible mistakes," he whispers.

Esther and Peter look at each other.

It'll be different now, Father swears in her memory. *It was your mother, all her idea; I should never have listened—but, but she's gone now. It'll be different, you'll see.*

But it had been too different; that was the problem. Esther could never forget Father had abandoned them. Peter could never forget the witch's face. He was terrified, and she was furious, and they were both traumatized, sparking with magic. They were too strange, too difficult, and one day, too much. One day, they'd woken up to a note in their father's place.

It's better for everyone this way.

"It'll be different," the man says, as Millie inches forward, as Kit slumps. He must suspect what Esther has known for years: fathers who leave only come back to disappoint you. But Peter, he'd needed to believe so badly. Even after the note, he'd been so desperate to believe.

I'll find him; I can do it. He's just upset. I won't be any trouble this time, though. I'll do better. I'll be good.

Peter, Esther is startled to realize, is crying.

Millie is, too. "Daddy," she says, stepping towards him—

But Peter's there, suddenly, kneeling between them.

"Don't," he begs Millie. "I was wrong before. I'm always wrong. Don't make my mistakes."

"Peter—"

"Hey, you can't—"

Peter ignores them. "If you're ready to forgive," he says, "then forgive. But don't do it just because you love someone. Love is a gift, not an obligation."

He does turn, then, meets Esther's eyes. "Choose them if they're right for you."

Esther can't speak.

The man in the doorway stands. "This place isn't your home," he says—but only to Millie, always to Millie. "I know you never wanted any of this. We'll find a new house, somewhere far away. Put all this misery behind us. You can be normal again, I know it. We'll be happy again. Marlene—"

But Millie steps back, squeezes Kit's hand.

"I'm Millie now," she repeats.

"Baby—"

"We choose Esther," Kit says, cutting him off.

The words burn, but only because no one's ever said them before and meant it.

*

LATER, MUCH LATER, there's a knock on the door.

The children are in bed, no nightmares yet. No telling how long that will last. Esther glances at her shotgun, leaves it where it is. Sits beside Peter on the stoop.

The siderails, usually chocolate, are now cinnamon sticks. Peter's favorite.

He reaches out, wondering...and then shudders and pulls back, bony arms wrapping tightly around his stomach.

It still feels like such a step.

"Thank you," Esther says.

"Don't thank—"

"Thank you."

Peter shrugs, eyes on the trees. "I owe you. More than I can ever give."

"I owe you, too—"

"No," Peter says, shaking his head. "You saved my life. You saved me, and I repaid you by locking you up—"

I'm sorry, I can't let you go. It's just till I find Father, I swear; it'll be better. I swear, I'm so sorry—

"I told you," Esther says unsteadily. "I forgave you for that—"

"The church cellar didn't like it," Peter pushes on, breathlessly. "It wasn't that kind of church; it wanted to welcome people, not imprison them. But you couldn't hear churches, so I broke the rule. I locked you in, just like—"

"Peter," Esther says, more firmly.

"I just didn't want you to leave me. And I couldn't come back here; you *knew* I couldn't come back here—"

She had, and that decision still haunts her, even if it'd been the one she'd needed to make. Esther couldn't keep chasing their father. She couldn't keep hoping that he'd change, that he'd remember love was meant to be unconditional. She wasn't the daughter he wanted. She wouldn't apologize for it, not ever again. Esther had needed to figure out who she was, who she could be; she'd needed to come back and face what had happened—but Peter hadn't been ready, and she'd known that. She'd made it impossible for him to choose her.

She'd known he'd be upset, maybe even furious, but she hadn't expected his devastation, his sheer panic. She'd never thought—

She was in that cellar for days before she finally escaped.

"I was so scared of being alone," Peter whispers. "I was so scared all the time, and I kept telling myself, I had to be stronger, I could hold us together, if I could just bring him back, if I could just make you both *see*—"

Esther takes his hand. "I know, Peter."

"I was the one who couldn't see. I stole your choice. You shouldn't trust me."

"But I do," Esther says, and it isn't a lie, not entirely.

He looks at her.

She ignores her own tears. "Some things are hard to separate," she admits, and he smiles softly at that. "Anyway, it's better today than yesterday. Isn't it?"

He nods. "I know you didn't do anything wrong. You don't need forgiveness, but I do forgive you, I should, I almost—"

Peter reaches out towards House again, this time making fingerprints in the cinnamon.

Esther's tired of dwelling. She's so damn tired of memories, of letting mistrust choose for her again and again.

"Come back tomorrow," she asks him. "We'll have dinner."

And Peter says quietly, "Okay."

To Balance the Weight of Khalem

R.B. Lemberg

WHILE A STUDENT refugee in Khalem, I discover the market by chance. It is the heart of the city—not the palace, not the high-end shopping streets, not the historical museum—the market is the heart of Khalem's people and their food. Thick lentil soups cook in old brass vats under perpetually dirty awnings; flatbreads glide through the air as they bake upon overhead oven belts. There's yelling and bargaining and stories and arguments; I thought I was fluent in the language of Khalem, but it turns out I'm only fluent in the smooth, dry speech of the university. The voice of the market fills me up like warm bread dipped in oil.

The honey seller lets me sample spoonfuls of honey: buckwheat, dark and viscous; the golden quince blossom; pear. *Have you gone to the sidewise market yet?* he says. *My brother has a stall there.*

Where?

Sideways, sidewise—I am not sure I understand the word. He gestures over his back. *Right there.* I cannot see anything. Just a wall.

THE SIDEWISE MARKET

I DO NOT have money to come back in daylight. At dusk, a copper coin buys me a grab bag of slightly overheated vegetables the merchants do not want to lug home. I come after closing hours.

When they start bombing the market, I stop going. But I need to eat, and I need to breathe the air of the sweet decay of the night, the winding stone streets squeezing in the stalls; the star-full sky veiled by the city's breath.

I return again and again. In the newspapers: the familiar
stalls of dry beans and fruit in their burlap sacks are gone; the
honey seller's face, stilled forever. I am hungry, increasingly
hungry; the dormitory rent is raised because of the war. My
stipend remains the same. Then it is reduced.

In despair, I apply to study abroad in Islingar. They will not
want me, but I have to do something. The application fees to two
universities eat up my stipend; I cannot apply to more.

One evening, I fall into the sidewise market by accident.
Too hungry to think much or notice where I'm going, I take a
wrong turn; pass under a stone arch I have not noticed before.
The other side is not much different, except it is quieter, as if
the night itself holds its breath. In the velvet folds of darkness,
I smell vegetables ripe with the day's heat, almost falling into
decay; slops and garbage and urine; above, the old fabrics of
the tents rustle softly, their dirt swallowed by the night. A lone
lantern sways above the only open stall. It is a simple, rickety
construction, a tray of worn wood under the awning whose
histories had been smoothed and devoured. On the tray are
onions, each globe perfect and golden, shining with some inner
light.

I sway on my feet; I have not eaten since the morning's single
egg; in my hand, the crinkly bag of bargain vegetables makes a
desperate noise. The owner of the onion stall has not moved all
this time. He is a person behind the light. I am afraid of large
men. But he smiles. There is nothing predatory in it. He is not
after my vulnerability, my aloneness; he is not after anything.
He is the jeweler of the market of shadows, when all the sirens
are resting and all the people have left. He is the inheritor of
crevasses into which gold has spilled and stilled, the magic of the
fissures of the world. So am I, I think, and wonder if it's true.

I shuffle on my feet, and slops and refuse squelch under
the only shoes I own. He says something. Perhaps something
as simple as, *would you like to buy some onions?* Perhaps he says
something else. *I am a golden king of loss, and leaving me you will
forever hunger for my jewelmaking craft, visible only in the warmest hour of
darkness.*

Where are you from? he says. I understand this much.

Raiga, I whisper. I do not much remember it. Cold, and big men threatening my father. Later, people standing in a long line, three streets long. A serpent of people dressed all in gray, their heads bowed under the stone heaviness of the air. We are trying to leave Raiga. My father holding my hand. We must obtain documents. But I can't, we can't. *Islingar is not receiving; you are out of quota.* I remember people slipping money to Islingar's representatives. My father's twitching hand. He does not have enough to give, to be counted in the quota of refugees allowed to flee Raiga's wars on a ship to Islingar. My father's face is ashen with defeat, like a curtain falling. He does not speak when the two of us walk back home. There isn't much home left. Three more months, and then gone.

Raiga, the onion jeweler says, and his smile brings me back to the sheltering darkness of the sidewise market. *Did you want to come to Khalem?*

I shake my head. *No, Islingar. But they did not want us.*

He does not say, *I'm sorry about the war.* How can we be sorry about a war that is not of our making? *I'm sorry you had to come from one war to another, from your war to ours,* but he does not say it; perhaps he does not even think it. I am not afraid. I should be, I think, but he does not mean me harm.

Do they have onions there? he asks.

*In Raiga? Yes, they do...*I've eaten onions since I was little. Onions split in half and roasted in a cast iron skillet. Onions cut into rings and battered in millet flour. Onions diced and browned to sweetness, then mixed into buckwheat kasha. I have not eaten since the morning's single egg. I do not eat much, now. I have no money; only the market and its darkness feed me, when I can come here at all; when the trolleys are running, when the sirens are silent. A bag of leftover vegetables for one copper coin—vegetables teetering on the tender, sweet edge of rot.

Do they have onions like these in Raiga? he says. The warmth of his voice neither pulls me closer nor pushes me away.

No, not like these.

Never like these, he echoes. *I make them out of this city. Like that piece of jewelry described in ancient books: Khalem of Gold. Nobody knows what it looked like, not even people who work at the historical museum—but I will tell you this: Khalem of Gold is an onion; each onion contains the city, and is reflected in it. They glow and are shaped by my carving hand, and so that the city can never be destroyed or forgotten.*

His fingers wrap around an onion. He lifts it to the lantern's lone light, and in the onion, I suddenly see: the goldwork towers and walls of the Old City; the broken bridge, jagged after a recent bombing yet still shining; rows of humble houses etched in ebullient metal; the curve and sway of the historical museum.

Would you like an onion?

I shuffle from foot to foot. I do not know how to tell him I spent all my money so I could eat something, and I will have to walk forty minutes to my dormitory.

Free, he says. *I'm sorry about the war.*

I reach out my hand, and he drops the city into it. It feels warm in my palm. I lose sight of the jeweled detail; my eyes see nothing but onion skin, layers and layers of it, brownish-orange and curling up, and underneath it, golden.

I do not remember how I make it back to the dormitory. I walk, the onion in my right hand, the bag of vegetables in the other. It is a long walk in darkness, but I am safe in the glow, or I simply do not remember.

My good knife was stolen a week ago. In the communal kitchen, I cut the vegetables into jagged pieces with a blunt table knife. I am so hungry that my hands are shaking; a stray motion of the knife grazes my finger. I cut—more tear apart—the bell peppers, the zucchini, and the eggplants; throw them with some oil into the pot. It is a deep blue pot. My father gave it to me. *A good pot for many things*, he said; *you can make soup or kasha or even braise fish*. But what I have are these vegetables, soft and spotted but still releasing an aroma of secrets and warm stone. The clove of garlic from the bargain bag has begun to rot. I scrape the bad bits off.

It is more than I've eaten in days, since I last dared go to the market. I steal a pinch of turmeric and a few peppercorns from the neighbor; it feels only fair after my knife disappeared, and it is night, and nobody will see me. Darkness has been my first line of defense for as long as I can remember.

The vegetables sizzle and sag, reminding me of another

life—a summer in Raiga, when my grandmother made sinenkie i belenkie—each piece of aubergine and summer squash perfectly cut with an unstolen knife. But mine is better. The vegetables smell of gratitude and secrets, of the sidewise market and words spoken in the dark.

I have not cut the magic onion from the stall. I look at it while the vegetables cook. Khalem of Gold. The onion does not come with chains, but I think about them now, chains glimpsed only from afar, from a ship, that one time before we landed—the chains of Khalem, upon which the city is balanced. This city, unlike any other, uncomfortable with its own weight and with the war; a city that must always and forever be balanced.

I spoon warm vegetables into my mouth straight out of the pot, swaying in the bare dormitory kitchen with its grayish floor tiles and a single forlorn ceiling light. We have almost been discarded, these vegetables and I, blemished and sagging and rich with the promise of rot.

I stand over the pot and eat. There is no point in leaving anything; it will be stolen. I eat until my stomach hurts. I eat until I've scraped every last bit from the pot, eaten everything except the onion.

I take the onion with me to my room, curl around it in bed. I do not know when I will eat again.

Leaving Khalem

On board the departing ship, I see the whole of Khalem clearly the first time. It is a carven globe of gold floating in the sky, tethered to the ground with ancient linked chains. The city shines in the evening's gloom—the humble houses and the arc of the museum's roof, and the palace, and the cratered bridge, the black pockmarks of recent bombings stark upon gold. One of the chains has been recently severed and repaired in modern fashion, clumsily, quickly, piling rough metal over the ruin of gold.

It begins to rain. The sheen of water softens the dark evening sky to a deep layered blue. The sea is shivering; wave after wave rocks the ship, but I am allowed to stay on the deck, grasping the railing with hands gone numb in the cold.

Ten years ago, when my family fled Raiga to Khalem on a similar ship, we were herded into a single windowless room belowdecks. We were not prisoners, but neither were we free to leave—a mercy of Khalem, who took us in when Islingar refused us. We found out later that people had died in Khalem, and the government needed more people to balance the weight of the city on its chains. It wasn't about offering us refuge, not directly. They had a need—the city needed to be balanced with our bodies.

But now, leaving Khalem and its glow, seeing it clearly for the first time, I grieve—for all I have seen and have not, for all the doors in the market that I could not open, doors that led to tiny eateries serving dumplings in fragrant green sauce and fried chicken hearts; and how I would smell them and look at the people—older, dressed simply, their faces wrinkled from work—dreaming that one day I would be like them, I would open a door and walk in, coins in my pocket, and order a millet flatbread with tart yoghurt sauce and a tiny glass of tea, and be full.

In my bag, the onion rests, safely wrapped in tissue-thin paper, together with my acceptance letter from one of Islingar's top universities. *Impressed by your record*—but I have excelled out of desperation to get the merit stipend and eat. The student papers to Islingar, too, are conditional. Conditional on my continuing unwavering excellence, my perfection, which will be judged and tested every year. The new university paid for my ticket, too: room and board in third class, with a possibility of a discounted upgrade, but I could not afford that.

I become at once queasy and elated from the motions of the ship, the salt spray in my face like a lattice of diamonds; all the stars of the night. The carved globe of Khalem recedes into the rain.

I HAD A CHOICE

BELOWDECKS IN THIRD class, I see the same windowless room and wonder if I am on the same ship that brought me from Raiga to Khalem a decade ago. I do not remember much. The smell of despair.

Somebody's grandmother sitting very still on a cot. She was translucent, taking as little space as possible; her eyes glazed with memories of two wars. Children crying. Somewhere, in the distance, a light.

I shake the memory away. On this ship, people are pressed together, but it does not feel as desperate. Children are crying here too, but grandmothers do not; I see an old woman stirring a soup in a pot. She looks so ordinary, her back stooped, her hair gathered and bound in a garish flowering kerchief, that I almost call out to her in the language of Raiga. She turns, and the greeting is swallowed on my mouth. She looks from under a forest of brows. Her eyes are sunken and dark. She is not translucent—rooted into the planks of the ship like a stubborn ancient tree. Her lips leaf through *daughter, son,* and settle on *child.*

Child, she says in the language of Khalem. *Child, what about the onion?*

I am clutching it, always clutching it in my pocket. The streets and gates and towers. Khalem of gold. She looks at it through the fabric. Looks at me, and suddenly I am afraid, and fear snakes like a wet wind around my torso.

I don't know what you mean, I lie.

Oh you know, child. There is a magic onion stall in the sidewise market of Khalem, where every globe is burnished and mellow like the city that was taken away from me, for even though I weigh more than you do, they cast my people out and let your people in to balance the chains of Khalem.

She stirs the soup in its pot: it is verdant and vivid, herbs and secrets ground first between her palms until their scent opens, then lowered gently into the simmering water. She has shaped millet-flour dumplings and set them adrift in the broth. The ladle with which she stirs is carved, and for a moment I wonder if my eyes betray me. Its handle is golden—an open-jawed lion—and the ladle itself is made of old dark wood. She does not cook this soup for the crowd that presses and sighs belowdecks. This is a memory that twists my stomach and makes me sway on my feet.

A magic onion stall, she says, *that once belonged to my family and now belongs to yours, once belonged to my father and now belongs to yours...*

Nothing belongs to my family. My voice is bitter. *My father owns*

nothing. He is very ill. He gave me his pot, but it was stolen in the
dormitories before I left. He gave me his knife, but that was stolen even
earlier. When my father fell ill, we could not afford to treat him. He told me
to leave Khalem while I still could.

She sways and stirs the green soup with her princely ladle, her
wizened hand gripping the lion by the waist. *You had a choice. A*
choice to stay or leave, she says.

Yes, that is true. I left Raiga with my family, but now I am
older and alone. I could have stayed in Khalem, I guess.

I collect a dry meal from the opposite side of the room. The
sea rations taste of nothing and smell like third class, warm and
smoky and sad.

ABOVEDECKS

THE SEA IS gray and sputtering, and I can no longer see land.
Fog has risen over Khalem, and the far-off Raiga can only be
imagined, a rough outline of loss.

I try to remember it. Pine forests, drops of amber sap at
my feet. It is always cold. Big men are threatening my father.
Standing in line; it is three streets long, made out of people
dressed in gray, their heads bowed under the heaviness of the
air. My father's hand is big and reassuring, but I wonder if he is
afraid. *We must obtain documents.* But Islingar isn't receiving.

On the ship bound for Islingar now, I check and recheck my
documents. These are not refugee invitations. Mine are student
documents with not much weight or rights, but my fingers touch
my pocket over and over. I've wrapped the permission to enter
in waxed paper, put it in my right pocket, sewed it shut. My
hand keeps touching, tracking the crinkly outline of the packet,
caressing it over the fabric. My fingers worry at the seams. Each
evening I finger the stitching open and check, then stitch it shut
again. My left pocket holds the onion.

NAYRA

THE GRANDMOTHER IS still there, in the third class common room
by the stove. It is an electric stove, white and battered, but I do

not see it connect to anything. Why is there a stove here, if the food is dry rations? I did not think about it before.

She stands in the same way, her stooped back to me. The ladle has transformed: its handle is a silvery seahorse with enameled eyes and the wood is mahogany. She is cooking a thick lentil stew in the manner of the markets of Khalem, spiced with turmeric and cardamom and leaves of amber. I am not hungry, for a change; my stomach is full of dry pieces of bread from the rations; but the smell of the lentil soup stirs me. I'd eat it forever. I'd ladle it with the ladle with the silver seahorse and the lion of gold. I'd scoop it with my bare hands and be burned.

I am Nayra, she says without turning.

I take too long to respond. I have had many names, but none of them fit.

She gives up. *Give me the onion, and I'll feed you.*

I can't.

Nayra stirs and stirs her pot, on the hot stove that does not connect to anything.

She says, *Twenty years ago the streets of Khalem were crowded with stalls. Every rounded fruit and root and vegetable had a carver, adorning the produce that grows on the slopes of Khalem. They were jewelers of everyday, for all they often argued. What did not sell was diced and stirred in burnished bronze pots, and then cooked low and slow while the cooler air spread its blessed breath over the tired city, the sellers swapping tales and ladling soup under the bejeweled net of the stars.*

And the onion stall belonged to your family? I ask.

Nayra turns to me, and her eyes are golden like story, like childhood. *One of the onion jewelers was my father,* she says. *There were many more. I no longer remember.*

I, too, don't remember much—not of Raiga, not even of Khalem. There is the ship, the semi-dark glowing closeness of it, and abovedecks, the fog and he wind.

Give the onion to me, Nayra says. *You don't need it.* But I do.

ABOVEDECKS AT NIGHT

I FIND A spot on the open deck from which to watch the sea. Nobody bothers me here. Not much can be seen in the darkness, but I listen to the incessant language of the waves. Above me, the stars dive in and out of clouds. In the depths of the sea I imagine its life—giant fish, red and gold and almost as round as an onion.

I take my onion out, cradle it in my hands. It has not begun to soften or rot. It shines like it shone in the dark sideways market. Its jeweled ridges feel soothing under my fingers—the streets and markets and homes of Khalem. My fingers trace the past of Nayra's story: stalls that line the streets, people selling all manner of things that are round and bejeweled—onions, figs, the purplish globe artichokes; oranges, not needing to be carved or otherwise adorned, for their skin has drunk from the sun.

My onion is glowing golden between my palms; I am occupied by its secrets. Only later, lying awake on my berth and trying to fall asleep, I wonder if I have heard, from a distance, a sigh coming up from the bottomless sea.

Night after night

NIGHT AFTER NIGHT I climb up to the deck and let my onion shine. In calmer weather, I hear the sigh from the sea, more pronounced now, and sometimes a shadow, as if of wings, rising and falling like a breath cradled and diffused by the wave. On stormier nights I hear nothing, and the deck hands send me below.

I have eaten my fill every day. I am not used to this—to eating this much, to eating so much dry bread, to not having anything stolen.

The shadow ray

IT IS RAINING. The night sky adorns itself in the sideways stitching of rain. The deck hands are sheltering elsewhere. I take out my onion—a familiar gesture by now—and raise it to my chest. My palms cradle the houses and streets of Khalem as its light ventures forth, golden and warm like a beacon.

Out of the sea, triangular wings rise, darker than the onion-gilt wave. Flitting between the ship and the water. It is a sea animal, a ray. It traverses the boundary space between the ship and the sea, the boundary space which is softened by spray and the sideways stitching of rain. Our eyes meet; it is human; human like me and like Nayra, and I do not know why I think this.

What is your name? I shout to the shadow in the sea. It sprays me with water, or maybe it is the ship's sudden movement, lurching away, and then it is gone.

THE MAID OF MURUR

LATER THAT NIGHT, lying on my berth, I count breath after breath to a hundred, but sleep does not come. I count the number of berths in this corner of third class, I count the people fast asleep, the wooden beams above my head. I count the knots on the beams and their patterns, I count the wet sound of steps coming closer and closer.

I stop counting and turn to see a pale-blue hand draw back the curtain. There are three more people asleep nearby, but the stranger is quiet; only the water trickling down their breast and hip makes a sound, like a sigh.

I am called the Maid of Murur. Her naked skin is pale blue, like the wave. She holds her ray skin neatly folded across the elbow. *And you?*

*I am....I am....*I turn my eyes away. *I can tell you what I am called in my documents?*

What would you like to be called? Her voice shivers. I sit on my berth and pat the place next to me, push the blanket towards her.

My mouth opens. *Belezal.* I have not expected this, never imagined that name could be mine. It is a Khalem name, the name of the great mythic artisan who fashioned the first bejeweled globe of Khalem out of gold; before everyone took up this form, before onions and figs and artichokes were carved to resemble his craft. It is said that his golden coffin hangs from the central chain of Khalem and balances it with its weight.

Are you a man?

I shake my head. *Neither this or that, you know. I heard I can be whatever I want in Islingar.*

My father wouldn't understand. The thought pains me, that I

kept it a secret from him for so long, that he'd think I was hurt in the war, that he failed to protect me. But I lost his knife and his pot, and that pains me much more than losing the name he had given me.

I stare at the small puddles on the floor, uncertain when the ray-person slipped away.

Hunger of a different kind

In the third-class commons, the rations-people mock me when I ask for more. The words are almost soft at first, but after a few days it intensifies; they call me a growing boy and a vulture of dry bread and they laugh with their I've-always-eaten-my-fill mouths. Nayra nods at me from the other side of the room. Her tireless arm stirs the pot.

You're hungry again, she says when I make it over. She is cooking onions today—onions sliced into thin rings and cooked translucent and golden with turmeric and cardamom. As I stand there transfixed, my mouth watering, she grimaces. *It's not the same. The onions that grow on this ship taste like water. Not like the ocean even, for that is full of salt and life. The water of the ship is sanitary and still, and it bloats these onions, steals any life and taste from within. What you smell is the spice.*

They grow onions here? It is hard for me to imagine, but she nods.

Even deeper within the bowels of the ship there are gardens tended by those of us who will never land.

Nayra stirs the pot, a familiar motion by now. Today the handle of her ladle is a bird made of silver, its feet transformed into chains wrapped around the wood of the spoon.

No matter how much spice I add, it will never taste like Khalem.

Nayra's gaze slides over my bulging pocket. I wait for her to ask again, but the only sound she makes is the stirring, stirring, stirring the simple pot on the stove which is not connected to anything.

You said that you will never land?

She sighs. *Not now. Not ever, perhaps.*

Islingar is not receiving?

Oh, I have the documents, Nayra says. *Documents for Islingar, a land where onions soak up even more water, a land that is tasteless and smells like nothing I know. No, child, I want to go back to Khalem.*

Belowdecks on my berth, I eat everything in the ration packet, but I am not full. I want to eat all the dry bread that scrapes the insides of my mouth and slides down my throat like a gravelly lump. I want to devour Nayra's onions, their bloated, watery taste softened by spice. I want to taste the ocean, drink the brine and the seaweed until we are safe on dry land. No matter how much I eat there is an emptiness in me, the weight of Khalem that can never be balanced by chains.

WORDS OF MURUR

I CLIMB ABOVEDECKS that night. It is windy, and the ship lurches; but I have become stealthier. I hide from the deck hands, my clothing blown this way and that by the wind. I am huddled in dreary cold wrappings against the gusts of water and wind. When I take out the onion, I doubt anyone will see me. Not the maid of Murur; not the ship hands, not even the stars in the overcast, punishing sky. Not even Nayra. *You do not need the onion,* she said. *My father was among the last onion jewelers of Khalem. Every rounded fruit and vegetable had a carver, adorning the pliant flesh with the slopes and streets of Khalem, adorning the graveyards and markets and chains that hold it aloft. You do not need it, but I do.*

I should have told her, *my father, too, used to carve—with his paper-thin knife made from my grandfather's razor, and with his big carver's tools. There is no natural magic remaining in Raiga, but the artists make it out of the fallen forests, out of memory. Out of wood they shape birds and streets and houses, carve protections and lions into the corner beams. But he found no wood in Khalem. It is a city of gold and chain, of stone and carved onion. When my father sickened—*

The maid of Murur is here. She sits heavily on the wet wooden boards by my side. Her naked human skin is glowing blue; her slippery ray-skin folded once more over her arm.

Your onion glows like a beacon.

I do not need it, I say.

Not even to call me out of the turbulent sea?

Maybe. To call you. I smile despite myself. *Why are you at sea? Because Raiga is at war.*

I know very little about Murur. A small country neighboring Raiga from southeast, for centuries swallowed and spat out by Raiga's conflicts.

Murur was pretty once. She shakes her head, and droplets of water fall on my hands from her seaweed-braided dark hair. *Pretty before all the wars. Now everything is rigid—the clothes, the words, the people. They do not want someone like me, and I'd rather be in the ocean than anywhere with my family.* Her voice goes mocking, shrill with pain. *You say you can love a person of any shape—then why* can't *you marry a boy?*

The way she says the word 'boy' makes me clench inside. She asked if I was a boy, but I am neither this nor that, at least not yet.

She looks at me, worried. Clasps my hand. *I do not mean you. They would not want you, just like they do not want me.*

Her hand on mine is warm and wet, and my feelings churn like the storm. At least she told her family who she was. I did not tell my parents, when I left. I was hungry and alone, and it did not seem possible to have that conversation in Khalem. I just hoped to be free in Islingar.

I say, *You can be whatever you want in Islingar.*

I do not have the documents. I am not even alive anymore, not in a way you are alive, Belezal. I do not even have a human name. I traded all that for the ray-skin. I did all that to be free.

She no longer has a human name; but my name—my name!—my name on her lips is like gold and salt water. The name Belezal is Khalem's heavy chain weighted with the shores that I wanted to reach all my life, as warm as a carved golden onion.

It is cold here, I whisper. *Are you not cold?*

A little. She scuttles closer to me, and I put my shaking arm around her shoulders.

It is cold here, I say again. My lips, too, are like ice. Soon we will wrap a single ray-skin around us and plunge into the sea. But I do not want to go there. I mumble, *Would you like to come down—to my berth?*

She does, and we do, and we drape her ray-skin over the berth's opening so that nobody can look.

THE POT OF EMPTY WATER

YOU SMELL LIKE the sea, Nayra says. *Like seaweed.* It's morning, and I've wandered over to her stove again after the rations-people refused me any extras. Back in the berth, my lover ate the last of my dried bread—stale and too salty, still better than sea snails and worms. Then she left. I am hungry again, hungry always and as long as I can remember.

Nayra gives me a knowing look. *Ah, youth.*

I look away. *She cannot come ashore with me.*

Nayra's wrinkled hand stirs a pot of empty water. The ladle is plain wood with no adornment, its handle worn thin by decades of work.

No documents?

I nod. *No documents. Where we come from, they do not want people like us.*

*But they wanted you in Khalem. And my father—my father—*Nayra's voice runs thin and bitter. Runs out.

My father, too, was a carver. I have thought of this moment, practiced the words, but I cannot quite say them now. *My father—in Raiga he was a carver of wood; he could have carved ships if he lived closer to the coast.* But the ships of Khalem are hammered out of sheet brass; they cannot venture far into the open sea.

This ship, Nayra says, *was made before Raiga and Islingar, made in the great isle of Selei before it sunk underwave, made when Khalem as we know it was only beginning, when Belezal forged the streets and the chains.*

That's my name. Belezal. A name made real last night on the lips of the shapeshifting ray of Murur.

A weighty name to carry, Nayra says. *A legacy of chains.* She is silent for a moment. *We were exiled from the city, my father and I, so your people could balance the weight of Khalem.*

She is bitter, but I stay by her side. I want to say, *I had nothing to eat there. We barely survived. My father is very ill, and even the knife he gave me was stolen. In Khalem, I could not be who I am.*

I do not say these words. They will not help.

I love the city, too. I do not say this either. I did not love it when I came and left.

I say, *I do not understand why the city needs to be balanced with our bodies. Our weight.*

Because it hangs in the balance.

Nayra relents and releases a small pouch that hangs around her neck; warms the spices before crushing them into the boiling water. They float, dissolving in that heat. She stirs the empty soup as I watch, and she ladles it—hot water, just water from the secret bowels of the ship, first sanitary-still and then vibrant, alive with Nayra's spices.

I take a sip, and it is the city: its markets and birds and crowded streets— For the briefest moment, I see it as it was in peaceful times. The jewelers of fruit and root and vegetable in their festive embroidered robes under aprons, and my father— my people—carving birds and reindeer into housebeams made of stone and wood; and small-statured people I have never seen carving jewels out of spice berries. All around are shouts and argument and song; good-natured cries and little brass-bells calling the market to dinner. Even the honey-seller is there, with his wax candles carved like the onion, carved like the city. I swallow, and it goes away.

Who are the jewelers of spice? I ask, and Nayra nods.

These people are called Khidi. They say they founded Khalem. It was their city before it was hung suspended in the air, before the weight of the world was balanced in it.

You do not believe it?

I do not know. She shrugs. *The city is always changing.*

I am sorry, I say. I am sorry for everything. My father's sickness, the war that spat us out of Raiga and into Khalem, the tumult and din of Khalem, the churning of the sea and this ancient ship that traveled it before our countries were real, before Belezal spun the chains of Khalem. I'm sorry we can come together only in memory shared with a spoonful of empty soup. I'm sorry my lover won't come ashore with me. I'm sorry I took a name too large for me to carry. I'm sorry that I am and am not a boy.

I tell Nayra, *I'm sorry you cannot go home.* I cannot, either. I do not know where it is.

TIDE

THE MAID OF Murur comes back in the night, when I am asleep in my berth. I blurt, *you do not need the onion to find me.*

I don't, she says. *But it is good to have the light.*

Her lips latch to mine, and the sea of her swallows me.

AN OFFERING

I BRING THE onion to Nayra the next day, proffer it in both my hands as I would give her the city. The strongest light.

I do not need it, I say, *but you do.*

She turns towards me. Away from the stove. The ladle is poised in her hand. It is ebony, crowned in a golden bulb of an onion. Did she hold it before I spoke? I don't know.

What made you change your mind?

I swallow. *I don't know.*

My lips move, soundless. *The onion jeweler gave me a gift; he did not need to give it. I can choose to give, too.*

And, *I am no longer sure this is mine.*

And, *You have been on this ship for decades. You cannot return to Khalem.*

This is Khalem.

Aloud I say, *I did not know you before.*

The ladle shakes in Nayra's hand. She kept asking me for the onion, but now I know that she did not think I would give her anything.

What about your lover?

I shrug, pretending indifference. *She can find her own way to me.*

Are you absolutely sure? But Nayra is already stretching out her hand.

I let the golden globe go. It is a gift, this Khalem of Gold, a gift I did not have to receive, or to give. But I did, and I am, because each jeweled onion contains the city and is reflected in it, and each carver carves the city and gifts it to those who need to remember it and pass it on for others. We may not understand Khalem and its chains and its weight, but we can remember it, so the city can never be destroyed.

Nayra lays down her ladle and takes up a paring knife. With slightly shaking hands she peels the city—its golden skin and the streets and its bridges and the curve of the royal palace. Memory sloughs off, revealing the white flesh inside. Her motions are sure now. She carves that up too, the onion beneath the skin, the meat and heart of the city, its hidden mechanical core—now only, and ever, an onion. My eyes blur. The smell in my nostrils is sharp and triumphant for a brief, bright moment.

I hear the rings fall onto the hot oil of Nayra's pan. My eyes are closed now, but I hear them. They sizzle at first. Then they hiss. Then they sigh as they sag. They are gentle and soft and translucent, caramelizing to brown.

Into the softness I think, *war has damaged Khalem. It is not the city of your youth.* But Nayra's eyes are closed. She is inhaling: the soft, yielding flesh is releasing the sun.

She says, *Do you have that dry bread?* I have eaten it all, but I manage to beg a few more pieces off a new rations-person. Nayra softens the bread with some oil and fries it, then heaps golden onion on top. Cuts it in half. She eats like a bird, in small pecks, her eyes closed and her whole body rigid, attuned to some inner vision. A trickle of tears runs down from the corner of her right eye; her left is dry.

I watch for a bit, and then I have to look away. There's the uneaten piece, heaped high with translucent brown onion. No longer my onion, the shining carved Khalem of gold. No, this is disemboweled. Dead.

As if I never received it as gift from the jeweler at his stall, as if it never gave me the strength to leave, as if I never made of it a beacon for the sea, as if it never held the city and its streets and memories and light.

Just a cooked vegetable.

I take a step back. Another.

Nayra opens an eye. *That's for you*, she says. *The second half. You should eat it.*

I turn away and run, all the way to my berth and the dark.

SILENCE

AT NIGHT I am on the deck. The weather is still and pleasant, and hosts of stars litter the sky. I stare out into the sea, but there's nothing. Not even a shadow of wings.

The next night I cup my hands like an onion and lift them, empty, to my chest. I have not gone to see Nayra. I have not eaten.

The sea is still.

A STORM IN THE SMALLEST SPACE

THE MAID OF Murur comes to my berth in the dead of the night. The ray-skin in her hand is dripping salt.

What happened, Belezal? Where is your beacon?

I shake my head. *I gave it away.* I shouldn't have, but—maybe I should have? The moment was clear and translucent like an onion gently softened by heat for a brief moment before wilting.

You gave it away? The maid of Murur's voice is thin, sharp.

I thought—I thought somebody else needed it more. Someone who cannot go home.

I, too, cannot go home. I thought—I thought you cared? Her lips tremble; her hair is seaweed trembling like a forest in the small space of my berth.

Nobody cares about me, she says. *My family, caring only for the shape they gave me, the order they imposed on me, the people who wanted the body but did not see me—the friends who turned away—the summons of war— the bitter embrace of the sea—*

And all the boys *you did not want.* I do not know what made me say that, and I do. Because she, too, would not see me unless I made clear that I'm not a boy, or at least neither this nor that.

She rises, wrapping herself tight in the slithery ray-skin, and I know I will lose her, and I do not want to lose her, and I have to lose her; I do not understand how this happened so fast.

It's not about you being a boy, Belezal. You should have asked me first about the onion—you should have asked me first about everything— Her voice is like a storm on the sea, carrying all the weight and anguish of water.

I want to hug her to me, but I can't. *No,* I say. *I shouldn't have asked you about the onion. It does not belong to you, or to me. It belongs to Khalem.*

I listen to the rapid beating of footsteps, then a splash, far away. In my hectic dreams later, an enormous shadow ray encircles the ship, and tightens; then lets go.

LEAVETAKING

A DAY BEFORE landing, I go to speak to Nayra once more.

I'm sorry about your lover, she says when I tell her.

I shake my head. *She did not want me. Not everything I am.*

Don't be so sure about that, Nayra says. In her hand, the ladle is all silver vines creeping up to a blossoming rose. *Sometimes it takes more time and more words than youth can afford. You have to exchange many words; they will lead you deep into each other's truths. You are not born with all the perfect words, especially if where you're born the words were not allowed. You need to make the words. Words and memories and food and touch. You have to be patient.*

I shrug. *I cannot be patient now. She is gone.* And then, bitter, *She just wanted the onion.*

Nayra smiles. I have never seen her smile before: like a tired window cracking open into a seascape of purest azure.

No, child. It is I who wanted the onion. She only wanted your light.

The words sink into me, glowing and golden; too painful to hold.

I change course. *You have the documents. Come ashore with me to Islingar.*

I cannot. She shakes her head. *Even though I cannot return, I must stay true to Khalem.*

I say, *I lived in Khalem for a decade, but I did not truly know it before I met you. Did not love it before we spoke. You'll carry Khalem with you ashore. Its spices and markets and truths.* And its love.

Nayra shakes her head. Then she pats mine. *Not yet.*

ISLINGAR

IN ISLINGAR I settle in the seashore town of Luga, home of the university. Excelling is easier now that they give me a stipend to cover my lodgings and food. I eat the tasteless fruits of Islingar, great slabs of bread cut thin and toasted to dryness.

I sit with my books by the window overlooking the sea. I nibble on dry bread and daydream of a great ancient ship made of wood and barnacle-covered; made in the isle of Selei before it sunk underwave, made when Belezal forged the streets and the chains of Khalem. In my vision the ship is enormous, larger than water and land. As it grows in my vision I hear, deep within it, the sound of Nayra's ladle making circles in the pot of soup.

I buy a blue pot and put empty water to boil on my electric stove. It is plugged in, and the low humming of it comforts me. I buy overpriced sumac and coriander, turmeric and cumin, and I stir the empty soup with a ladle made of wood. The spices here are not as potent as Nayra's; they hardly taste of anything. I add more and stir, always keeping an eye on the horizon. There is no ship I see, and no gigantic ray.

I begin to add lentils and vegetables to the pot. The zucchini and onions are waterlogged here, barely tasting of earth, but I can afford them.

In time, I buy larger clothing and marvel at how easy it is both to find and to buy these sizes. When strangers ask me where I'm from, I say Khalem.

THEY WERE JEWELERS OF EVERYDAY

MY FATHER SENDS me a package over the sea. It is his own carving knife, thin and sharp, made from my grandfather's shaving razor. My father cannot hold it anymore, much less carve.

The package tarried for three months before reaching Islingar. There is no letter—confiscated in customs, perhaps. The binding is torn and the back address smudged, but the knife arrives safe in its wrappings, still holding a razor-sharp edge.

It takes me four days to find a good onion. The store onions of Islingar have no luster, but a middle-aged woman sells me a good one from a communal garden patch. It looks slightly tarnished and does not quite glow, but it smells like the dark and golden streets of Khalem's sidewise market.

When I sit by the window to carve the onion, my hands shake. I lost the first knife in the dormitories, but the knife I hold is dearer even. Why did my father send it? Because he thought me his son, even though I said nothing; to inherit his knife and my grandfather's, or because he thought I should inherit them as a daughter? What was I? Neither this nor that, a person who was brought to Khalem and left it, a person always looking back to the sea? Did it truly matter why my father sent me the knife? It is of Raigan make. I hold it, the handle warm with my touch and older than my life, older than all the wars I have known. It has traveled from Raiga to Khalem and then out of Khalem oversea, like I did.

I carve—hesitantly at first, then with abandon. I am a carver in the lineage of Khalem but I am also a stranger to it. A stranger everywhere. I carve as my father would carve—birds and reindeer and trees; I carve as Nayra's father would carve—streets too wide, imprecise, the bulbous roofs of Khalem's inner quarters, the curve and sweep of the museum. I carve things of my own: a harbor, much like this one in Luga, which cannot be found in Khalem. A ship, which neither of our fathers have seen. And then I am out of onion.

My creation is dull and clumsy, uneven. The images I saw so vividly in my mind are shapeless gouges and slashes. If the maid of Murur only wanted my light then what I made is crude and feeble; it cannot compare to the great work of the carvers of Khalem or to my father's craft. It cannot call anyone out of the sea. It cannot do anything.

A SUMMONS AND A WAVE

WHEN I SENSE her presence by my side, I think I am dreaming. But the maid of Murur is real, her blue skin glowing with pinpricks of light. Her ray-skin has transformed into a studded leather coat. She wears a white men's collared shirt beneath it, and a pair of sharply pleated trousers, in the latest fashions of Islingar.

Did I call you?

You did. She smiles, and her mouth is lit by a row of small, sharp, white teeth. *And I decided to be called.*

I want to reach out to her, touch her tide-starry hand, but I cannot, not yet. The depth of words that Nayra spoke about is missing.

I tell her, *I need to be—I need to be what I am, even if it's a boy. I am neither—or both—and one day I may be entirely a boy, or not, but I cannot—I cannot have you tell me I'm special and different from other boys, so if you cannot have a boy, it will not work.*

She puts her hand on mine, soft and heavy, breaching the boundary between wakefulness and dream. *I'm sorry I said that. Thing is—it's not about you or any other person, boy or not. It is because—of what they wanted me to be. I'm good with a boy and a girl and a person who is both or neither, a person of any shape, as long as they do not want me to change who I am.*

Why would I want to change you? I blurt. *You are perfect.*

Her hair shadows my face, runs down my body in star-drops of water and light. Words, Nayra said, words to get to the deep still core of ourselves; but we touch and words scamper while our waves crush relentlessly, gently ashore.

A CHAIN OF WORDS AND SOFT ONION

WE TALK IN the night. How she came to the ship after I disembarked, her ray-skin draped over her arm and dripping tears in the third-class commons; how Nayra gave her my half of the old piece of bread and leftover onion. How she ate it, the ancient city and all its heart and its wars, its kindness and cruelty and its sacrifices.

A piece of Khalem is in her now as it is in me, a memory golden and sharp like a chain that balances both of us.

It is easier to find the right words now that I've lived for a while in Islingar, my lover says. *I have even picked up my name again. Gabi.* She waves her fist fiercely towards the sea and beyond it, Murur. *They do not get to take it away from me, not anymore.*

But I am here only provisionally. Even if I'm excellent in my studies, I cannot stay here forever.

I do not ask Gabi how she got her documents.

A MORNING IN LUGA

IN THE MORNING, she is still here, sprawled asleep in my bed. The onion I carved flickers on the kitchen table, barely there, but she found me. All what is needed is my light.

I slice up my clumsily carved onion into a pan with some oil and soften it gently with sumac and cumin. The jewelers of everyday in Khalem carved their unsold produce each night and cooked it for a big communal meal; tomorrow I will find another onion and practice until I am truly a carver.

Nobody's watching, but I look around anyway, before unplugging my stove from the electrical outlet in the wall.

There is no change. The stove hums gently, the warmth of the heating element cooks the onion base. I add lentils and rice and water and set it all to a gentle simmer. My ladle is wood, but as I look, it sprouts a handle of silver. It is a chain. A chain of Khalem holding tight to a ship that forever travels between all the shores, a ship more ancient than wars, a ship that saves us and drowns us, a ship that traversed the waves a thousand times for those of us that do not have a place to go, so we must always be going places.

I know that one day we will see it again, my lover and I; see the ancient barnacled ship fill our vision and expand. We will run down to the harbor, Gabi in her jacket of ray skin and I in my big Islingar clothes. We will hold hands and run breathless beyond the customs tower, race barefoot to the pier. The air will be too bright and too green, full of smells of dry seaweed and wind.

We will climb the rusted, ancient chains of the ship, go down to third-class where the stove hums as softly as mine and an old woman of Khalem stands motionless by a big pot of water. We will ask our elder to come ashore with us, or maybe we'll tell her we are ready to come on the ship once more. We might never be allowed to enter Khalem again, might never find home, but we'll balance the weight of each other.

I will not stop carving until it is so.

Acknowledgements

"If You Take My Meaning" by Charlie Jane Anders was originally published by *Tordotcom*, February 26, 2020.

"A Voyage to Queensthroat" by Anya Johanna DeNiro was originally published by *Strange Horizons*, August 2020.

"Rat and Finch are Friends" by Innocent Chizaram Ilo was originally published by *Strange Horizons*, March 2020.

"Salt and Iron" by Gem Isherwood was originally published by *Podcastle*, May 2020

"The Currant Dumas" by L.D. Lewis was originally published by *Glitter + Ashes*, edited by dave ring.

"Everquest" by Naomi Kanakia was originally published by *Lightspeed*, October 2020.

"Portrait of Three Women with an Owl" by Gwen C. Katz was originally published by *The Future Fire*, February 2020.

"The Ashes of Vivian Firestrike" by Kristen Koopman was originally published by *Glittership*, May 2020.

"To Balance the Weight of Khalem" by RB Lemberg was originally published by *Beneath Ceaseless Skies*, March 2020

"Thin Red Jellies" by Lina Rather was originally published by *Gigonotosaurus*, February 2020.

"Body, Remember" by Nicasio Andres Reed (*Fireside*, November 2020)

"Escaping Dr. Markoff" by Gabriela Santiago was originally published by *The Dark*, March 2020

"The Last Good Time to Be Alive" by Waverly SM was originally published by *Reckoning 4*, edited by Danika Dinsmore and Arkady Martine.

"Monsters Never Leave You" by Carlie St. George was originally published by *Strange Horizons*, June 2020.

"The Wedding After The Bomb" by Brendan Williams-Childs was originally published by *Catapult*, April 2020.

"8-Bit Free Will" by John Wiswell was originally published by *Podcastle*, November 2020.

About the Authors

Charlie Jane Anders is the author of a brand new young adult space opera, *Victories Greater Than Death*. Her writing advice, *Never Say You Can't Survive*, comes out in August. She co-hosts the *Our Opinions Are Correct* podcast.

Anya Johanna DeNiro was born in Erie, Pennsylvania. She received a BA in English from the College of Wooster and an MFA in Creative Writing from the University of Virginia. She's also a 1998 graduate of the Clarion Workshop. Her short fiction has appeared widely, in venues such as *Asimov's, Strange Horizons, One Story, Interfictions, Catapult,* and *Shimmer*. She's the author of two collection of short stories, both published by Small Beer Press, *Skinny Dipping in the Lake of the Dead* (2006) and *Tyrannia* (2013); and a novel, *Total Oblivion, More or Less* (2009) (as Alan DeNiro). She's also been shortlisted for the O.Henry Award, and a finalist for the Crawford Award and Theodore Sturgeon Award.

Innocent Chizaram Ilo is Igbo. They live in Lagos and write to make sense of the world around them. Their works have been published or are forthcoming in *Escape Pod, Granta, The Guardian, Al Jazeera, Catapult, Fireside Fiction, Reckoning Press, Cast of Wonders, Strange Horizons, BBC Culture* and elsewhere. They are the winner of the 2020 Commonwealth Short Story Prize (African Region) and a finalist of the Otherwise (formerly James Triptree) and Lambda awards.

Gem Isherwood is an author of speculative fiction whose work is often influenced by folklore, fairy tales and the Gothic. She lives on a small island in the middle of the Irish Sea populated by fairies, ghosts and cats with no tails. You can find her on Twitter @GemIsWriting.

Naomi Kanakia is the author of two novels (*Enter Title Here*, Disney '16) and *We Are Totally Normal* (HarperTeen, '20). Additionally, her stories have appeared or are forthcoming in *Asimov's, Clarkesworld, F&SF, Gulf Coast, The Indiana Review*, and *West Branch*, and her poetry has appeared in *Soundings East, The American Journal of Poetry*, and *Vallum*. She lives in San Francisco with her wife and daughter. If you want to know more you can visit her blog at www.blotter-paper.com or follow her on Twitter at @rahkan.

Gwen C. Katz is a bisexual author, artist, game designer, and Nazi-puncher who lives in Pasadena, California with her husband and a revolving door of transient animals. Her first novel, *Among the Red Stars*, tells the story of Russia's famous all-female bomber regiment known as the Night Witches. She's published around a dozen short stories in venues like *Glittership* and *Curiosities*. Some of her favorite artists include Leonora Carrington, Remedios Varo, and Leonor Fini, the three women who loosely inspired this story. Find her online at gwenckatz.com or on Twitter and Instagram at @gwenckatz.

Kristen Koopman is a graduate student, writer, and nerd. Her interests include blatant escapism, overanalyzing anything and everything, playing with her dog, and consuming enough garlic to kill vampires at twenty paces. Other stories of hers can be found at *Kaleidotrope, Toasted Cake*, and forthcoming in *It Gets Even Better: Stories of Queer Possibility*. She is definitely not two smaller Kristen Koopmans in a trenchcoat.

R.B. Lemberg is a queer, bigender immigrant from Ukraine, Russia, and Israel to the US. R.B.'s novella *The Four Profound Weaves* (Tachyon, 2020) is a finalist for the Nebula award. Their novel *The Unbalancing* is forthcoming from Tachyon in 2022. You can find R.B. on Twitter at @rb_lemberg, on Patreon at patreon.com/rblemberg, and at their website rblemberg.net.

L.D. Lewis is an award-winning SF/F writer and editor, and serves as a founding creator, Art Director, and Project Manager for the World Fantasy Award-winning and Hugo Award-nominated *FIYAH Literary Magazine*. She is the author of *A Ruin of Shadows* (Dancing Star Press, 2018) and her published short fiction includes appearances in *FIYAH, PodCastle, Anathema: Spec from the Margins, Strange Horizons,* and *Fireside Magazine*, among others. She lives in Georgia with her coffee habit and an impressive Funko Pop! collection. Visit her website at ldlewiswrites.com and follow her on Twitter @ellethevillain.

Lina Rather is a speculative fiction author from Michigan, now living in Washington, D.C. Her short fiction has appeared in venues including *Lightspeed, Daily Science Fiction,* and *Shimmer*. Her debut novella *Sisters of the Vast Black*, about nuns living in a giant slug in outer space, was published by Tor.Com Publishing in October 2019. When she isn't writing, she likes to cook, go hiking, and collect terrible 90s comic books. Find out more about her and her writing at linarather.com or on Twitter @LinaRather.

Nicasio Andres Reed is a queer, trans, Filipino-American writer, poet, and essayist whose work has appeared in venues such as *Strange Horizons, Lightspeed, Uncanny Magazine, Fireside,* and *Shimmer*. He lives in Tagaytay, in the Philippines, with four dogs, some family, and the occasional uninvited monitor lizard. You can find more of his work at nicasioreed.com.

Gabriela Santiago has previously been published in *Clarkesworld, Strange Horizons, The Dark,* and *Lady Churchill's Rosebud Wristlet*, among others. She is also the founder and curator of the science fiction cabaret Revolutionary Jetpacks, centering the futures imagined by BIPOC, queer and trans, and disabled artists. Follow her at writing-relatedactivities.tumblr.com or @LifeOnEarth89 on Twitter.

Waverly SM is a speculative fiction writer preoccupied with apocalypses, impossible choices, and the ambient trauma of living in the world. They're a 2019 Lambda Literary Fellow whose work has appeared in *Reckoning 4, Stim: An Autism Anthology, Lucent Dreaming, SAND,* and *Lucky Pierre Magazine.* They can currently be found trying to approximate the anchorite lifestyle in Oxford, or more expediently at www.waverlysm.com.

Carlie St. George is a Clarion West graduate with stories in *The Year's Best Dark Fantasy & Horror, Strange Horizons, The Dark,* and multiple other magazines and anthologies. When not writing about fairy tales and the families you make for yourself, she talks a lot about movies and television on her blog My Geek Blasphemy.

Brendan Williams-Childs is a speculative fiction writer originally from Wyoming. His work has appeared in *Nat. Brut, Catapult,* on NPR, and in various anthologies, including the Lambda-nominated *Meanwhile Elsewhere: Science Fiction and Fantasy from Transgender Authors* and *Glitter + Ashes: Queer Tales of a World that Wouldn't Die.*

John (@Wiswell) is an ace/aro writer who lives where New York keeps all its trees. He is a finalist for the 2021 Hugo, Nebula, and Locus Award, and his fiction has appeared in *Uncanny Magazine, Nature Futures,* and *Cast of Wonders.* This story was inspired by his lifetime love of games as a medium for entertainment, narrative, and social bonding. Dragon Quest is every bit as much a reason he's a writer as *The Hobbit* is.

About the Editors

Cherae Clark is the author of *The Unbroken*, the first book in the Magic of the Lost trilogy. She graduated from Indiana University's creative writing MFA and was a 2012 Lambda Literary Fellow. She's been a personal trainer, an English teacher, and an editor, and is some combination thereof as she travels the world. When she's not writing or working, she's learning languages, doing P90something, or reading about war and [post-]colonial history. Her work has also appeared in *FIYAH, PodCastle,* and *Beneath Ceaseless Skies.*

Charles Payseur is an avid reader, writer, and reviewer of speculative fiction. His works have appeared in *The Best American Science Fiction and Fantasy, Lightspeed Magazine,* and *Beneath Ceaseless Skies*, among others, and he's a six-time Hugo Award finalist and two-time Ignyte Award finalist. His debut short fiction collection, *The Burning Day and Other Strange Stories*, was published by Lethe Press (2021). He currently resides in Eau Claire, Wisconsin, with his herd of disobedient pets and husband, Matt. He can be found gushing about short fiction on Twitter as @ClowderofTwo.

About the Press

Neon Hemlock Press is an emerging purveyor of zines, queer chapbooks and speculative fiction. Learn more about us at www.neonhemlock.com and on Twitter at @neonhemlock.